"Are you afraid of me?"

"Absolutely not, and yes, with everything in my heart and soul," I blurted without thought.

He chuckled, and looked directly at me for the first time in several minutes. "I'm not sure that qualifies as an answer—it's more like a contradiction."

"Up is down, remember? Besides, everything about you is a contradiction." Pondering my word choice a little more carefully, I added, "You won't hurt me. How I know that, I can't say. But the ways you make me feel, Haden—that's what frightens me. I know you'll be my undoing." I stepped towards him but he stepped back.

"Who was your first kiss?"

Heat rushed into my face. I flattered myself by thinking maybe he wanted to kiss me. I wished he wanted to kiss me. "I haven't . . ." Squeezing my eyes closed, I began again. "I haven't been kissed. Yet."

"Why?"

I rolled my eyes at his innocence. "You obviously know I'm not like other girls. I'm shy and I don't spend time with boys. My father is strict and—"

"That's not why."

He thought he knew me so well. "Fine. You tell me why I haven't been kissed."

I regretted the words and my tone instantly. What if he told me what I already knew? That I was lacking. Not interesting or pretty enough.

"You were waiting."

FALLING UNDER

GWEN HAYES

NEW AMERICAN LIBRARY

NEW AMERICAN LIBRARY

Published by New American Library, a division of Penguin Group (USA) Inc., 375 Hudson Street, New York, New York 10014, USA • Penguin Group (Canada), 90 Eglinton Avenue East, Suite 700, Toronto, Ontario M4P 2Y3, Canada (a division of Pearson Penguin Canada Inc.) • Penguin Books Ltd., 80 Strand, London WC2R 0RL, England • Penguin Ireland, 25 St. Stephen's Green, Dublin 2, Ireland (a division of Penguin Books Ltd.) • Penguin Group (Australia), 250 Camberwell Road, Camberwell, Victoria 3124, Australia (a division of Pearson Australia Group Pty. Ltd.) • Penguin Books India Pvt. Ltd., 11 Community Centre, Panchsheel Park, New Delhi - 110 017, India • Penguin Group (NZ), 67 Apollo Drive, Rosedale, North Shore 0632, New Zealand (a division of Pearson New Zealand Ltd.) • Penguin Books (South Africa) (Pty.) Ltd., 24 Sturdee Avenue, Rosebank, Johannesburg 2196, South Africa

Penguin Books Ltd., Registered Offices:
80 Strand, London WC2R 0RL, England

First published by New American Library,
a division of Penguin Group (USA) Inc.

First Printing, March 2011
5   7   9   10   8   6

 REGISTERED TRADEMARK—MARCA REGISTRADA

LIBRARY OF CONGRESS CATALOGING-IN-PUBLICATION DATA:

Hayes, Gwen.
Falling under/Gwen Hayes.
p. cm.
ISBN 978-0-451-23268-7
1. Demonology—Fiction. 2. Supernatural—Fiction. 3. Dreams—Fiction.
4. High schools—Fiction. 5. Schools—Fiction. I. Title.
PZ7.H31458Fal 2011
[Fic]—dc22   2010039897

Set in Adobe Caslon • Designed by Elke Sigal

Printed in the United States of America

*To Hayley Nicole, who will always be the little girl I love
and who is becoming the young woman I so admire*

ACKNOWLEDGMENTS

I'd like to thank my Sequim Middle School librarian, Jo Chinn, for nurturing my love of YA books. It was her passion for reading and her sense of humor and fun that got me through a few of those "iffy" years.

Thanks also to my critique partner, Ciar Cullen, for encouraging me to carry on when I had no idea what this story was, only that it scared me to write it. Also responsible for the mayhem are Bria Quinlan and Jodi Meadows, who understand about cheese and other necessary things.

My cover, my extraordinary cover, is a testament to the genius of the art department at NAL. A million thanks to Oceana Gottlieb and her crew, to Dana France, and to model Tara.

A special shout-out to Kat Sherbo, who makes all things possible, and to Jan McInroy, for her superhero copyediting skills. My undying gratitude goes to my phenomeliscious agent, Jessica Sinsheimer, who does all kinds of important things for me, but tells me about only the fun ones, and to Anne Sowards, who is so cool she makes me want to write things just to impress her. Seriously.

And, of course, thank you to my family. Their support made this dream a reality for me, and I am blessed beyond all reason to be surrounded with so much love. Also, thank you, Travis, for holding my hand through it all. I love you more.

fALLING UNDER

CHAPTER ONE

Everything changed the night I saw the burning man fall from the sky.

I'd been reading well past a reasonable hour, the white eyelet quilt tented over my iPhone to block any escaping light even though my father was already tucked away in bed dreaming of new ways to make me safer.

The cell phone was a compromise—I added extra music lessons to my scarce free time in exchange for a phone. It was win-win for Father; the few hours a day I wasn't with him or sheltered in the safety of my pink and ivory room, decorated by a prestigious designer to gild my cage, I was now instantly accessible. In addition, there were now even fewer hours in which I might find trouble. He didn't know I could read e-books on the phone; he didn't even know what e-books were. Father just thought he'd finally broken me of reading by flashlight.

It would never have occurred to him that I hadn't been broken—I'd graduated. Every night I went somewhere new and pretended to be someone else—someone interesting—on the device he'd purchased to control me more than he already did. A priceless freedom to a girl with a strange British accent living in the small town of Serendipity Falls, California, under her watchful father's thumb.

But the burning man falling from the sky pulled me from my faraway world. My gaze wandered to the window an instant before he appeared. And then, slowly, like a feather caught on a light breeze, he willowed past my window, turning his grotesque head towards me, his mouth open in a silent scream. He was more than *on* fire. He *was* fire.

Orange and red flames braided together in the shape of a man, but it was his eyes that caused me to suck in my breath and hold it as I ran to the window. His eyes, scared and imploring, told of a darkness and agony I couldn't begin to understand.

I leaned farther into the window, the glass surprisingly warm from his brush past it. Like I touched a trace of him. As he completed his unhurried, torturous descent to the lawn, he kept his gaze locked on mine. Beseeching me for something I couldn't give as the flames consumed him. So many things I should have felt, wondered, or worried about, yet I just watched, fascinated and compelled to see him to the end.

He landed in the yard, still burning alive. My father's pristine lawn would be scorched.

He'd be so disappointed.

Afraid to leave my perch, I was unsure what to do next. Surely what I was seeing was a figment of my overactive imagination. A dream caused by too much reading and not enough sleeping. But what if he suffered while I did nothing?

I turned and ran, as quietly as I could, through my room, down the stairs, and finally out the back door. The dew-covered grass beneath my feet reminded me of my state of undress. The nightgown felt thinner and more revealing than what my father had intended when he approved its purchase.

I shivered, not with cold but with nerves. The flames of the burning man sputtered and cooled, revealing charred bones and hunks of flesh. Yet he moved and groaned.

I sank to my knees, horrified that God would be so merciless as to let this poor human being endure such misery. The scent of cooked meat triggered my gag reflex. Strips of bumpy, burned flesh covered his bones here and there, but . . . his eyes . . . his eyes remained whole and lucid, giving him the garish appearance of a Halloween corpse.

The smell of sulfur stung my nose, making it hard to breathe. Yet the burning man continued to rasp and sputter.

How could he? His lungs had been incinerated.

For the first time, I noticed I still held the phone. Stupid girl. I should have dialed 911 a long time ago. I'd just pressed the 9 when he spoke.

"Don't bother."

I whimpered at the sound of his raspy, inhuman voice. "You need an ambulance."

The skeleton gurgled a bit, the sound grating and raw. "Too . . . late. I don't have much time."

He shouldn't have had *any* time. I looked to the sky, but there was no sign of smoke or anything else falling. He groaned again.

"I . . . I'm sorry." Lame, stupid girl. "I don't know what to do. I . . . wish I could make you more comfortable."

"You must be so frightened." He whispered now, slowly yet with a carefully measured cadence. "I'm sorry you had to see this."

How could he worry about my comfort right now? "Do you want to . . . um . . . pray or something?"

"No."

His answer came too quickly, too vehemently.

"You'll stay?" he asked—no, implored. "I have no right to ask it of you, but . . . I'm afraid to be alone right now. Will you stay . . . until . . ."

"Of course."

Moisture from the cold, wet grass seeped into the material of my nightgown, promising ugly stains in the virginal white shroud. I already felt the weight of yet another of Father's disappointments.

"Do you want me to ring anyone for you? To say good-bye?"

"There . . . is . . . no . . . one." His whisper weakened with each word.

No one to mourn him? I forced myself to look him, death, in the eyes, and leaned closer, blocking out the revulsion of his grotesque appearance. His last vision should be of someone caring that he died. Someone mourning him. He raised his bony fingers as if to touch me and I steeled myself not to flinch as his hand, still smoldering, neared my face.

He rattled and spoke his last words. "Worth . . . the . . . fall."

His hand dropped, and the grass sizzled beneath it.

Then his body turned to dust, leaving only a blackened scorch mark on my father's lawn.

I rolled away from the sunlight streaming through my lace curtains and burrowed my head under the pillow. It was a dream. It must have been. Burning men don't fall from the sky. Skeletons don't speak one minute and turn to dust the next.

I rubbed the sleep from my eyes and stared at the ceiling. I was going to have to look. Resigned, I walked the distance from my bed to the window, and it seemed to stretch farther and farther away, the way things do in nightmares. I touched the glass first—it was cool, of course. My fingers splayed on the window and I leaned into it, looking down, hoping to find the perfectly manicured lawn I'd known just yesterday. But the perfection was marred and the grass seared where he'd lain. The burning man.

My heartbeat sputtered and restarted, thumping wildly and faltering with its own rhythm. My mind raced to find an explanation that didn't include a fiery cadaver with scary eyes and a lonely soul.

What kind of . . . people . . . fell from the sky? Aliens? Fallen angels? Skydivers?

Maybe his plane crashed. But none of that explained his ability to talk with no lungs . . . or skin, or organs, or . . . No. I must have dreamt it. There was no other explanation. Best to put it out of my mind. Nightmares had no control over me and there was nothing to fear.

Besides, nothing happens in sleepy towns like Serendipity Falls. That's why Father bought a house here. His commute to the city wasn't bad, a half hour unless the fog blanketed us in. He did whatever it was barristers do in their offices all day and made it home for supper almost every evening.

He'd chosen this town precisely for its lack of drama, I reassured myself as I grabbed my pink robe off the hook. What devilry ever befell a girl in a counterfeitly cheerful Victorian house? Surely the heavy cornices and gingerbread trim were wards against all things evil.

It wasn't until I turned on the bathroom light that I remembered what day it was.

The familiar numbness that got me through this day every year painted itself over me. One foot in front of the other, one routine, then the next, lather, rinse, repeat. I'd go downstairs, drink my orange juice, take a vitamin, walk to school. It was just a day, after all.

Father would already be gone to his San Francisco office. It was easier that way, at least in the morning. Not having to face each other meant not having to acknowledge the significance of the day, this day.

The anniversary of my mother's death.

I struggled with my hair. The wild curls preferred to be loose and resisted the taming of elastic bands or clips. The wildness of my mane—a curse, according to my father, who'd tried unsuccessfully to convince me that I should style it shorter and sleeker—was a gift from my mother. The wildness of my heart was yet another unwanted motherly inheritance. Father tried to convince me that I should live carefully, and the struggle to rein in my spirit, as well as my hair, kept me battle-weary day after day.

Wanting to please Father, I always pushed back my impulses. He needed me. Sure, he could be gruff and impossibly strict, but I was all he had. Things would have been different if my mother hadn't died, but there was no sense going down that road. Especially today.

I sprinted down the stairs and then chastised myself for the recklessness since Father wasn't there to do it for me. I took the vitamin he'd left out, drank the juice he'd poured, and ate the biscuit—I mean cookie—only after I'd first double-checked that he'd actually left, and then made sure no stray crumbs would give me away. I avoided the greeting card left on the center of the polished table for as long as I could.

My hands shook as I opened our one exception to completely ignoring that this day existed.

> *Happy 17th Birthday, Theia.*
> *Love, Father*

I put the card in my pack, grabbed a sweater, and walked to school.

Nobody at Serendipity High extended me birthday wishes because that was the way I wanted it. My friends, now that I had them, shot surreptitious glances at me all day, but respected my request. I was lucky for their friendship; my life had been so different only four years ago, when we had first moved to the States.

Life in London had been even lonelier. Our estate had been a cold place, steeped in Alderson history but not love, not laughter.

After all the years of homeschooling with a stodgy tutor, I had been surprised that Father had given in and allowed me to attend a public school when we moved to America. Surprised and grateful, until I realized that the strange girl with a funny accent was not going to be welcomed easily into a small school with cliques already firmly in place.

Everything about me was different from my American peers, starting, but certainly not ending, with my accent. Not having spent much time with my British peers either, I was as awkward as a foal taking its first steps when it came to interacting.

"Earth to Thei."

I blinked at Donny across the cafeteria table. "Sorry. What were you saying?"

Donny—Donnatella to those who dared call her that—rolled her eyes and stole another Tater Tot from my lunch tray. "I asked if you had figured out your prison-break plans for this weekend."

Father preferred I not spend much time with Donny. Which, when I was being honest with myself, I realized was part of the appeal. Donny was irreverent and maybe a little wild.

Okay, make that a lot wild. Why she wanted to be friends with me, a girl who worked so hard at being completely boring, was a mystery. Whenever I asked, she would reply with a comment about liking my hoity-toity accent, and then she'd wink at me mischievously. She'd taken me under her wing during a particularly bad experience in my PE class that first year, and I would do anything for her.

Donny's family was the kind I used to dream about. They lived in a much smaller house, but it was a lively, almost-too-loud house. Someone was always laughing . . . or yelling. It was never quite clean, but there were always good things to eat and someone to listen to how your day was. I even envied her for her little brother, as mischievous and destructive as he was, and for her parents, who didn't put up with much but did it with a sense of humor.

Also, I envied how comfortable she was in her body. A couple inches taller than me, mostly due to her legs, Donny exuded this aura of confidence about her appearance that I would never have. Everything she wore was chosen carefully, as if to exhibit her assets. Her brown hair was layered around her face to draw attention to high cheekbones, and the part was on the side, accentuating her proud forehead. She always wore earrings that peeked out when her hair moved—a whisper that there was more to see if you took the time to look.

"Why is it so important that I go to this club with you?" I asked. Donny was very social, whereas I was not. She often had her own plans on the weekend that didn't include me, and I was more than okay with that.

"Because you need to get out more. I swear to God, you are going to explode one day if you don't vent a little wickedness now and then. Does your father know what happens to daughters of overly uptight and strict parents when they get their first taste of freedom at college?"

"No, what?"

"*Girls Gone Wild*, that's what."

The thought of me flashing my breasts to a camera in exchange for a trucker hat made us laugh so hard we couldn't breathe. The funniest part was that we both knew Donny would do it for a stick of gum.

Our third musketeer, Amelia, joined us as the giggling

subsided. As usual, she was dressed in what Donny liked to call "rebellious goth." Ame liked the alternative styles of the emo/goth kids—but she hated black and dark colors. Instead, she looked like a rainbow with skull and spider accessories. "What's the laughing about, or do I want to know?"

"You don't. Trust me." Donny patted the bench next to her. "Ame, help me convince Theia that she needs to cut loose with us this weekend." She bit the tip of her pizza, the cheese stretching a mile before breaking. Only Donny could make that sexy. When I ate pizza, I cut it into bite-size pieces.

Ame unpacked her lunch from the reusable tie-dyed sack she brought every day—she was very conscious of her carbon footprint. "Theia, if you don't cut loose with us this weekend, I will have to listen to Donny bitch about you all night and it won't be any fun at all. *And* I won't have anyone to talk to when she ditches me for the first pretty boy who comes along. You have to come."

Amelia wasn't joking. Donny really enjoyed her pretty boys. Amelia, on the other hand, had pined hopelessly for the same bloke since he'd moved to our school in seventh grade, the same year I did. She'd been stuck in "just a chum" purgatory for four years, but refused to tell him how she felt or give any other boy the time of day.

Ame carried herself differently from Donny. Donny was catlike and slinky, while Ame was more like a happy puppy. She bounced a lot and used her whole body when she spoke. She was also beautiful, but you couldn't tell her that.

Now that Amelia had let her hair grow back to the shiny black-brown it was naturally, and not the brittle blond she'd been trying to keep it, Donny and I both felt like she was the prettiest of all three of us. Amelia, however, saw only flaws with the features we thought made her exotic and outstanding.

Ame was born in Korea and adopted by a family perhaps even whiter than my own. Most of the time, I think she handled the diversity well. Sometimes she acted like we didn't see her wishing away her heritage. Other times, though, she talked about going to Korea someday, not so much to find her birth parents but just to walk where her roots had once been.

But when it was just the three of us together, roots were never an issue.

Donny put her hands together as if in prayer. "Pwetty please, say you'll come with us on Friday. You will love this club. It's the only under-eighteen club I've ever been to that didn't make me worry about our generation. It's actually fun. And not lame."

"I have nothing to wear to a dance club." And I didn't. Father's personal shopper chose my wardrobe according to a strict outline of recommendations—none of which included anything that would be suitable for dance clubs.

"I have your outfit all picked out," Donny answered a little too gleefully. "Oh, yeah, and Sandra Dee called; she'd like her sweater sets back."

That was low, but not wrong. Father's shopper believed thinking outside of the box meant three-quarter sleeves in place of long ones. And I have bottoms in every shade of khaki ever made. You know, for my wacky, carefree days.

All the same, Donny was not to be trusted as a replacement for the shopper. "Your clothes won't fit me, Donny. Your legs are a mile longer than mine."

"All the better to wrap around a boy with. Speaking of—"
She paused so Amelia and I could groan.

Donny really was certifiably boy crazy. I had no such aspi-
rations. Aside from my accent and "strange" English ways, my
real boy problem had less to do with my looks and more to do
with my upbringing. As in: Father says no. I'd been segregated
from boys my whole life, not allowed to have coed parties even
as a child. And dating was out of the question.

I was untouchable.

He just wanted me to be safe, and he worried that boys
would make me reckless and distract me from my music
studies—which were far more important to him than they
were to me.

I love the violin, truly I do, but I'll admit to sometimes
being bored by all the work involved in maintaining my skill
level. However, musical proficiency is important.

To Father.

It didn't matter to him that I was beginning to feel less
joy in the music. The more he pushed, the less I cared. In fact,
I preferred playing modern music but could do so only when
he wasn't home. Because modern music wasn't respectable. It
didn't pay tribute to the deep roots of my family tree.

Aldersons were to be the best at whatever they did. Father
proved that daily at his workplace, or so I heard from his col-
leagues at the picnics every summer. His company had trans-
ferred him twice to the States to fix its sorrier offices—once
the year he met my mother, and again when I was thirteen. He
was also unbeatable at racquetball and sailing. I was to follow
in the grand tradition of all the Aldersons before me and excel.

Whether I wished to or not.

Donny continued, ignoring our groans. "My sources in the admin office tell me we are getting fresh meat tomorrow. All the way from New York City. God, I hope he's cute. We need new cute at this school."

Amelia picked at her salad. She hated salad but was on what Donny dubbed a foreverdiet. "We only need *new* cute because you have exhausted the population of *already-here* cute. Take it easy on the new guy, will you?"

"He's probably a sneetch anyway," Donny said.

"Sneetches" was what we called the in-crowd at school, the haves as opposed to the have-nots. We named them from a Dr. Seuss story in which the Star-Belly Sneetches, who were born with a green star on their bellies, thought they were better than all those who had no green star—or in this case green money.

By current standards, I possessed all the right accoutrements to be a sneetch, except the ones that would have made me want to be one. Much to my father's dismay, the children of his business associates and fellow golf club members were not the chosen brethren of his daughter. Of course, he never helped me get accepted, since he resolutely shielded me from their activities and social situations, but try telling him that.

Donny pulled out her compact, checking for nonexistent damage before fourth period. "Amelia, if you tell me you want the new guy, sneetch or not, I'll stay away from him. But you have to promise to actually talk to him. Not just pine from afar. Reruns are boring."

"I'm not even remotely interested in the new guy, but thanks for the offer. I know how hard that must have been for you."

Donny started on me next, but I held up my hand. "Halt. I am not remotely interested in the new bloke we haven't seen yet either." On a whim, I asked them both, "Did either of you hear anything about a plane crash last night? Or maybe a meteorite?"

"Did you have dreams about aliens probing your secret places, Thei?" Donny asked, again much too gleefully.

"No, I— Never mind."

The bell rang, reminding me that my fourth-period class was on the other side of campus, but at least it smelled better than the cafeteria. We had to wait for a pack of sneetches, several of them in cheerleader uniforms, to file past our table. As per their social custom, they made no eye contact with those of us without *stars upon thars*.

When one of the varsity basketball players tried to pass without even seeing us, Donny drew the line. "Hey, Bill, did I ever tell you how much it meant to me that you made sure my needs were still met that one time you couldn't get it up? That makes you a real gentleman."

Of course, Bill did no such thing. Oh, he really did have a problem—but he left Donny to finish things for herself when he didn't bring his A-game.

He grunted, someone muttered, "Bitch," and all was right in our world.

By the end of the evening, I was wiped out. I practiced for two hours after school with my new tutor, who knew within ten minutes that I was better than he was. So, like anyone with an overinflated sense of self, he punished me with futile exercises and extra practice time.

Dinner was a somber affair, as usual. Muriel, our house-keeper and cook, tried to sneak in a cakelike dessert to appease her own guilt at my lack of birthday celebration, and Father read his paper throughout the meal, stopping to tell me to "Sit up straight" and "Stop fidgeting so much."

"Father," I began cautiously, "I'd like to spend the week-end at Donny's."

"We'll see," he answered. And that was the end of the discussion.

I'm not sure how my mother could have fallen in love with him. He was so cold. And worse, I think he was trying to make sure I turned out as icily perfect as he was. Sometimes I felt the crystals forming inside, etching a pattern of frost on my heart, and I thought it would be easier to follow his path than diverge from it. If I was careful and cautious, dutiful and obedient, perhaps I could stop the wayward longings I had. The ones where I thought, *There has to be more.* More than this uncomfortable silence at a table too large for the two people who ate here every night.

But if there was more, Father wanted none of it. He re-tired to his study and I retired to my fancy decorated cell, finished my homework, looked at my violin and considered playing it for an hour, and then put myself to bed with no hope of falling asleep.

But fall asleep I did. I think. And that was when every-thing got worse.

CHAPTER TWO

I awoke in the dark yard, kneeling in the dewy grass near the site of the burning man without any recollection of leaving the house.

Father would be irate to find me outside in only my nightgown in the middle of the night. This impulsive behavior was what he'd been guarding me against all my life. He'd bellow and grumble and tell me I would end up just like my mother. And then, as soon as the harsh words escaped his mouth, he would regret them and walk away. A new necklace or tickets to the ballet would appear on my vanity table the next day.

Father was nothing if not predictable.

A fog had rolled in, displacing the sense of familiarity of my own backyard. Though it was the dead of night, the moon glow dappled the trees, creating longer shadows than I remembered.

And there was music.

The muted strains of orchestral music captured my interest because they weren't coming from the house, but from deeper on the grounds. My father's yard was vast, and his only in that he directed the workers to its upkeep. Father didn't sully his hands with the soil, yet spent much of his time inspecting the lawn for flaws.

The grass and I had a lot in common.

Though we lived in the Bay Area, the grounds looked distinctly British, just as my father liked it. The lawn surrounding our stark white home was a passion—the only one he'd allowed himself. The hedgerow alone took hours of shaping by his workers. Interspersed like hidden Easter eggs were special English roses he'd had cultivated. They weren't very hardy and didn't often make it, but some were still there—you just had to look hard to find them.

I kept walking. The closer I got to the music, the stranger the surroundings became. They may have been the same plants and shrubs I'd grown up with, but the shadows distorted their shapes and made them ominous. I'd never noticed how many thorns the garden had—or how the vines twisted and held the lattice in a stranglehold.

I began taking shallower breaths and my heart beat faster and faster.

No matter how far I went towards the music, I got no closer. It always seemed "just over here" a little more, and I carried on farther and farther until I realized I was in a maze of shrubbery. A labyrinth.

Only there shouldn't have been one on the grounds.

Turn back. But it was too late. I tried, but the path changed as I walked and I had the sensation that I was walking towards the middle of the maze instead of back to my house no matter what I did.

The haunting strains of an unfamiliar melody filtered through the branches. My trained ear picked the musicians out to be a quartet. The tune captured a gothic mood and was rising to a crescendo when I arrived at a gazebo alight in candles.

I should be panicking. Yet the pull was so strong that like a moth to flame I carried on.

Cautiously, I made my way up the steps. The candles were tied to thorny branches, eerie yet beautiful. I rubbed my arms, but the shivers continued. A nightgown was little protection.

"I'd always hoped you'd come, but I didn't dare expect you."

My breath hitched at the masculine voice. I whirled towards it instead of away, like a smart girl would have done.

The young man bowed deeply. "Theia."

He wore an old-fashioned gray suit, with tails on the jacket and a black cravat pinned with a symbol I didn't recognize. His dark hair was thick and looked so soft I had to resist the urge to touch it. Looking into his dark eyes was like falling into the stars, making me feel weightless and disoriented.

"Who are you?" I asked, at odds and embarrassed that he was dressed so formally while I was dressed for bed.

"I'm so happy you've come," he answered. "Now the celebration can commence."

I stole another look at him. He was taller than me and the cut of his jacket could have distorted his figure, but I didn't think it did. Broad shoulders and a tapered waist, like that of an athlete. His face was perfect . . . but not. Unearthly, yet beautiful.

He clapped his hands twice, and the spans of green grass surrounding the gazebo ignited instantly with candelabras and torches, illuminating what appeared to be a party in progress.

A jeweled pewter goblet was thrust into my hand, and I surveyed the scene in wonder. Tables sheeted in red and black cloths were laden with food and drink. The revelers, costumed in silk and lace, smiled garishly at one another and carried on muted conversations without moving their lips, their faces made up like those of lurid clowns.

The orchestral quartet drew my gaze as they started a haunting new song similar to the one that had led me to the gazebo. But it wasn't the song that held my attention. It was their appearance. Much like the man standing next to me, they were dressed formally—black tuxedos and top hats. But where their faces should have been, instead they bore only flesh with no features.

I gasped in horror. "What is happening?"

I turned to my host, and his face clouded briefly with what looked like regret. Quickly, he returned his debonair mask over his features. "You look lovely."

I wanted to scream or cry with frustration. I was frightened by what I was seeing, what I was feeling, but instead I answered, "Thank you."

He smiled and it was beautiful and horrible what I saw in it. Hope that should not be born and desire that could never bear fruit. Whether they were my feelings or his, I did not know.

My fingers relaxed on the stem of the goblet and it slipped

through my hands. In slow motion, the cup fell to the ground, spilling bloodred liquid throughout its descent.

I awoke in my bed, my nightgown stained red.

I leaned against the lockers waiting for Amelia to fetch her binder. I was so tired they needed to make a new word for tired. Every time I blinked, I swore the backs of my eyelids were made of sandpaper.

Being friends with Donny, who worked in the admin office and *knew* things, also meant Ame and I got lockers in the Main instead of over the hill and dale where other juniors floundered between classes. It was auspicious considering that usually only seniors and sneetches were able to snag the coveted location.

The Main was really the *old* high school—a two-story brick monster. Several decades ago, they expanded the campus, adding buildings that made it really hard to get to class on time because they were spaced so far apart. The closer you were to your senior year, the more classes you had in the Main. Also housed in the Main were the library, admin services, the student store, and the student lounge—aka Sneetch Central—in the corridor outside the library.

"I have play practice after school tomorrow if you want to come over after," Ame said, then stopped. "You're really pale. Are you sure you're okay?"

Nodding, I pushed off the bank of lockers. "I just haven't slept well the last two nights."

She dug in her pocket and handed me a quartz crystal. "This one restores energy. If you can keep it on your skin, it will work better."

I nodded, pretending I believed her.

"I'm serious," she said, reading my ambivalence. "I even bathed it in the healing powers of the waterfalls."

I didn't want to patronize her, really I didn't. But I didn't believe all the stuff about the "mystical" waterfalls like she did.

Our town, Serendipity Falls, was named for the nearby waterfalls of the same name. They were our town treasure— our tourist bait. Not only were they gorgeous, but there were several old legends attached to them, enchantment being one of them. Water nymphs, healing powers, love potions—the pool fed by the cascading water was said to have all that and more.

"Put the crystal in your bra," she suggested, knowing I would do no such thing. "How are things with your dad?"

"Same as always, I guess."

Amelia always felt it was incredibly sad the way my father overcompensated for my lack of a mother. She made excuses for his irrational behavior based on his losing his one true love. I guess she's the romantic of our trio. Donny pretty much thought my father was the devil. It never occurred to me to think of him one way or the other. Father was who he was.

My mind wandered back to my strange dreams from the last two nights. They were, of course, dreams. Though I wouldn't rule out sleepwalking, as I now had two ruined nightgowns that proved I'd been outside. Which was really disturbing. I thought maybe I should ask Father's secretary to make me a doctor's appointment. Sleepwalking outside was dangerous.

As we walked down the hall, I pulled the band out of my hair to ease my growing headache and finger-combed my curls. As we passed the windows of the admin office, time blurred into slow motion. I shivered and a rush of cold seeped into the marrow of my bones as if someone had just stepped on my grave. And danced on it as well.

It was him.

He'd traded his coat and tails for jeans and a tight Abercrombie and Fitch tee, but it was him. I would have known him anywhere.

I blinked slowly, believing he was a mirage. A very handsome mirage. But I didn't have the power to dream cute boys into life. When he didn't disappear, part of my heart sang and part of it worried that I'd never be the same again.

He looked right into my eyes. He didn't smile, but he didn't drop his gaze either. Life carried on around us, but we were trapped in a different moment than the rest of the students in the crowded hall and office. The noisy corridor suddenly quieted, like someone had clicked the MUTE button. Though he didn't physically move, I *felt* him take a bow, deeply, like he had the night before.

Oh, I never would be the same again.

His presence in my waking world stirred all my senses. Still in slow motion, I kept walking, warmed wherever his eyes touched me. When I finally dropped eye contact, the world caught up with me—or the other way around.

Ame grabbed my arm. "Are you all right? You look like you've seen a ghost."

"Please keep walking," I squeaked.

She slung a protective arm around me and ushered me into the nearest bathroom. I slumped against the wall, trying to catch my breath, but my lungs didn't want to work, and I exhaled when I should have inhaled.

"What is wrong with you? Do you need the nurse? Should I call your dad?"

I shook my head, which did nothing for my already poor balance. "No. I just need a minute."

The door burst open and the surge of energy that always followed Donny came in with her. "Oh, my God. Tell me you saw him. He is undeniably . . . hey . . . what's wrong?"

Amelia answered. "She just freaked out. It was the weirdest thing. We were walking down the hall and everything was fine. Then she—"

"You saw him, right?" My voice sounded foreign to me—desperate. I still wasn't breathing right. "The boy in the office? He was really there?"

"The smokin' new guy? Yeah, I saw him—" Donny's face lit up. "Oh, wow! Finally you get the hots for someone. I was beginning to think you might sway the other direction, if you know what I mean. This is great. I mean, I'm a little perturbed that I don't get him first—but, you know, I'm willing to sacrifice one boy for the greater good if it means you'll finally get laid."

"You are the opposite of classy, Donny." Amelia was still rubbing my arm. "Is that what this was about? Love at first sight?" Ever the romantic.

"Oh, Jesus, Ame." Donny opened her purse, pulling out makeup. To me, she said, "We are going to get a little color back on your face and then you are going to talk to Hottie McTightPants before some other ho snags him."

"Wait. There's more. . . ." Ame and Donny exchanged glances, worried glances. I guess I was being a touch dramatic, but who wouldn't be? "I had this really weird dream last night. And *he* was in it."

"You dreamt about him. Oh, that's wonderful. You're so lucky." Amelia practically swooned. "It's like a fairy tale."

"You're so retarded." Donny thrust her purse at Ame and pushed her to the side so she could grab both my shoulders. "Tell me all about the dream. Was he kinky?"

"No, he wasn't kinky. Well, maybe he was—I don't know, he was kind of weird . . . but you're missing the point. I dreamt about him *before* I saw him."

Amelia was going to need a chair. "That's so amazing. Maybe you knew each other in a former life and you just now found each other again." Amelia wasn't just a romantic; she was also a metaphysical junkie. Tarot cards, dream interpretation, crystals, past-life regression—if it made it to the shelf of the metaphysical bookstore, Ame was a rapt pupil.

Donny wasn't fazed by my revelation—or Ame's. "He's probably been in town a day or two before he started school. Maybe you saw him when we were getting gelato or something."

I exhaled and the tension whooshed from my body. "You're right. I'm sure you're right." That made much more sense than dreaming up a guy from thin air. Which reminded me of the burning man, and suddenly I felt not good again. "I feel like my life has taken a turn for the strange."

Donny was applying blusher to my cheeks even though I tried to move my head away from it. "Stop squirming. Deciding you like boys doesn't mean your life is getting strange. It means you're finally growing into your hormones. Let's go out there and get him, tiger."

She and Amelia each grabbed an arm and took me into the hall, despite my dragging feet. Once we got to the office, my heart plummeted. He was surrounded by students—two of them cheerleaders, one of them holding his new schedule, obviously ready to show him to his class. As much as I hated to admit it, he looked natural at the center of the beautiful people.

"Oh, God," Amelia said, scrunching her face. "He's crawling with sneetches."

How long could my heart keep falling? It just dropped further and further, turning everything around me to a shade of gray. "It doesn't matter." I said it, but I didn't mean it.

Everything about him suddenly mattered very much to me. Too much. The hole where my heart used to be ached. I didn't think I'd ever seen anyone so attractive. I willed his dark eyes to look at me. I wanted to pull the other girls off him and be the only girl he shared that smile with. I wanted to know his dreams, his secrets . . . his name.

Donny gave me a little squeeze. "I'm as morally opposed to the sneetches as you guys are—but let's cut him a little slack. He's new—he doesn't know how vile they are. Plus they probably descended on him like a pack of wolves on a rabbit."

At that moment, the rabbit looked up and right into my eyes. He wasn't helpless prey. Far from it. His eyes were nearly black and made him look more dangerous than any predator in the forest. An involuntary shiver racked my body—he actually smiled at my reaction. It wasn't a happy smile, or even a pleasant one. It was an expression of pride, like he'd accomplished a strategic move on the chessboard. Or maybe trapped Bambi in a corner.

I became spoils of the hunt.

Even as he looked at me, he looked through me. And then he put his arm around a sneetch and whispered something in her ear without dropping his gaze from mine.

And I felt it.

I gasped at the sensation. As surely as if I were the one standing next to him, I felt his breath against my face, hottest near my ear.

He watched her.

Theia didn't move like the other students. She considered every movement carefully, as if she was concerned that her body might do something without her. Like she was always reining something in.

The kind of control he would never have.

She dropped books off at her locker, glancing over her shoulder occasionally. No doubt she felt his presence. He checked his impulse to get her attention. He didn't know if he could stand another interlude like the one this morning. Not without losing control.

He half hoped she would untether her hair again. The amber and honey curls were such a contradiction to her carefulness. They caught the light, spinning the colors in a whirling dervish of caramel and brown sugar.

Instead, she left the band around her ringlets, pulling the hair tautly away from her oval face. Her eyebrows were highly arched over her wary eyes, eyes the color of slate. The depth of her eye color changed with her emotions. Sometimes her eyes reminded him of the seas violent with storm. Other times they were as gray as a cemetery headstone.

He closed his eyes. Whatever had made him think coming here was a good idea abandoned him just as surely as his good sense had. Last night had been a mistake. One he hoped he'd be strong enough not to make again. She had no place in his world, just as he had no place in hers.

He hung back but kept her in his sights, wishing that his weakness didn't make him feel like a common stalker. Even that would have been better for her than he was. Safer.

There were things to be done and his purpose was clear. He couldn't afford this distraction; the price would be more than he could bear, and it wouldn't be his alone.

For her sake, he needed to end this dalliance quickly. If she hated him, all the better.

But still he watched her. The heart that he wasn't supposed to have blossomed in his chest, reaching for her even though the rest of him knew it could never be. Would never be.

His carefully planned strategy had changed because of her. He would spend his last breath making sure he never tainted the one true thing he'd ever really known.

The usual silence of dinner with Father had given me the opportunity to push my food around my plate listlessly and relive the moment when the new boy, whose name turned out to be Haden Black, touched me without touching me. No matter how hard I tried to put it out of my mind, the feel of his breath against my ear as he whispered to another girl kept me riveted to the same memory, over and over. The way he looked at me while he did it . . . I could have sworn he knew what he did to me.

Even as he frightened me, he intrigued me.

Thankfully, he had been easily avoided for the rest of the day. We had only one class together and our desks were on opposite sides of the room. Not that I hadn't been hyperaware of him, but at least I couldn't see him.

Father took a business call at the table. He rarely did that. Sometimes when I watched him talk to strangers, I noticed he didn't look so much like my father. With me, he carried himself so severely, so guarded.

When he spoke on the phone, even though he was businesslike, he relaxed. His features softened. His brown eyes warmed. My father had impeccable taste in clothes, his hair, though thinning, still had a bit of wave and only a little gray, and I always thought his hands were almost elegant the way he used them in conversation. But it was only when he wasn't talking to me that I thought he might actually be a handsome man.

"Please pass the carrots," I said when he finished his call.

Father shot me a perplexed glance as he handed me the bowl. For all our estrangement, he knew my eating habits, and carrots were never my favorite. Mostly I just wanted a reason to interact with him.

"Thank you."

"Hmmm," he answered.

Perhaps it was the lack of sound sleep that clouded my judgment, but a small ball of anger fizzed in my chest at the way he treated me, and I wanted to provoke him into something—anything—besides this stoic cordial acquaintance association we had. So I asked, "Did my mother like carrots?"

He reacted, like I'd known he would, as if I had slapped his face. Shock paled his skin, and then red replaced it. "What does it matter what kind of food your mother preferred?" He punctuated each word with a punch of mettle. Father didn't appreciate things that came out of nowhere.

"I just . . . I just want to know her better."

He'd recovered himself and masked his face in cool indifference once again. "I loved your mother, Theia. It pains me to talk about her. She did not like carrots, as I recall." Father wiped the corners of his mouth, though it wasn't necessary, as he ate with a precision that a surgeon would envy. "Your mother didn't like much that wasn't junk food."

I'd gotten that from her, my love of junk food. That made me smile.

Father pushed away from the table. "Perhaps if she'd learned to take better care of herself, you could be asking her these questions."

My smile was quickly replaced with a tug of longing at my heart. He'd known that would hurt. I deserved it, I suppose, for bringing her up. My mother was a forbidden subject unless to provide my father a cautionary tale in order to bring me to heel.

He blamed her for dying. I suspect he blamed me for killing her.

He left me sitting alone at the table, though I was no lonelier than I had been when he was still in the room.

I resolved to practice violin for an hour after dinner. I promised myself an hour of whatever I wanted to play instead of what had been prescribed for me to practice. Getting lost in music meant I wouldn't have to think about my father, the burning man, my strange dream, or Haden Black.

As a child, I took to music quickly and with what seemed

to everyone else very little effort. I could never explain to them that the hard part of playing the violin was not the notes or the finger placement, or even the calluses. It was the pieces of me I had to sacrifice when I pulled the songs out. When I played for myself, I belonged to the song, and the song became the *real* Theia. Without a tutor or an audience, my own world opened up. A world richer than the one where I lived. A place where I didn't feel bound to expectations or fault. When I played for others, the opposite was true. The songs I played for them weren't to unlock my world; instead, I disappeared in a way, and was able to open up theirs.

It was a heady thing, to be told as a child that I touched people so deeply. Strangers. I'd been told I was gifted, but so often it seemed that what I was given was a gift for others.

And so I used to long for the time alone with my violin, to escape and release the girl I wanted to be from her captivity inside the girl I really was. Used to. Lately, I no longer felt compelled to make my own music, but the last two days had wearied me. I needed a holiday from me.

As the sun sank into the horizon, I played from memory the melancholy tune that had lured me into the labyrinth the night before. I'd chosen the sunroom off the kitchen, with the wicker furniture and ferns, because it had the best view of the setting sun; I'd chosen the song without realizing I'd done so until I'd been playing for ten minutes.

By then, I also realized I was crying. Real tears rolled down my cheeks, plopping onto my violin, but I didn't stop playing. The song took root inside of me, like an invasion. Each note I played felt like I was searching for something; if I could whittle to the core of the song I would have it. Yet the more I played, the more mysterious and elusive whatever I was searching for became.

As I played, I became one with the song and unburdened of my life. The further I reached for the tune, the more the world fell away. Suddenly, I walked through the hedges and smelled the night air. A waking dream. Part of me knew I was still in the house, but part of me had been set free.

I stepped on a twig and it snapped beneath my foot. The noise startled the birds that had been hiding in the hedge and hundreds of black-and-white doves ascended from their perches at once. The sound of the multitudes taking flight thundered deep in my ears, and the mass of the birds covered the moonlight. Leaving me in the dark.

I covered my head and crouched low, trying to shield myself from the swarm. The lack of light disoriented me and chilled the evening by several degrees. That the moonlight was warm in my dream struck me as odd. My heartbeat accelerated and so did the song. It got faster and faster until the sound made me dizzy.

"Theia, stop at once!"

I was back in the sunroom, sweat pouring off my body. My father stood in the door, bellowing at me to stop playing.

I couldn't pull myself out of it, even though he bade me stop. My whole body jerked, and what I played sounded more like noise than music, but I couldn't stop. Faster, faster. I must have looked like I was having a seizure. My violin started to smoke—that was when Father crossed the room and forced my arm still.

"Theia, what the hell are you doing?" He wrenched the instrument from my hand and I slumped into the chair.

I couldn't answer him. I couldn't even be sure I was really in the room with him. I'd been possessed by something. Something unforgiving in its quest to take over my life.

My father stared at me for a few seconds. I wonder what he saw, what he thought. I'm sure my face was flushed and my eyes were wild. A person doesn't play an instrument so fast that it begins to smoke without her appearance changing too.

Maybe I'd imagined the smoke—it couldn't really do that, could it?

I met his eyes.

"Theia," he began, and then guarded his face again. "For heaven's sake, sit up straight."

And he left the room.

CHAPTER THREE

T hat night, the labyrinth wasn't a hedge of green, but instead walls of twisted branches barbed with thorns, and no signs of vegetation . . . or life. The gnarled, sharp sticks were plaited together so tightly that no light poked through the walls, but some of the sticks stuck out and scraped my skin if I passed too close.

A new song pierced the night air. In the thrall of the music there was no escape, not for me, but still I walked slowly, each step carefully choreographed, wary of stirring up anything like the birds I'd encountered earlier. I wrapped my arms around myself, with no other protection from the chill or the razor-sharp branches. I didn't really want to be there. My fascination with Haden Black notwithstanding, the nocturnal adventures scared me. I shouldn't have been so lucid if I were only dreaming. And if I were sleepwalking outside, I worried I could really hurt myself.

I think Father knew all along that I had the capacity for this kind of trouble. That must be why he'd always tried to tamp down my natural inclination towards being free-spirited like my mother. Maybe he was right to try and stifle this predilection—just look what I'd done when left to my own devices.

The lure of the maze's center pulled me too strongly to be denied, like an echo of my own heartbeat. When I reached the clearing, I searched for my host—half hoping and half dreading his reappearance. On a dais, the same faceless quartet played their haunting, moody song. In front of them, a ballroom floor of sorts showcased pairs of ghoulish dancers. They were costumed in silks and lace, the ladies' hair in elaborate updos and cascading curls. The gentlemen, all very graceful, were also decked out in formal wear of black tuxedos with jewel-toned cummerbunds and ties.

But their faces . . . each was unique in a completely horrible way. Some were fleshless skeletons, bones with empty sockets. Others were worse, with one feature malformed or missing completely. Noses like beaks, mouths where noses should be, eyes set too far apart—and yet they danced beautifully, as if they were enchanting and not horrifying. As if it were perfectly normal that a gaping mouth should open to two sets of gnarled teeth.

I wished I could unsee the dancers and their morbid expressions. So far nobody had even glanced at me, a fact I was grateful for. Then the dancers parted as if invisible walls had moved them away from the middle.

Him.

My pulse pounded so hard, my skin rippled. I tried to breathe in deeper, but I couldn't fill my lungs with enough air.

It was as if he commanded all the oxygen, like a vacuum or a black hole. Around him, his cheerful ghouls danced merrily.

Tonight he wore a top hat, which he removed with a flourish when he bowed, reminding me of a wicked Mr. Darcy. He was definitely mischievous—and dangerous. Due to my strict upbringing, my etiquette was impeccable, so of course I curtsied in return and then felt stupid and childish.

The heaving of my chest suddenly embarrassed me. I didn't wear a bra to bed and his smile suggested that he could see that very well from his spot in the middle of the parquet floor. Crossing my arms over my chest would have been even more obvious, so instead I stood still. Very, very still.

I swallowed as he replaced his hat and slowly paraded past his morbid partiers. They smiled at him adoringly—at least it was similar to smiling—and quickly filled in the middle, never missing a step of their intricate waltz.

Haden stopped in front of me, the material of his formal black suit shimmering like the night sky. "Theia, a pleasure to have you in our company once again."

His voice caused rolling shivers up and down my spine. "Who are you?"

In response, he only smiled while his gaze roamed my body.

"I saw you today . . . at school."

He cocked his head. "Did you, now? Would you like to dance?"

He stepped towards me, and I instinctively moved back a step.

"No." I shook my head, and he laughed the way adults laugh when a child amuses them. Despite the chill in my bones, my skin flushed white-hot. "I don't . . . dance. I don't know how anyway."

"Then we shall teach you. You of all humans should be a wonderful dancer."

"Humans?"

"Forgive me. I slipped, didn't I?" He gave an exaggerated shrug. "Still, dancing will be natural to someone like you."

"What do you mean, someone like me?"

"I've heard your violin, Theia. It sings like an angel in your hands."

Had he been to a concert? Had I seen him before, and that was why I dreamt about him before I met him? Though that explanation seemed safer than any others I'd conjured, I knew it wasn't real. None of this would be explained by easy coincidence, and that knowledge made me shiver.

I swallowed around the fear that had settled like a ball in my throat. "Playing music and dancing to music are two different talents . . . Haden."

He pretended he didn't hear me say his name. "Nonsense. Two different instruments, perhaps."

"I'm not an instrument."

Haden stared at my lips until I felt them tingle. "You pluck music from your soul and feed it to your violin."

"But—"

He circled me. The heat that trailed him wrapped around me like ribbons, as did his scent. I tried to place the spice but couldn't name it.

The second time around, I followed him. As if there were a Maypole between us, we circled slowly, our eyes locked.

"Hold your arms out to the sides." I did his bidding without thought. "Look into my eyes and move with me," he commanded.

He didn't touch me like the other couples waltzing, yet he moved to the same steps they did, graceful and lithe. And I moved with him, tenuously at first. His eyes anchored my spirit to his, and my body followed along.

Still without touching, we relaxed our arms and faced each other palm to palm as we moved into the throng. The energy between our hands sparked, charging the air around us and causing the hair on the back of my neck to rise.

And I danced.

The sensation of my spirit's freedom should have overwhelmed me, undone me. But I danced. I didn't care that I wore a white cotton nightgown at a formal boogeyman ball. I didn't care that I danced with the devil. Instead of sensible fear, I rejoiced at the physical freedom I'd never known.

And I fed the music to my body.

It was not so different from when I lost myself in my songs, except that I felt it in more than my heart and head. My body felt so alive. I could feel the blood flowing through my veins, keeping rhythm with the percussion of the orchestra.

The menacing connection between Haden and me strengthened. As long as I looked into his eyes, I knew exactly where his next step would take me. My heart stuttered briefly, and when it regained its rhythm I knew it had synced its beat to his.

The expression on his face softened and appeared to me unguarded for the first time. "Did you feel that?" he whispered.

"Yes," I replied. How had I not seen how young he looked before? He was no older than me. And certainly not menacing.

"Don't." His curt voice cut into me as if he'd just called me a name.

"Don't what?"

"Don't fall under." He closed his eyes and turned his head away, breaking the link.

I tumbled through darkness, awakening in my own bed with a stranger's heart beating in my chest.

Amelia had a plan.

It was awful.

We'd been sitting at our usual bench in the cafeteria. As per unspoken custom, I'd given my sensible, nourishing, homemade lunch to Donny in exchange for her cafeteria hot lunch. She thought I was weird, but I never got to have greasy American food anywhere near my father.

And then, holding a folded piece of notebook paper in her hand, Ame blurted out her brand-new plot to hook Mike Matheny, the object of her undying love.

Donny grabbed said plan out of Ame's hands and looked at it in disgust. "What the hell is wrong with you?" Donny asked her. "Quit pretending you are seven and just go tell him you want to jump him. Stop messing around with notes."

Ame grabbed the paper back from Donny. "It's not a note. It's a poem. Everything is not about sex, you know. Haven't you ever wanted romance in your life?"

"Not if it means I tread the same three feet of water for four years." Donny and Amelia argued like an old married couple, but there was never any venom in it. That was part of their charm. Donny hugged Ame with one arm. "Sweetie, you know I adore you. You are beautiful, funny, and smart. Any guy would be lucky to have you. If Mike Matheny hasn't figured that out by now, he's not smart enough to be with you."

I hugged Amelia from the other side. "You really are beautiful, funny, and smart. And I really like your poem too."

"So you guys don't think I should give him the poem?"

Donny groaned and pretended to throw herself on the table and bang her head.

I squeezed Ame's shoulder. "We just think that passing him anonymous love notes—er . . . poems—is too . . . um . . . subtle."

She sighed and pulled her heavy braid over one shoulder so she could play with the ends of it. "Well, I like my plan." Each of her fingernails was painted a different color.

"Amelia, it's not a plan; it's a cop-out. Are you going to put boxes on it so he can check yes or no?" Donny hadn't lifted her head from the table, so her words were muffled.

"Oh, I'm sorry. I should totally take your advice and just throw myself at him. It works so well for you. Where's your boyfriend, Donny? Oh, that's right. You don't *have* a boyfriend."

Donny sat up. "If that was supposed to hurt, you missed. I don't want a boyfriend. Why buy the cow?"

"Huh?" I asked.

"Why buy the cow when you can get the milk for free. My grandma told me that when she didn't like how short my dress was in the prom pictures." Donny waggled her eyebrows at me. "I think she meant I was giving it away, but it works better for me this way."

"Ame, have we convinced you not to slip anonymous sonnets in his locker yet?" I wished she would just talk to him.

"No. Besides, you're one to talk."

My cheeks warmed. "What do you mean?"

"I couldn't help but notice you scoping the halls for fresh sneetch all day."

"I—"

"*He's* only been here two days," Donny answered for me. "Not his entire high school career. Nice try, Ame." She pinned me with a glance. "Not that you are off the hook either."

I stuck my tongue out at her.

Haden Black had proven to be very elusive today. I knew he was at school, and I knew every time he was near because the air around me would still, like the world was rearranging itself to accommodate him in it. I'd look up and catch a fleeting glimpse of him, and then the atmosphere would return to normal.

What I would do if I saw him was still a mystery. I mean, I'd dreamt he was some sort of ringmaster in a macabre circus. And that we waltzed without touching. And that our hearts beat as one.

I don't spend a lot of time talking to boys, but even I knew that was too much too soon.

Not to mention that I suspected that my dreams weren't dreams and that it really happened, and that weirdness was befalling me at every turn.

Eager to pretend that all was normal, I frowned at Ame's salad. "Do you want half my burger?"

She shook her head.

"You're not fat," I argued, getting my retort in before she had a chance to say hers.

"I'm not skinny either."

Amelia wasn't petite, not like her American mom, who wore a size two and was as blond as a supermodel. Ame still held on to a layer of baby fat that made her look utterly huggable to me, but to her it was the mark of total failure.

People gravitated to her because she was kind to everyone. She was also so much fun—quick to laugh and open to new ideas and experiences. There were a lot of boys who circled around her, smart enough to notice how she glowed, wanting to be close if she'd let them. She didn't seem to understand there could be potential for more than friendship with any of them. She only noticed Mike Matheny not noticing.

Ame's phone beeped. "Omigosh, I almost forgot," she said after she flipped it open. "I have a tarot reading tomorrow after school. You guys should totally come. Madame Varnie is supposed to be amazing. Maybe she could do all our cards."

"Madame Varnie? Are you serious? She sounds like someone you'd find in a circus tent." Donny didn't have much patience for Amelia's psychic readings. "I don't even understand why you go. Half the time you come back cheery from an *unfortunate* reading because they tell you your future isn't set in stone, so if it's bad, no worries. Why bother getting it read if it isn't necessarily accurate anyway?"

Ame sighed. "Because I like getting in touch with my intuition."

"But you're not," said Donny. "You're getting in touch with someone else's intuition with no promises of precision. Not to mention you could be saving the money you spend on fake intuition for your very real college tuition."

College tuition was a big worry for Donny. Her family couldn't exactly stash the money away for it every month.

"Hi, Donny." A sneetch in a letter jacket stood in front of our table. Willingly.

Ame's eyebrows were almost touching, she was grimacing so hard. "Gabe Erickson?"

Gabe smiled at Donny, his white teeth gleaming under the fluorescent cafeteria lighting. I wondered what he looked like in black light.

Donny very pointedly did not say "hi" back. She did stretch out her legs, plop her Uggs onto the bench, and yawn.

"I brought you this." He held out a paperback. Gabe's sandy brown hair lay in a perfect wave on his forehead like a commercial for the ideal teenaged boy.

"You brought me a book." Donny wrinkled her nose. "Why?"

"It's *Catcher in the Rye*," he explained.

"So?"

Gabe's flawless tan pinkened. "Well, I heard you say that you lost yours. And we need it for English. I had an extra copy." He pushed the book towards her again.

Donny looked at Ame and me for guidance, and we both shrugged. She exhaled loudly and took the book from him like she thought it might have teeth. "I wasn't planning on reading it anyway, but thanks. I guess."

He smiled.

She looked at us again when he didn't depart.

"I don't want to keep you from your important duties, Gabe. Don't you head up the swirly brigade? 'No freshman left behind' and all that?"

Gabe's smile faded. "No. I'm not . . . never mind. See you around."

Every now and then, Donny lets her vulnerable side show through the mask of derisiveness she usually wears. This wasn't one of those times. She kept up her front while she watched him walk away.

"That was weird," Ame said, a masterfully understated appraisal of the encounter.

"But nice," I added.

Donny glared at me. "Never trust a sneetch, little girl."

Obviously, U.S. history was not my strongest class. Though I was born in the United States, after my mother's death, Father and I returned to England until business brought him back when I was thirteen.

I tried to keep up but often got confused. I had to learn so much that the other students took for granted; so much of it was already part of their popular culture. And Father was the opposite of helpful when it came to anything American. Donny called him Ameriphobic.

Mr. Frank, the history teacher, partnered up the class for a project. This was never a good thing. Mr. Frank didn't understand about the chasm between the star-bellies and the rest of us. He also didn't comprehend that pairing me up with anyone at all was bad, but pairing me with a boy dropped my IQ into single digits.

As he read the matchups out loud, my skin prickled with heat and my ears began ringing. Because there were only two names I was listening for and I hadn't heard either yet.

Please, God, no.

"And lastly, Theia and Haden," he read from his notes.

My nerves danced like they were trying to get out of my

skin. I turned slowly towards Haden's chair, trying to swallow and trying not to look like I wanted to pass out.

He stared back at me, his face unreadable and his dark, dark eyes as mesmerizing as ever. The rest of the class left their seats, making their way to their respective partners while we sat staring at each other.

I wished he would smile, but then I remembered the way he had smiled at me in the hall—the wicked, knowing smirk that made me even more self-conscious than I already was. No, it was best he didn't devastate me.

He raised his brow as if to question and indicated the now-empty desk in front of me. I nodded and pivoted back in my seat. A few seconds ago, my face could have fried an egg, but now my skin was suddenly stone-cold and clammy. We were doomed to an F on the project. I didn't see a way around it.

I didn't look at him but knew when he sat backwards in the chair. Instead, my full attention went to the deep groove scratched into my desk. The air between us fizzled. Did he feel it? I tried to catch my breath, but the more I tried to inhale, the more I felt consumed.

"Are you going to be okay?" he asked.

"Sure," I answered as if the room hadn't shifted sideways in the last thirty seconds. I forced myself to look at him. He wore a sapphire blue button-down shirt with a slight sheen and well-worn jeans. The shirt molded to his frame and begged to be touched.

My heartbeat filled my ears, at first a rapid staccato rhythm that resolved into a deeper, resonating thump, like too much bass in a car stereo. I was aware of my blood being pulled in and out of my heart the way the moon directs the tide. And then the pounding hiccuped and the beat was no longer my own again.

Did he feel it too?

I knew the rest of the world was moving right along, time was inching forward, and lives were being led all around me, but I was in the eye of the hurricane as far as all of that went. Timeless and still, we regarded each other over the empty desk between us.

His eyes were fringed in lush, dark lashes and his lips were rich, plump, forbidden. I imagined kissing them and my tongue swept across my mouth as if he were whetting my appetite. He hissed and reared back in his seat, shocking us both with his reaction and flinging us back into the present.

I was mortified.

"Look, I haven't even read the chapters yet. Maybe I should do that first and then we can talk about the project. Okay?" Haden asked, his voice sounding tinny and a little fake.

I nodded. It made sense. After all, he had just started school here. Of course he needed to catch up. Still, disappointment tasted like dry popcorn and caught in my throat. He turned around, and I stared at his neck, wanting to crawl over my desk and kiss him there. His nape turned red in the spot where I stared and he picked up his stuff and moved back to his desk. As if he knew what I was thinking.

And couldn't get away from me fast enough.

CHAPTER FOUR

Awakening in the yard again made me angry.

I didn't ask for this. The ghoulish nights and humiliating days seemed unfair. It wasn't as if the life I led directed me to this point. Nobody worked harder to stay out of trouble than I did, so why did it stalk me in my slumber?

The labyrinth beckoned, and as usual I responded. Though foliage had returned to the thorny sticks, the atmosphere was no friendlier. In fact, the path was trickier and I encountered more dead ends despite the strong pull of the center. Topiaries of life-size humanish forms startled me and red eyes watched me from deep inside the bushes. My nightgown stuck to my body where I perspired despite the chill.

I wondered what would happen if I refused to continue. Would I wake up from a bad dream or would the conse-quences be more dire? Though the fiends had yet to threaten me, they weren't cuddly and sweet either. Something told me that crossing the creatures of nightmares would mean very bad things for me, and that, for the moment, they tolerated my existence here because Haden desired my appearance.

Except that maybe he didn't.

I kept going because I needed answers. If this was a dream, what was my subconscious trying to tell me? And if this was real . . .

I coughed as the smell of smoke filled my nose. The closer I got to the core, the warmer the air became, until at last I reached the clearing.

A bonfire had replaced the parquet dance floor. Tonight there were no dancing ladies in finery and jewels. In fact, there were no clothes at all, aside from a hat or two, because there was no flesh at all.

Animated skeletons reveled around the fire in a circle, laughing raucously. They creaked and rattled as they moved, the sound unsettling and dreadful. Many of them drank from cups, and the liquid would spill from their necks and ribs as they swallowed.

One of them noticed me, and a hush fell over the crowd until they all moved at once to get a better look, craning their necks. The sound was a horrifying symphony of cracking and clicking. I was too afraid to run, too afraid to cry out, too afraid to blink. A soft mew escaped my throat and the backs of my knees quivered.

From behind me, a male voice said, "If it frightens you so, why do you keep returning?"

Why his voice calmed my fear, I can't understand. It touched me like a blanket fresh from the dryer, warm and soft. My nerves stilled and he stepped around me so that we were facing. He smiled and it devastated me, tearing at little pieces of me I didn't know I had until he began shredding them.

"What are you, Haden?"

He made a careless gesture with one hand to his boneyard and they resumed their party. Mollified, I guess, that my company wasn't unwelcomed. The scraping noises of all of them moving at once again sent shivers down my spine.

"What do you wish me to be, Theia?"

"I wish you to be . . . honest." Because I didn't know what else to wish for.

"Do you?" He tilted his chin and appraised me. "I'm not certain of that at all."

"Please."

"Honestly?" He bent at the waist and spoke softly in my ear, his voice low and warm. "I find you absolutely enchanting."

The tremors traveled from my ear to my toes, with an interesting side trip that made me glad I'd remembered to wear a bra to bed.

I looked for the lie in his dark eyes, but found an earnest expression instead. He straightened regally and stepped back, decreasing the intimacy between us.

It was then I noticed he wasn't in his formal attire this evening, though what he wore could hardly be considered modern. His oversize white shirt was rumpled and untucked from his breeches, like he'd just stepped off a pirate ship.

The skeletons' rabble-rousing grew louder, but the grinding of their joints hurt my head and I rubbed my temples.

"I'm not sure you should be here, Theia."

That made two of us. "Where is here?"

"This is my world." He gestured to the creatures surrounding the bonfire like a ringleader at the circus. "My legacy."

"Why am I here? How did I get here?"

"I wish I knew." He pinned me with an intense gaze, one that should have frightened me. Instead, it electrified me. "You have the way of moonlight about you. Like you're made of silvery beams of light." Upon further inspection, he added, "You don't belong here."

His words felt like a cut across my chest. Everything was so contradictory. "You don't want me here, then?"

"Is that what I said?"

"You talk to me in circles."

"I suppose I do. You are no better, my little lamb. Tell me, why are you here?" He ushered me back into the maze and away from the bone party, stopping in a large corner by a fountain alight with candles.

"I don't know—I thought you did. Am I dreaming? What about school? You pretend you don't know me. And what about the burning man?" The questions came out on a rush of air. I must have sounded like a lunatic.

Haden, if it was really Haden, responded to my barrage with, "The burning man?"

I exhaled loudly. "You answer questions with questions."

"You don't like me."

"I don't *know* you."

"I don't think you'll like me any more if you get to know me either. This place, it blooms from your presence like a flower to the sun. But it isn't good for you. I wish one of us was strong enough to keep you away."

I stepped towards him, not consciously, but yet there I was. "So you do want me here."

"Theia," he warned, "you were made for something else. This is not your destiny." He sat on a bench that I could have sworn hadn't been there a minute ago. "Falling under the spell of it will only bring you heartache."

"I'm not dreaming, am I?"

"Do you think you are?" I rolled my eyes, and he chuckled at my reaction. "Sometimes the answers are more questions. Sometimes down is up." He reached to the foliage and plucked out a black rose, though I hadn't noticed any flowers on the bushes before. He inhaled the scent and then held it to me.

I placed my fingers gingerly on the stem until I noticed there were no thorns and accepted his offering, not sure that I should have but unable to resist all the same. "Thank you." He hadn't let go of the stem and we both stared at the flower between us. A strange sensation overtook me and I spoke without thought. "I can feel your heartbeat, Haden."

He loosened his grip on the rose. "It's hard to imagine you don't belong when the pull is so strong. You may have to be the stronger of us."

"I don't know how to be strong. I don't know how to be anything."

He clucked his tongue and dismissed my comment. "You know more than you think."

"I'd like to know where we are." I sniffed the rose, startled that the scent wasn't like any flower I'd smelled before. Instead, it bore a spicy fragrance with vanilla undertones. It smelled like Haden.

"Maybe it doesn't have a name." He flashed his trademark grin. "Maybe it's different things to different people."

"I think it's a dream."

"Maybe for you it is." He reached for my hair but stopped himself. "Maybe you should wake up."

And then I did.

I sat up, stunned at the sunlight and not as stunned as I should have been to find a long-stemmed black rose atop the pillow next to me.

Donny handed me her blended mocha drink. "Hold this, will you?" She bent at the waist and fluffed her fingers through her hair. Whipping back up, she reminded me of a supermodel with perfectly tousled mink tresses. "God. My mom switched shampoo and my hair is so flat now, it's driving me nuts."

"Your hair looks fine." We were waiting for Amelia at our usual spot in front of the Main. My mind kept traveling back to the rose and to Haden, trying to make sense of either and failing miserably.

Amelia eased down next to me and plucked the mocha from my hand, handing it back to Donny after she'd taken a drink. "Don't forget we have Madame Varnie after school today."

"Ugh. Can't we get our wisdom teeth removed instead?" Donny answered, and then she sat up straighter. "I spy, with my little eye . . . fresh sneetch at nine o'clock."

Right before she said it, the left side of my face had warmed as if the sun was shining on it. Quickly, I bent over and pretended to dig through my bag on the ground and stole a glance. Sure enough, Haden was headed straight for us.

Whatever I was looking for in my bag became really hard to find. I rummaged through it, cursing at my stupid inability to act like a normal person. No way was I making eye contact. It's not like he would stop before he reached us either. Our spot just happened to be a bench close to the front doors.

My face got warmer and warmer and my search for the elusive object in my bag became ludicrously intense. When Haden stopped directly in front of my bag, my gaze made the slow journey from his feet up. Hunched over my schoolbag, I was at eye level to his crotch and I couldn't help but rest my gaze there just a second too long, as if my skin weren't already on fire with the blush from hell.

Imagine my surprise when he crouched to my level. "Hey, partner."

Chai tea. That's what he smelled like. A little exotic, a little sweet. His features softened, waiting for my response, but I couldn't form one. His lips were so close that I could barely restrain myself from tasting them, which was an unlikely and unwelcome thought, but it traversed my mind anyway.

Donny resumed her practiced slouch, and Ame sighed slightly. Their presence offered me a little courage and allowed me to speak, finally. "Did you, um, finish the reading?" My father's voice in my head chastised me for the "um."

"I did. Maybe we can work on some of the questions at lunch?" He smiled. I was unprepared for my reaction to the most potent weapon Haden had in his arsenal—a real smile, one that reached his eyes. One genuine emotion was enough to unravel my life from the security of everything I'd ever known.

For seventeen years, I'd tried to live Father's way. Each

step measured, my words carefully chosen. In his fortress of fears, I grew up—but not strong. I yearned to replace the hole in his heart left by my mother, so my life never belonged to me. My own heart was my weakest muscle, never exercised, never even flexed.

Suddenly, I understood that it still miraculously worked. And it was full. So full it felt like rays of sunshine were bursting through my chest, poking out of me in radiant splendor. Haden spellbound me and life changed to Technicolor. In his smile, I felt the bindings that tethered my spirit rip away.

I wanted to be reckless. I wanted to be like my mother. I half expected the campus to erupt in song and a choreographed dance number.

"I'll meet you in the library," was what I answered, though what I wanted to say was much more prolific and would have been a great deal more embarrassing.

"I can't wait," he said, blushing so gently I may have imagined it. He stood slowly, unfurling, never losing eye contact with me. He maintained the connection even when assailed by Brittany and Noelle, the cheerleaders from his first day. They flanked him, draping themselves over him, and touching him like I never had.

"There you are," Brittany said, stroking his arm and pointedly ignoring the rest of us. "We have a surprise for you."

Brittany held up a basket of muffins and Noelle dangled a thermos from her finger.

Something changed. A foreign expression moved over his face, like a thief stealing my most prized possession. The unnamed spicy aroma that usually surrounded him singed, and I smelled sulfur instead. Haden slipped his arms around

Britney and Noelle and barely nodded a good-bye to me as they walked away.

My radiant heart shriveled into a tiny, dry raisin. How could I be so stupid? My father deserved extra credit for at least trying to keep me away from boys, since I obviously didn't understand a single thing about them. Haden was probably laughing and telling the Sneetch Association how I practically swooned at his feet. They'd be chuckling at my naïveté while they complained about how hard it was to find good help these days.

I was a joke.

"Stop it." Donny followed the trio into the building with her eyes. "He's being a jerk. Don't you take his shit personally."

"I'm not."

"You are too. The air left your tires as soon as those girls showed up. I'm so tired of them. All of them. They suck. They think their daddies' money makes them special and it doesn't."

Ame disagreed. "It certainly makes their boobs special. Noelle is in my PE class. Two weeks ago, her girls were B students—they look like C-plus at least now."

Donny snorted. "Oh, my God. You're right. What kind of parent pays for a boob job for a seventeen-year-old? Mine won't even pay for highlights."

My barely Bs tightened at the thought of going under the knife. Not even to get Haden's attention would I do that. If that was what he wanted—tears stung my eyes—if that was really what he wanted, my heart was breaking.

"Don't you cry for him," Donny warned me. "He's not

even worth a single tear. He's a cartoon who thinks he's a man."

I nodded. She was right. Sneetches are not tear-worthy.

Ame flipped open her cell. "Crap. We're all late for class."

"Are they ever going to fix the bell so that it actually rings once in a while?" Donny drank the last of her coffee and tossed the cup.

The school bell had been off all year. Sometimes it rang for no apparent reason; most of the time it just didn't do anything at all. Most teachers stopped letting us use the bell as a tardy excuse by winter break.

"Hey, guys. Hi, Donny."

We all looked up in surprise at the source of the voice. Gabe of the always perfect hair had joined us.

"What do you want?" Donny asked. To be fair, I still hadn't seen him be anything but nice.

"Nothing really." He shrugged. "I guess we should go to class, huh?"

"Ladies first," she snapped, gesturing for him to go ahead of us.

"Are you always such a bitch, or do you save it up for me special?" he asked.

Ame and I exchanged wide-eyed glances.

"This is level-one bitchery, asshat. Stick around if you want the real show."

He muttered under his breath and started walking towards the door that we should have gone through five minutes ago. Donny crossed her arms and glared at him until he turned around and yelled, "I'll save you a seat in English."

Before she could retort, he flashed a smile and took off running up the steps.

A trace of a smirk crossed Donny's face before she asked, "What the hell is going on around here?"

I half expected to be stood up in the library. I promised myself not to be let down if he skipped the study session. And if he did show, I would remain aloof and unconcerned with anything but our mutual grade.

Instead, Haden was already asking me a question as he slid into the chair across the table from me. "Who exactly are you, Theia Alderson?"

He stole my breath, frazzled my senses, and interrupted my heartbeat. Now he wanted me to be coherent? I found myself staring at his Adam's apple to avoid his eyes. "I'm just a girl."

Haden's clothes, though completely different from the kind he wore in my dreams, fit him very well. A white collar poked out of the V-neck navy sweater, crisp yet somehow casual. His jeans, as I remembered from my too-close encounter that morning, were also dark navy, but were distressed and fit him to showcase his lean lines.

Completely at ease in a lazy pose that reminded me of Donny's slouches, he regarded me for what seemed a very long moment. "I've asked around about you."

"Oh?" I tidied the papers in front of me. *Why was he asking about me?*

"Tell me, how does the only girl who hasn't lived in this town her whole life *not* have any kind of status at all? Nobody knows anything about you. It's like you're a ghost."

"More like a nonentity." The words slipped out.

"I find that hard to believe." Haden leaned forward, encroaching on my space, throwing me off balance. Lord, the smell of him made me tingle. "The guys in this school must be first-class morons. Your accent alone should make them all mad for you. The pretty English rose."

"I've noticed that most young men here are easily distracted by . . . other kinds of girls." I blushed violently. I hoped he'd be humane enough not to mock me for it.

Haden smirked. "I started to wonder if maybe I was the only one who could see you. 'Isn't she that girl who plays violin?' was the most I got out of anyone."

I shrugged. He could stop anytime. I didn't need to be reminded how very unseen I was. "We should tackle some of these questions."

"I just wondered how the most beautiful girl in school manages to fly so far under the radar."

I sat back in my chair. "Now I know you are teasing me."

He smiled, not the kind that disarmed me completely, but one that signaled a shift of power all the same. "The other girls, they try very hard to sparkle. You—you just glow without any effort at all."

I bit my lip. Knowing I wasn't the most beautiful girl in school didn't change the elation I'd felt when he said I was. Haden was out of my league, I knew that. If I was going to begin the kind of games boys and girls play in high school, I should have started with a nice boy who didn't make me feel like Little Red Riding Hood alone with the Big Bad Wolf. I wanted so badly to believe he thought I was special that I was willing to pretend I didn't know better.

"Nothing to say to that?"

"I can't think of anything to say that won't sound stupid. I don't have much practice with—"

"Compliments?"

I nodded. Compliments. Boys. Conversation. Seduction. You name it, I was inexperienced.

"Do I make you nervous?"

I nodded again.

"I suppose, in the long run, that's probably a good thing."

"Haden?" I asked hesitantly.

"Yes, Theia." He leaned forward again, smiling at my agitation. I couldn't help but smile back a little.

"Does anything make you nervous?"

He cocked his head to the side, measuring me and his answer carefully. "Not very much. Why do you ask?"

"I suppose I just want to get some equal footing. You seem to like to keep me off balance."

His grin turned wolfish. "I suppose I do. It's not a good idea for you to be too comfortable around me anyway." He raised an eyebrow like a well-accomplished villain. "I'm not a very good person."

"You want me to be afraid of you?"

He shook his head. "I want you to be smart." His voice was so low I instinctively leaned closer.

"Are you so very dangerous, then?"

The distance between our faces grew shorter with each breath. "I'm not like the other boys," he teased.

"I'm glad," I whispered.

Haden sighed and his eyelids lowered, his gaze resting

on my lips. "I'm serious, Theia. You'll never be safe with me."

"If you are about to tell me you are a vampire that glitters in the sunshine, I will—"

He laughed, a chuckle really, but it wasn't practiced. It wasn't an emotion he put on to impress me or anyone else. It encouraged me to want more of him.

His hand traced the table near mine, and I spread my fingers out in hopes of an actual touch. He pondered our closeness very carefully, it seemed. I wished very much to know what he was thinking.

Our moment was broken by a female voice. "Haden?"

We sat up, and I blushed eighteen shades of red while he answered, "Hey, Brittany."

Disappointment and humiliation twined around my insides while looking at Brittany. She was perfect in all the ways that counted when attracting a boy. She shimmered in the right places and stayed matte in the others. Sixteen going on twenty-three on the outside, while portraying a wholesome, family-values girl on the inside. Maybe that was her outside too, though. I don't know what she was on the inside. An enigma. She wasn't very nice—but you never saw her being overtly ugly either.

"My locker is stuck. Can you come help me?" She was already pulling him by the hand. The look she shot me had territorial written all over it. "We're all going to Hootenanny's after the game. Can you come?"

Hootenanny's was our small town's answer to TGI Friday's and the place the sneetches loved most in the world after sporting activities. Donny, Ame, and I avoided Hootenanny's, preferring the smaller, less frequented places in town.

"Of course I'll help you," he answered. "We'll work on these later?" he asked me as he was being led away.

"Right."

He walked backwards a few more steps and brought Brittany's hand to his lips without taking his eyes off me.

My hand tingled where he kissed her.

And the bastard knew it.

CHAPTER FIVE

Later that afternoon, Donny reluctantly pulled her car in front of the cute bungalow Ame pointed to on the right. "I really think this is lame," she said, complaining one more time in case either of us was unsure how she felt about this visit to the psychic.

Amelia smoosh-hugged her across the seats. "I know you do. Thanks for coming with me anyway."

I couldn't help but smile at Amelia's barely contained excitement. She clapped her hands, the sound muted by her rainbow-print fingerless gloves that striped their way up her arm. I looked at my bland beige-on-beige outfit and pursed my lips.

I wasn't exactly all-in on this little adventure, but it was a distraction, and I needed one desperately. Haden had tangled my insides with his pretty compliments followed by total disregard.

And then there were my dreams.

We'd had a substitute in history, so we watched yet another war film. My skin felt heated the entire hour, but I didn't dare turn to see if Haden was looking at me. After class, he disappeared into the hall before I managed to sling my bag over my shoulder.

I was disappointed and relieved at the same time.

Donny and Amelia were still talking in the front seat. I realized I'd been daydreaming again.

"Don't expect me to spend money on this scam," Donny reminded Amelia. "And don't tell me to have an open mind. I'm open to new experiences—just not ones that include me paying some fraud to tell me things I already know about myself."

"You're the most open girl in our whole school," Ame teased as she threw open her door and bounded out of the car.

"I don't think she meant that in a good way." Donny met my eyes in the rearview mirror. "C'mon, English. If I have to go in, so do you."

I nodded my assent, but was much slower to exit the vehicle than Amelia, who was already halfway up the sidewalk to the door.

She hurried back and grabbed our arms as we rounded the car. "Would you guys hurry up?"

We made it to the front porch, our arms straining at the sockets. Ame punched the doorbell and bounced on the balls of her feet while we waited for Madame Varnie to answer.

Since I had no expectations of what Madame Varnie looked like, I have no idea why I was so very surprised at her appearance. To say that she stunned the three of us into silence when she opened the door would be an understatement.

I suppose the first thing that stood out was her lilac turban that matched the shapeless shift she wore. The shiny fabric formed a large beehive on her head, and in the middle of it was a glass eye the color of peacock feathers and surrounded by fake jeweled beads. It was about twenty-four inches of nonsense, but unfortunately, not the oddest thing about her.

Madame Varnie's face was overly made up. Too much powder, too much shadow, and too much lipstick were spackled onto a face that was distinctly neither middle-aged nor female, as the costume seemed to suggest. Instead, Madame Varnie was very clearly a younger man in drag.

"Well, hello," *she* said, in a breathy, effeminate voice.

Amelia squinted very hard at the person in front of us. "Um. Madame Varnie, I'm Amelia. I have an appointment. I've brought my friends—I hope that's okay."

"Of course, dearie." Madame opened the door wide and ushered us into the house.

Amelia bounded in with no hesitation; Donny and I, however, had to silently dare each other inside with our eyes. The first room we encountered—the living room, I supposed—was filled with moving cartons in various states of packing or unpacking. I couldn't be sure which.

Madame led us into another area of the house through a beaded doorway. This room was considerably less transitory than the other. I had to credit Donny for yesterday's observation; it did have a circus tent feel to it. Fabric was draped artfully across the ceiling, billowing in shades of purple and red. White lights stretched around the perimeter of the room like stars against the dark wall. In the center of it all, a small table covered in blue velvet held an iridescent crystal ball. It was nearly the size of a basketball and rested on a pewter holder.

Donny released an exasperated sigh. "The only thing missing from this big top is the amazing fire-eating dog woman," she said under her breath.

The ambience was excessive, but it wasn't off-putting. I rubbed her arm, reminding her to behave. We were here for Ame. She nodded, probably recalling all the times we'd accompanied her on boy-scavenging expeditions that really didn't interest us.

Madame Varnie sat Ame in one chair and brought another to the table. I saw another chair against the wall and helped myself. We crowded around the small table, with Ame between Donny and me and Madame across from us.

"Miss Amelia, what type of divination are you most comfortable with? We can do tarot or the crystal ball . . . or I can just read your hand," Madame Varnie stated in her falsetto.

I could *feel* Donny grimace at her fake voice even if I couldn't see it. The tension in the small room ratcheted up. Even if Madame was not a true psychic, she must have felt the disdain coming at her across the table.

"Cards, maybe?" Ame answered.

I shuddered. The images on tarot cards always frightened me. Even Amelia's Hello Kitty deck. She tried to read our futures with them sometimes, but had to use a book to look up the meaning of each card. By the time we were half done, none of it made sense to anyone and we resorted to eating chocolate and painting our nails for the rest of the evening.

Madame Varnie did not have a reference book. "What is most on your mind, Amelia?" Madame began shuffling the deck, the sound of it making my toes curl. I don't know why I hated the cards so much.

"You're the psychic," Donny blurted out. "*You* tell us what's on her mind."

"Donny!" Ame shouted. "You're being rude."

"I'm sorry. I just don't buy this. Mrs. Doubtfire here is going to ask you leading questions and then you'll be so impressed when he comes up with profound insights into your character."

I was embarrassed for Ame. This was important to her, but Donny was a raging guard dog when it came to protecting us. There wasn't anything she wouldn't do for us, and I couldn't count the times I'd relied on her saying the things I just couldn't work up the courage to utter myself.

Ame gasped a protest, but the psychic only smiled. "It's all right, Amelia. Your friend only has your best interest in mind. We should all be so lucky to have someone so valiant on our side."

Donny crossed her arms in front of her defiantly. Madame Varnie sat back and removed the turban from his head, revealing the messy blond spikes he'd hidden beneath it. He couldn't have been more than twenty, but it was hard to tell under the makeup.

In his own voice, a hundred octaves lower than "Madame's," he spoke directly to Donny. "A lot of my clients like the show. They wouldn't take a guy like me seriously—they need the theatrics and the entertainment value. They don't want to know I spent the morning carving waves with my surfboard before I read their future." He shrugged. "I'm leaving town soon anyway, so I don't really care if you see me."

"Are they running you out? Lynch mob maybe?" Donny asked and then offered, "Come to think of it, I did see a sale on pitchforks at the hardware store."

He laughed. "No. Let's just say the vibe in Serendipity Falls is no longer as welcoming to people who can see the truth. Plus, the waves are bigger down the coast." He paused. "I'm the real deal. Give me your hand and I'll prove it to you."

Donny stared at his hand with the same expression on her face as when Gabe tried to give her *Catcher in the Rye*. "I don't think so," she intoned.

"You're not being fair, Don," Ame said, clearly upset. "Give him a chance."

Donny lanced Amelia with a look that promised retribution was in her future and then thrust her hand at the half-crossed cross-dresser, palm up. "Fine."

Instead of looking at the lines on her palm, he turned her hand over and back a couple of times, inspecting it like he was picking out a good melon. "The girl that sits behind you cheats off your tests."

"That's all you got? Tell me something I don't know."

"I'm not reading the girl, I'm reading you. The reason I know she cheats is because you purposely wrote down three wrong answers so she'd get them wrong, and then changed them at the last minute after the bell. Geometry, I believe."

Donny snatched her hand away and didn't have a snappy comeback for once.

Ame looked at her and then at me with wide eyes before stretching her arm across the table. "My turn, Madame Varnie."

He took her hand gingerly. "You can just call me Varnie, sugar, if you like. It seems a little less ridiculous under the circumstances."

Ame blushed. So he was a sweet-talking, cross-dressing, fortune-telling . . . surfer?

While he inspected Ame's hand, it struck me that no matter what we called him, it wouldn't make this situation less ridiculous. Donny, however, was still being quiet, likely trying to work out how he'd managed to extract that information about her. I'm sure she wouldn't allow for him to really be psychic yet. Her mind must have been churning like mad to find a plausible excuse.

"Miss Amelia," he began, and though his words conveyed a Southern accent, he didn't have one. "Why didn't you try out for that part in the play?"

She swallowed hard. "What—what do you mean?"

"You would have been an amazing Liesl. They would have picked you."

"You didn't try out?" Donny asked her. "I thought you were going to."

Amelia had spent weeks constantly practicing for *Sound of Music* tryouts. It had gotten to the point that Donny and I had memorized all the lyrics and the scene she needed to read just from being in her presence.

"I changed my mind." Her voice, shrunken and small, made me sad.

"Why?" I asked.

"The other girls who were trying out were so good. I

didn't think I had a chance. Not really. I mean, one girl looked so much like the actress in the movie, I was really surprised she didn't get the part." She picked imaginary fuzz off her arm warmer. "Who ever heard of a Korean Liesl?"

Donny pulled Ame into her shoulder. "You're such a dummy. The only one who cares about that kind of stuff is you. You nailed that song every time you sang it."

I glanced across the table and found Varnie staring at me strangely. I didn't know how long he'd been doing that, but he didn't look away after I caught him. "I think we should use the cards for you," he said, his forehead furrowing into worried wrinkles.

"I'm not—"

"Yes, let's do that." Amelia sat up from leaning on Donny, eager to change the focus back to something metaphysical.

"Just relax," he told me as he shuffled. "Try to think about nothing at all."

That was strange. All of Amelia's tarot books had told us to focus on a question or a problem.

I inhaled deeply. The oxygen relieved my poor lungs, leaving me to suspect I'd been taking very shallow breaths since we'd arrived.

He stopped shuffling, even though he hadn't asked me to direct him to stop. The first card he placed on the velvet cloth sent a shiver through me. It was red—bloodred—with a black-cloaked figure and scythe in the middle.

It was the death card.

Ame reached for my hand and squeezed. "Remember, it's a visual representation of transformation, not necessarily death."

I nodded, and he flipped the next card.

It was the same as the first.

Ame clutched my hand tighter and goose bumps invaded my skin. There should only have been one death card in the deck.

"That's impossible." Varnie paled under the already white makeup still on his face.

The hair on my arms lifted like it was trying to get as far away from me as it could. I couldn't tear my eyes away from the identical cards, though I wanted to. My fight-or-flight instinct was begging me to run away, but I was glued to the seat.

Varnie slapped another card on the table like he was angry that his cards were betraying him. Again, the same card appeared. He recoiled.

Donny stood up, pushing the table for leverage and it wobbled. "We're leaving."

I couldn't take my eyes off the cards.

Donny tapped my shoulder. "Come on. He's a con artist. He obviously stacked the deck to scare you into giving him more money for a reading."

I raised my eyes to Varnie's. He was more scared than I was.

"I didn't do this," he said. "Someone must have come in and messed with my deck. . . ."

As his words trailed off, we realized he didn't believe that any more than we did.

"I need a beer." He pushed away from the table and strode out.

I didn't want to be in the room with the cards, so I yanked Ame with me and got up too. Donny grabbed my other hand.

By the time the three of us were back in his living room, he had a beer in his hand and was pacing. Varnie was full of pent-up energy. Whatever had happened in there was not good. Not good at all.

"I'm so glad I'm leaving this godforsaken town," he murmured to no one in particular.

"Where are you going?" Ame sounded lost.

"Away. Far away." He stopped pacing and pointed his beer at me. "You might think of doing the same."

"Are you old enough to be drinking beer?" Ame asked.

All three of us swiveled our heads to look at her.

"What?" she asked defensively.

Varnie wiped his mouth with the back of his hand, smearing his lipstick. "Sugar, we've got a few more important things to discuss than California liquor laws."

Ame crossed her arms over her chest. "That means no, you're not. How old are you anyway? It's hard to tell with all the . . ."

"Maybelline?" Donny finished for her. "Ame, focus." Donny tugged her hood on. "We're leaving."

"I'm nineteen," Varnie answered.

Ame walked right up to him and peered into his eyes like she was looking into windows of a house. "There's something strange about you," she murmured.

"Ya think?" Donny answered. "Can we go now?"

"There's something strange about everyone, Miss Amelia," Varnie said quietly.

"What happened in there?" I asked, pointing to the room we'd left. Though I was quite sure I didn't really want to know.

"Look, girls . . ." When Varnie had our attention, he looked uncomfortable, like he didn't know what to do with it now that he had it. "This town is changing. There's a bad mojo and it's getting worse."

"What the hell are you talking about?" That was Donny. Of course.

"Bad juju," he answered, without really answering at all. "Darkness is gaining."

"I've felt it too," Amelia whispered, her eyes shining and trained on Varnie.

Donny, not as rapt as Ame, countered his logic. "Bad *juju* is forcing you out of town?"

Varnie sat on one of the moving cartons, his legs splayed in a most unladylike position under his skirt. "It's hard to get clear here anymore. There's a lot of stuff I just don't want to *see*. I can't get grounded." He looked right at me. "Some energy is feral." Why was he looking at me when he said that? "There's a lot of stuff happening in this town that you don't know about. Bad stuff. It's practically a beacon to things that go bump in the night."

His attention went back to Ame. "It's been getting worse over the years. I used to think it could be stopped, but I'm not so sure anymore. The purveyors of dark . . ."

"You can drop the act, Varnie. We don't believe you." As if Donny's bravado could undo the fear and the shivers that were affecting us all.

"So, what happened in there?" I repeated, nodding towards the room I hoped never to set foot in again.

"It's *you*," he answered. "Something about you."

"What do you mean?" Ame asked.

"Something is attaching to her. Something dark and dangerous. It wants her. It wants her very badly."

Me? The death cards. I thought of the three of them lying across the table, and then I thought of the skeletons and the ghouls in my dreams. My vision clouded until it was just a small pin of light. The pounding of my heart rushed into my ears, filling my head with the roar.

I sat down quickly to avoid falling. Donny and Ame joined me on either side, supporting my back.

I was obviously letting all these strange events get to me. There had to be a reasonable explanation. What would my father say?

He'd chastise me for getting involved with this esoteric gibberish. He'd get the doctor to prescribe me a heavy sleeping pill to avoid future sleepwalking, and then he'd remind me that boys were a foolish waste of my time.

I began to breathe easier. Yes, of course. This was all a series of unfortunate exaggerations of my too-fertile imagination. If only I'd listened to Father—

The afternoon sun was dimming, forming long shadows on the walls. I felt cold even though the temperature hadn't changed.

"So you're running away," Amelia accused Varnie. "All this is happening . . . to Theia and to our town . . . and you're just . . . leaving?"

He held out his arms like "what you see is what you get." "Look, my whole life I've had to hide that I'm different. When I was nine, I spent eighteen months in the psych ward until I smartened up and told the doctors the visions were gone." His voice lowered a little. "I was just a kid, ya know?"

He let his eyes drift closed while he composed himself. "I've been running a long time, sugar. The only one who's going to look out for Varnie is Varnie." He pulled off his clip-on earrings. "The stuff I've been seeing around here lately I can't *un*see. I'm spooked. And you should be too."

"Me?" Ame asked.

"You're so busy pretending to be an amateur that you've passed by the realization that you're talented. I'm kind of sorry I won't be around to watch you discover it."

"Good God. That's it. We are out of here." Donny got up and pulled Ame first, and then they both reached for me.

"Maybe we should let him finish," Ame argued even as she headed for the door.

"I think Madame Varnie has done enough damage for the afternoon, don't you?"

Varnie didn't even get off his box. I waited for him to say something—explain or console or anything—but he just sat on his box and let us go.

When Donny dropped me off in front of my house, she repeated one more time that he was a fake, a phony, and that he rigged that deck to scare me. I nodded and pretended to agree with her.

The problem was that Varnie was correct. Something about me wasn't right anymore. Something had attached to me in my dreams and wasn't letting me go.

Part of me didn't want it to.

CHAPTER SIX

Something tickled my nose.

I opened my eyes, surprised to feel the sun warm on my face. As I eased onto my elbows, I was startled to find Haden, my dream Haden anyway, lying beside me on a bed of soft green grass. He held another black long-stem rose, and he traced a lazy pattern with it on my arm.

"I thought you would never wake up." He grinned and his eyes lit with mischief. He was dressed in his Regency-era finery again, though I noticed that today his fingernails were painted black.

My very own goth Mr. Darcy. Jane Austen would be so proud.

I bent my legs so that I was hugging my knees, uneasy about the afternoon with Varnie.

Haden smiled and presented me with the onyx rose.

It was hard to imagine this as dangerous when Haden smiled at me like that. Feigning shyness, I glanced away in an effort to hold against the strong tide of longing.

My dreamscape was very different in the sunshine. We were on the bank of an unfamiliar river with no labyrinth in sight. Instead, it looked as if someone had painted nature with Easter egg dye. Each blade of grass was a different shade of green—from hunter to turquoise. Oddly shaped flowers sprouted in small patches and mushrooms the size of footstools grew in primary colors with patterns like polka dots and zigzags on them.

The water in the swiftly flowing river was the color of a blue raspberry Slurpee from 7-Eleven. I wanted to dip my feet in, but like everything in the land of my dreams, it made me wary despite its enchantment.

"We're alone," I announced aloud as the thought crossed my mind. Not a ghoul in sight.

"I felt the need to be selfish of your time," he answered.

I ignored the remark. I'd had enough empty flattery designed to tease me into his games. "I like it here. It's beautiful." I pushed myself up and strolled to the river's edge.

Haden joined me on the bank, standing near yet not touching. Never touching. Feeling self-conscious of my nightgown, even more so in the light of day, I hugged myself tightly. Without looking directly at him, I gathered my courage.

Before the words would form, Haden offered, "I know you have questions, little lamb. What if we traded answer for answer?"

"What do you mean?"

"That's your first. I mean, I'll answer a question for every question you answer me. My turn now. When did you begin playing music?"

I regarded him with a sideways glance. "I don't remember ever *not* playing the violin. I found my mother's in a chest when I was three."

My mother hadn't been a virtuoso by any means, but I'd been told she enjoyed playing occasionally. She'd listened to violinists on CD, especially while she was pregnant with me. My father didn't talk about her much, but he used that story to coerce me into extra practice now and then.

It was my turn for a question. So many things were unknown to me, where to start? "Are you real?"

"Yes," he answered. His voice, rough like gravel, surprised me. I peered at him closely.

I wanted to look at him forever, I decided. It was foolish, I knew that. Appearances meant nothing, and they seemed to mean less lately, in this place. Things that should be beautiful were raw with the kind of horror normally reserved for Halloween.

But Haden was different. He could have been a model, but there was a quality to him that film could never capture. It wasn't his dark eyes or sable waves of hair that drew me to him. He was mystifying with his wicked charm and roguish charisma, of course, but it was his loneliness that pulled me the hardest, I think.

Perhaps I was the only one who saw it. Maybe I made it up. But Haden Black was the loneliest person I'd ever met.

I wasn't sure he understood what I was asking. "I meant are you real here? Is this place real?"

He waggled his finger at me. "I know what you meant, but it's not your turn now."

"Well, then ask me something."

He shook his head. "I don't know what to ask first. I want to know it all. Everything." His lips quirked into a shy smile and he looked earnestly at his feet.

Even though I'd promised myself I wouldn't fall for his head games, he sounded so convincing. Everything inside me wanted to believe him. And as the water rolled past us on the sunny riverbank, part of his veneer faded. His body language changed—he seemed reticent and suddenly unsure of himself.

"So ask," I prodded, a little in awe that somehow, despite all logic, the power dynamic of this relationship was suddenly in my favor.

"What is your favorite food?"

"Ice cream."

"What flavor?"

I shook my head. "Tsk-tsk, Haden. It's not your turn."

"Have pity on a poor bastard, Theia." There again was the smile. The one that filled me to near bursting with a sudden joy.

"All right, strawberry. My turn." Giddiness fizzed like root beer in my stomach and spread from there until I felt effervescent. "When we're at school, in the other world . . ." I was tempted to say "real world," but the lines were so murky. "Do you remember this place and what happens here with me? Do both these worlds collide for you like they do for me?"

The reticence ate him up, and his good humor vanished. "I'm not sure this was such a wise game after all."

The wind kicked up from nowhere, sending a bitter chill

down my gown. And then it was gone just as suddenly as it gusted.

"Is that what this is? A game?" I asked.

"You've already asked your question."

"You didn't answer."

"No, this isn't a game." He loosened his cravat.

Oh, but it was. The *game* frustrated me. Questions I needed answers for and answers that begged for a question hammered at me from inside my head, but I had to wait. Wait my turn.

The silence lingered like an aftertaste for too long. Restlessness built the agitation in me until it was a living thing—a third person in this conversation.

Finally, he asked, "Are you afraid of me?"

"Absolutely not, and yes, with everything in my heart and soul," I blurted without thought.

He chuckled, and looked directly at me for the first time in several minutes. "I'm not sure that qualifies as an answer—it's more like a contradiction."

"Up is down, remember? Besides, everything about you is a contradiction." Pondering my word choice a little more carefully, I added, "You won't hurt me. How I know that, I can't say. But the ways you make me feel, Haden—that's what frightens me. I know you'll be my undoing."

The air grew more still than naturally possible, as if it were expecting something. "Oddly, that is exactly what I would say about you." He caressed my face with his gaze. Adoring me, memorizing me. He stopped on my lips, remaining too long.

My turn again. "Why don't you ever touch me?"

A wall went up, an invisible shield that locked him away from me. Not to be seen, but surely felt. "It's not a good idea."

"Why?" I stepped towards him but he stepped back.

"It's my turn. Who was your first kiss?"

Heat rushed into my face. I flattered myself by thinking maybe he wanted to kiss me. I wished he wanted to kiss me. I hadn't expected the question, and I'm sure he knew the answer. "I haven't . . ." Squeezing my eyes closed, I began again. "I haven't been kissed. Yet."

"Why?" Haden stepped out of his invisible shielded zone before he remembered himself, like he'd wanted to reach for me. "Why ever not?" he asked, but then remembered his own rules.

Encouraged by his bewilderment, I asked, "Why is it a bad idea to touch me?"

"You obviously know I'm not like other boys. It's not meant for our worlds to mix this way."

"Yet here we are."

"You forgot to answer me. Why haven't you been kissed?"

I rolled my eyes at his innocence. "You obviously know I'm not like other girls. I'm shy and I don't spend time with boys. My father is strict and—"

"That's not why."

He thought he knew me so well. "Fine. You tell me why I haven't been kissed."

I regretted the words and my tone instantly. What if he told me what I already knew? That I was lacking. Not interesting or pretty enough.

"You were waiting."

My blood surged, and I watched his lips now. Studied

them. Like they were the answers I sought. "Are you going to kiss me?"

"No."

The slap of rejection wounded me, and I reeled back. I had to turn my eyes away. I couldn't let him see how much hurt he could inflict upon me with just one word.

"You were wrong." The weight of his hands settled on my arms *psychically*, though he hadn't put them physically on me. It was a poor substitution, but once again, I met his eyes and was dazzled by the earnestness I saw there. "It's true that I never want to hurt you. But I can't promise you that I never would. I want to kiss you, Theia, but I won't."

"I want you to." I ached for him. The longing, like a vine, coiled around me and stretched out towards him, wanting to twine us together. I needed more than a psychic touch.

I needed him.

"I can't." He ground out the words even though he moved closer to me.

We were close enough to make it happen right then. I angled my head slightly and whispered, "I want you to be my first."

Our bodies tried to make the decision for us, bringing us impossibly close, our breath mingling and hearts thumping in unison.

"You're so beautiful," he whispered. "Sometimes I day-dream about your heart-shaped mouth for hours."

His will was breaking. It chipped off him little by little. He desired me and, surrounded by his scent, I desired to lose myself to him completely. Nothing else made sense but this.

Yet he fought a war with himself, even though I offered myself freely. The anguish in his eyes triggered a flash of something I'd seen before. Something recent . . . something . . .

I gasped and stumbled backwards.

I'd seen the suffering in those eyes once before.

"You're the burning man."

CHAPTER SEVEN

The impact of waking so suddenly sent me scrambling out of my bed before I even realized I was awake. I glanced around my room wildly, trying to make sense of where I was. My heart slammed against my rib cage like a trapped animal desperate for escape, and I trembled violently as my conscious self met up with the rest of me.

There would be no more sleep for me that night.

After my pronouncement, Haden had recoiled from me in horror. In the blink of an eye, he disappeared—reappearing several feet away and telling me to wake up.

Haden could not possibly be the burning man. That man had died in front of me, and I had watched him turn to dust. If that had even happened. Everything was so confusing. Up is down, down is up.

What I couldn't discount was the bone-deep awareness

that Haden had suffered and that somehow it had something to do with me.

I couldn't sit still. It was too late to try for more sleep, yet too early to get ready for school. The walls felt like a cage, and I suddenly hated everything in my room. Oh, I'd never really liked it much—it was fine for a catalog but not for a real girl. But now it mocked me. Where were my posters, my dirty clothes? A small concession was given by way of a corkboard with a few snapshots and movie tickets. The rest of the room was staged perfectly for a photo shoot or a real estate tour.

Empty of anything that defined it as real.

That was how I felt sometimes. I existed in a world made for show, not depth, not feeling.

And then along came Haden.

Haden stared at the bathroom mirror instead of going to class. The face looking back at him was what they saw when they looked at him, but his reflection lied. If they knew why he was here . . . what he planned to do . . . they would see him as he really was.

A monster.

He'd been waiting for this chance his whole life. To experience humanity. To be a part of it, to understand the feelings he'd been born with but never allowed to express. And now on this devil's errand, he'd learned there was one more human experience he hadn't known he was capable of.

A guilty conscience.

Haden cut class.

Disappointment colored my world gray again, and I

worked solo on the chapter questions we were supposed to be doing together. If I could forget about him, even for a few minutes, I could get some work done. My mind was not swayed by the logic, though, and instead I thought of nothing but Haden.

I wondered if we shared the same dreams. And then I chastised myself. Just because I dreamt of falling down the rabbit hole like Alice didn't mean I'd really found a gothic Wonderland at night. As real life put distance between me and my dreams, I found it easier to accept the difference.

Of course I dreamt about Haden. He was unreasonably handsome and the first boy to encourage conversation with me. I had a crush. I dreamt the boy I had feelings for had feelings back. And while I was at it, I exaggerated a little danger to add to his appeal. Honestly, it was more pathetic that I tried to make it more than it was.

In between classes, I stopped at the water fountain in the Main. As I waited my turn, I kept an eye out for Haden—but the lack of tingles and goose bumps probably meant he'd cut the rest of his classes too.

The student at the fountain finished and as he turned, I realized it was Mike Matheny, the one true love of Amelia. He was cute, I guessed. Like most in our school, he was a jeans-and-tee kind of guy. Not long ago, he'd shaved his head in solidarity when his wrestling coach began chemotherapy, but it was growing back now. He'd never had hair as nice as Gabe's, of course, but most humans didn't. He was still handsome, if a little . . . vacant.

As per my usual custom when confronted with a boy my age, I cast my eyes to my shoes while he passed me. I thought of Ame. How her crush had lasted years with no reward or even acknowledgment. Was her commitment to him courageous or just . . . lame? And was his oblivious nature a scam? Was he just trying to be nice or did he really not know how much she'd pined for him all these years?

An unusual sentiment flashed through me.

It wasn't fair.

It wasn't fair that she invested so much energy—so much of her heart—for nothing. She deserved to have someone in her life, a real boyfriend. One of us should have a crack at happiness. It wasn't fair.

"Mike," I yelled before he'd gotten too far.

He looked back at me, confused. And who wouldn't be? It was well-established that Theia Alderson did not socialize with boys. But Ame deserved a chance, didn't she?

"Amelia is coming over after school to study trig. Can you come?"

"Um."

My tongue felt thick, but I persevered. He was just a boy. If I could waltz at a zombie creature party, I could converse with a boy I wasn't even interested in. "Monday's test is supposed to be brutal. We're hoping massive amounts of caffeine and cramming will help."

"Um. Okay." He answered, still clearly perplexed.

As was I. I think I just wanted something to work out for someone. I didn't dare hope I stood a chance with Haden. Maybe I would invite Gabe too and not tell Donny until she got there. Wouldn't that be something?

I wrote down my address on a corner of notebook paper and tore it off. As I handed it to him, I sensed the heat of a stare on my back. I began turning towards the source when all the locker banks on either side of the hall opened and slammed violently at the same time. The momentum of the sudden force made some of them swing back and forth several times, smacking a few students who'd been caught unawares while they were retrieving their books. My adrenaline spiked, and Mike and I exchanged confused glances.

People came out of the classrooms to see for themselves what had caused the noise. A teacher blamed the wind and guided students back into class; another badgered those of us who hadn't yet gotten that far. I blinked and saw Haden at the other end of the hall, staring at Mike.

"Are you okay?" Mike asked me.

I nodded with very little enthusiasm and the bell rang. Instead of a short burst, the sound grew sharper and louder. Those of us still in the hall covered our ears. The noise was hideous and it felt like an electric screwdriver boring holes into the bones of my jaw.

I couldn't think clearly, the screech obliterating my thoughts, and judging by the other kids pushing their way to the door, it was affecting everyone the same way. Mike grabbed my sleeve and we ran towards the exit.

We got outside and kept running. All of us had to get away from the shrill screams. Had to. The clamor was so disorienting that I couldn't remember where I was going or what I was doing. As several of us spilled into the street, traffic horns blared and the smell of burned rubber assaulted my nose. The constant barrage on my eardrums gave me vertigo and nausea gripped me tightly, but I didn't dare stop yet.

When I got far enough away that I could uncover my

ears, my hearing was filtered as if I were deep underwater. Kids were falling down around me, and I'd lost track of Mike sometime after we'd gotten outside. I choked on the bile burning my throat and searched the mob for my friends. And for Haden.

Across the street, people threw chairs out of second-story windows to get out. There were emergency ladders, but students were panicking and dropping off them too soon in order to escape the whining din that sounded like hell had opened up and screamed.

And was still screaming.

We, the refugees who'd managed to escape, wandered around dazed and unhearing across the street from campus. The bell had been bad enough, but the mass exodus bruised and battered us too. Kids were crying and trying to call their parents even though they couldn't hear them on the other end of the phone. They held their phones and mouthed words into them. Maybe they yelled. I could hear nothing anymore.

Emergency vehicles came from all directions and barricades went up. We'd practiced similar situations before; evacuation and lockdown drills were mandatory in the American schools. But I'd always assumed I'd be able to hear the directions from the crew sent to save us. Instead, everyone was confused. *Were we okay?* How do you answer that?

I found Donny and Ame in time to be shuffled onto a school bus headed for the emergency room. We squeezed into one seat and held hands. We didn't bother talking, since none of us could hear. We clutched one another, and the weight of unspoken fears filled the bus like a balloon with too much air. The vibrations of the wheels tickled my eardrums, but very little sound got through. I'd never heard of an entire school being stricken deaf. Who would have thought it was even possible?

As we pulled away, I searched for Haden in the crowd not yet on buses, almost relieved when I couldn't find him. Part of me wondered if he'd had something to do with the disaster—which was crazy.

Part of me remembered Varnie's warning, though, too.

My ears popped a couple times and the pain doubled me over. Ame's gentle hand rubbed my back until I felt her body racked with what must have been the same pain. I concentrated on shallow breaths and trying to stay conscious. I thought of my violin and what my life would be like without music.

In between the popping sensations, it seemed like as we got farther from the school, my hearing was returning little by little, yet only certain pitches were audible. By the time we got to the ER, they had set up an outdoor "lobby" to evaluate the seriousness of each student's wounds—those who were bleeding and broken were guided into the hospital. The rest of us, who were in varying degrees of pain as our hearing returned bit by hurtful bit, had to wait it out under the tents.

Time passed in a blur. I had to keep my eyes on the ground because the rapid motion of the emergency workers made my vertigo worse. I don't know how long I'd been there when my father appeared in front of me, his mouth drawn into a firm line and his forehead creased with worry. The tears burst out of me then, and I propelled myself into his arms. He clutched me in an awkward yet very firm hold and I leaked tears and snot all over his cashmere sweater. He didn't let go until the tears stopped. The last time he'd done that I was seven.

Father sat me back in a chair and went looking for a doctor. He looked older than his fifty years, more solemn than I'd ever seen him, and I'd rarely seen him anything but solemn. I couldn't tell what they were saying, so my gaze wandered to the rest of my schoolmates. Everyone had withdrawn into as little space as possible in their seats. Parents were beginning to show up now, and that was the only thing that seemed to bring us all out of our frightened states. Moms and dads were suddenly all-important again. Like when we were kids. We were counting on them to know what to do, how to fix it. How to keep it from happening again.

I scanned the crowd for Haden once more, wondering what his parents looked like. What they did. A slight breeze caressed my cheek and I turned towards it—stunned to see Haden ten yards away. He watched me with an expression that looked a lot like guilt.

I eased between the covers of my bed and sighed, weary of the heaviness of my limbs. *No more thinking*, I promised myself. *No more puzzling out the inconsistencies and trying to make sense of the nonsensical.*

Muriel had spoiled me with homemade chocolate lava cake, my favorite. Father didn't reprimand me when I ate a huge ramekin of it in place of supper. He didn't read his paper at the table either. We didn't speak much, even though my hearing was mostly returned. But it wasn't our custom anyway. It was a companionable silence.

After the cake, I soaked in the tub until the water had long lost its warmth. For once, the girlish traditional night-gown was a comfort. And the room I had begun the day hating seemed welcoming and friendly. Familiar. Safe.

As I reached for the light on my nightstand, Father knocked on my door.

He wasn't a frequent visitor, and frankly, he looked ridiculous amongst my things. The frills and pinks against his austerity would have been amusing in a comedy, were it not my life.

Father perched on my bed in an uncomfortable-looking pose. "Do you—that is—is there anything else you need?"

I'm afraid I blinked in response. It was so unusual and so unlike him.

"Theia," he said, his face going ashen, "is your hearing getting worse again?"

I shook my head. "No. No, I'm sorry. I didn't mean to worry you. I think I'm just overtired."

He breathed easier. "Very well. I'll let you rest." He stood as if to leave, but stopped. "I'm very glad that you're feeling better."

"Thank you."

"I'll let you rest," he repeated.

"Good night, Father."

He nodded and crossed the room in much longer strides than he had on the way in.

"Father?" I called to him before he passed through the door.

"Yes?"

"Thank you for . . . coming today. And for checking on me now."

"Of course." His answer was matter-of-fact, but his voice cracked slightly.

That night there were no dreams. None that I remembered anyway. I awoke refreshed and with no lasting effects from my temporary deafness.

I awoke to the petals of black roses strewn across my bed.

CHAPTER EIGHT

In the morning, a lonely stillness cupped the quiet house in its hands. Father wasn't home; I knew it even before I saw the note. His absence weighed heavily on my senses. It had been nice, despite the awkwardness, to be visited by Father last night. The strange things happening to me seemed less scary. My life wasn't as precarious and disjointed, and I'd felt like a safe child again.

Muriel didn't work for us on the weekends. I wouldn't have minded the distraction of her that morning. She was the opposite of my father—all soft hugs and easy tears. She always smelled like lemons and brown sugar.

For want of something to do to keep me from thinking, I pulled out my violin, but was unable to coax a single note from it. After putting it away, I considered reading, but the words couldn't hold my attention either. I was restless and because of it, the stillness of the house ceased being lonely and instead became oppressive.

I powered up the computer in the study, determined to wrest back some of the control I felt I'd abandoned since the night I saw, or thought I saw, the burning man fall from the sky. I Googled "waking dreams" first. Bypassing personal journals, I found a medical site that spoke of sleep paralysis and began to relax even though the word "paralysis" was frightening. A medical explanation of my symptoms, one that didn't indicate poor health or psychotic imbalance, was very welcome indeed.

It all seemed to fit quite nicely. In the old days, there were folktales that explained the phenomenon. A woman— sometimes a hag, sometimes a beautiful demon—would kneel on the chest of a man and paralyze him, taking his life force or some such. Sometimes she was called Mara—as in "nightmare." The man couldn't move until she let him up.

But really, it was explained easily by modern medical facts. Sometimes people were unable to transition smoothly from deep sleep to wakefulness. In a deep sleep, the body relaxes the muscles so as not to flail about and hurt himself while dreaming. A person who becomes lucid while in this sleep state will not be able to move, and it is during this time that hallucinations occur. The mind is awake, but the body is still locked in sleep.

I sighed with relief. Though my dreams *felt* real to me because I was partially awake, I had never really left my bed. Excellent.

And then I thought of the rose hidden in my drawer and the petals on my bed this morning. They could not be explained by sleep paralysis.

Not ready to give up, I next Googled "lucid sleepwalking,"

though where I would have found a black rose while sleep-walking I couldn't say. I wouldn't know where to get one even while conscious, and Father certainly didn't cultivate them on the grounds. Unfortunately, the most relevant Web sites agreed that sleepwalkers don't remember their fugue states, and I remembered every detail of mine very vividly.

I wasn't prepared to abandon the explanation entirely. The Internet is not the most reliable source of information, after all. The things I saw on my sleepwalking travels must have worked their way into my dream state. I nodded at my own rationalization and searched for "black roses." It was then I learned that black roses don't exist in nature.

That was impossible. I'd held the rose, smelled its strange fragrance; it was right now drying in a drawer. The petals were not silk or man-made. The flower was real, and yet it could not exist.

Questions swirled around my brain and I found myself thinking about denial. I squeezed my eyes closed, accept-ing what I'd been trying so hard to reject. There was no use pretending.

A memory nagged at me. I hadn't been asleep in the sun-room while playing the violin a few days ago, and Father had clearly seen me while, in my mind, I was in the labyrinth. If I was somehow traveling to another place, why wasn't the rest of me going too? I typed "out-of-body experience" into the computer.

The scope of results was too large. There were so many different beliefs—astral projection, spirit walkers, soul travel-ers. I had to close the window. I thought of Varnie. He was likely my best source of information.

I showered and dressed in record time. Now that I'd decided to embrace getting educated, I was in a hurry to do so. I was giddy on my walk across town. I even promised myself not to flinch if he wanted to read the cards again.

Bounding up the steps of Varnie's house, I reminded myself of Ame with her endless enthusiasm. A huge weight had been lifted off my shoulders knowing that I would soon understand what was pulling me towards Haden—or Haden towards me. I knocked on the door and leaned to look in the picture window of the front room. The boxes were gone.

Dread frosted over my previous optimism. The house looked empty. I muttered a string of words I'd learned from Donny and sat dejectedly on the stoop. Varnie had made good on his proclamation of leaving town. I rose and sent one more dejected look at his front door.

As I accepted the inevitable, I noticed the white corner of an envelope sticking out from under the welcome mat. I toed it the rest of the way out. It had my name on it. I scooped it up and sat down on the step again, tearing into it before I remembered I was an Alderson and above that kind of unseemly behavior.

My hands shook as I read Varnie's unfamiliar scrawl.

Theia,

I'm sorry I missed you. I knew you'd come back (see, I told you I was the real deal), but things were just too dicey for me to hang around.

I wish I had all the answers you need. I really don't know what is going on with you. The problem with being a psychic, even a very good one, is that you can't

always control what is visible and what remains in
the shadows.

You, little girl, are shadowed more than anyone
I've ever met.

I've tried to get a clearer shot of you, but I just
can't. All I can tell you is what I said the other day.
Something wants you, and badly.

You'll need a talisman. It won't protect you, but
you'll need one just the same. Talk to Miss Amelia.
She'll be able to help you with that.

Good luck to you. And your friends. I wish I could
stick around and help, but I'm not sure I could do
much for you anyway. In other words, I'm too scared
to hang around and find out.

Varnie

I walked around town for an hour, letting Varnie's words criss-cross my brain over and over again. Donny texted me for a coffee date, but I wasn't ready to talk yet and she knew me so well that I wouldn't be able to hide what I was feeling, so I declined, claiming homework.

I hit the side roads then, so Donny wouldn't see me on her way to the coffee shop. She texted me again to remind me we were going dancing at Chasm that night and that I wasn't allowed to bail. And then once more to tell me she'd run into "that sneetch with the book" again. This time, she'd let him look down her shirt before she "accidentally" spilled her mocha on his trendy tennis shoes. I sighed as I typed "LOL" even though what I meant was "Poor Gabe."

I figured I should go home or ask Amelia what Varnie

meant about a talisman, but I just didn't want to yet. I was scared and angry and confused. I didn't want to talk about it—I didn't even want to think about it. I just needed a break from my own life.

A huge pickup with muddy flaps passed me, then stopped and came back at me in reverse. My heart caught in my throat. Haden rolled the passenger window down.

It wasn't exactly the vehicle I'd expected to see him drive. He seemed more like a sports car bloke. Something low to the ground with too much chrome and shiny paint. Instead, this behemoth truck dwarfed me with its size and excessive show of masculinity.

"Theia?" Haden hit a button and I heard the door unlock. "Do you need a ride?"

I glanced around furtively. "I'm not really sure where I'm going."

"So hop in," said the spider to the fly.

Doubt settled in my stomach. The warnings of Varnie and my father swirled together into a slow-cooked stew of unease. I barely knew this boy—and what little I did know of him was not comforting in the least.

"I don't know." To be honest, I wanted to get in, despite the possible danger. Maybe because of it. "Okay." I decided. "Thanks."

I hesitated at the door. A person of my height needed a stepladder to get into his truck, but I managed to hurl myself in without breaking any bones. "Where are you going?" I asked as I slammed the door behind me.

Haden flashed me a grin. "You ever been stumping?"

"Er . . . I don't even know what that is."

"It involves muddy logging roads, four-wheel drive, and holding on to the 'oh, shit' handle above your door." His grin was infectious, but his words scared me. He gentled his tone. "You don't have to go. I can drop you off someplace else. It's just something that I like to do. It makes me feel . . . alive, I guess." He gestured to the forestry road sign. "You in or not?"

What I was in was a lot of trouble. The thought of stumping terrified me, but so did everything else. This fear had its appeal. Haden offered me a respite from the void inside— something tangible. I could cling to the handle above the door and know, for the first time this week, exactly what was scaring me. "I'm in."

He smiled. "You sure?"

I nodded. "I'm sure."

Serendipity Falls didn't boast any malls or box stores. We were a small place, about five thousand in population. What we lacked in sophistication we made up for in nature. Close to the mountains and the beach, not to mention the falls, the high school kids had lots of opportunity for getting away from stress caused by school and parents. My friends and I usually chose the beach, but a lot of guys, like Haden, liked the hills and the nonmaintained forestry roads.

His truck climbed the winding dirt road up a long incline, and my mouth was already dry. Haden's hands were sure on the wheel, and his mastery of the curves gave me some measure of ease, but not enough to remember to breathe on my own.

"Do you do this a lot?" I asked, careful to avoid any conversation that might actually be what I wanted to talk about most. About the roses, and the dream, and whether I was insane or if he was actually haunting my sleep. About whether he had anything to do with the school bell. For the next hour, I just wanted to live for the minute I was in.

"Not as much as I'd like, but as often as I can." There was joy in his tone; Haden thrived on his adrenaline and the whine his truck made before he shifted. "Back home, I used to take the truck out to get away from my mom when she drove me crazy. It makes everything else seem far away, you know?" He looked at me, tying my stomach in knots. "You understand, I think, the need to just stop being what everyone expects and just *be?*"

"I'm not sure I've ever really done that," I answered honestly. "My father's been pretty good at drumming that kind of behavior out of me. I hear his voice in my head even when he's nowhere near."

Haden nodded, his knuckles whitening as he gripped the wheel harder. "My mother—she's the same way. She's very controlling. I'll never be what she wants, but it doesn't stop her from trying. But when I go stumping, I can't hear her. You'll see."

He turned off the "main" road onto what looked more like a bike trail. Something obstructed the road, but instead of slowing down, Haden went over it hard, jostling me against my straining seat belt. My heart caught in my throat and he hooted like a hillbilly.

He laughed at my expression. "Are you going to be okay?" he asked, echoing the question he'd asked me days before.

"I think I left my stomach back there."

"Should I take you home?"

I clutched the handle resolutely. "Absolutely not."

Excitement coursed through my veins, replacing the fear for a blessed change.

Haden laughed. "Are you ready for some real fun now?"

With my other hand, I tugged my hair band loose. My father would have called me "my mother's daughter" but I didn't even care. "I'm ready."

We flew, and each time we landed it felt like someone put me in a rock tumbler. Pretty soon, I was making my own *Dukes of Hazzard* exclamations. I never imagined myself ever yelling "Yee-haw!" before, but I loved it. Adrenaline tasted sweet like ambrosia, and I was loath to go home. For the next hour, I didn't measure my words, my steps, my feelings. Alive in the moment, what I felt was joy. And terror occasionally, but mostly joy.

Haden dropped me off in front of my house. The first boy ever to do so. It was nice, to feel normal.

"Thank you, Haden. I really had a good time."

"You look . . . flushed," he answered.

Haden looked flushed too.

The cab was suddenly full of all the things I hadn't said. Questions I hadn't asked.

He hurried to fill the silence. "Maybe next time you can drive."

"Oh, heavens no," I answered. "I'd kill us both."

I'd meant to be flip, but Haden winced and quickly looked out the driver's-side window. I watched him retreat just as he always did. "I have to go," he said without looking at me. "See you around."

His dismissal stung. "Sure," I murmured and opened my

door. I had to jump to reach the ground. It felt like a very long way down.

I didn't think to look at the caller ID on my phone when it beeped an incoming call. I assumed it was Donny calling about our plans for the night.

I never expected to hear a young man on the other end.

"Theia?"

"Yes?" The voice was familiar, but not overly so.

"It's Gabe. From school?" As opposed to all those other Gabes I knew.

"Er . . . hello, Gabe," I responded warily.

"Cheerios."

"Excuse me?"

Gabe exhaled nervously into the phone. "Isn't that something you guys say in your country? Cheerios?"

The conversation spiraled downwards from there, once I explained that some people did say "cheerio" as a greeting, I supposed. After more awkward ums, ers, and ahs were exchanged, Gabe ended a lengthy silence with, "You're probably wondering why I called."

"The question has occurred to me, yes."

"Your friend . . ."

"Donny," I supplied.

"Yeah. Look, I don't make a habit out of trying to get information about a girl I like from her friends, well, not since sixth grade anyway. It's just, she's being . . ."

"Difficult," I answered.

Gabe chuckled. I liked his voice; it was deep and sincere—

confident. I liked Gabe for all the same reasons. He continued to discuss Donny, alternating between reverent adoration and sublime irritation. At some point, I realized I was walking around the room and laughing and talking to a boy on the telephone and feeling completely at ease.

"Does she ever . . . talk about me?"

"She very adamantly refuses to discuss you most of the time." I softened the blow with, "I think that's a very good sign."

"Yeah?"

"Yeah."

Donny would have killed me if she'd known I was talking about her. Gabe would be good for her, though. I knew it in my heart. "We're going to Chasm tonight. If you're . . . around."

"Yeah?" he answered.

"Yeah."

"Thanks, Theia."

"Cheerios, Gabe."

Later that night, I momentarily wished to be back on the dance floor with the ghouls rather than staring at the dance floor filled with my peers. The thump of the bass jarred my musical sensibilities, which I admit are quite sensitive. My mind raced to pick up strains of harmony and melody, but all I could feel was the *thwomp thwomp thwomp* in my chest.

You would think we'd have been more guarded with our hearing after losing it for those hours yesterday. Instead, I think we all reveled in the abuse of our eardrums.

Donny nudged my bare shoulder. "So how did you really get out tonight? What did you tell Daddy Dearest?" She'd mastered the art of speaking in a tone I could hear above the music. I wasn't as fortunate.

"I said 'good night,'" I yelled, feeling foolish. By nature, yelling wasn't something I did, and certainly not well. My voice cracked. "Father's flight got bumped, so he won't be home until morning."

"Don't tempt me like that. I might keep you out all night." Even as she spoke to me, she didn't look at me. Donny's eyes were studying the scene, looking for someone—I wondered if it was Gabe. "Stop fussing with your hair," she chided me.

She wasn't even looking at me—how did she know? "I can't help it. It feels weird."

She'd styled it for me, of course. I was, for all intents and purposes, a creation of Donny that night. My hair felt big to me—but I had to admit, she'd arranged my curls into something of a masterpiece and the freedom from hair restraints not only felt good but also loosened my spirits a little.

My makeup was an altogether different experience. Shellacked and powdered, I protested her heavy hand, but my objections were dismissed. As were my protests about the red halter shirt she put me in, claiming it was a dress. If my future included a street corner and a pimp named Ice Money, I'd be ready.

As there was already one streetwalker in our group, Donny went with very little makeup, braided pigtails, and what I can only guess was an outgrown school uniform. She was quite a bit taller these days. The combination stunned just about every guy that looked at her.

Every so often, I tried to blend back into the wall and Donny would pinch me. For the first time ever, I wished she would ditch me for a pretty boy. If Ame had been there, at least the punishments would have been meted out between the two of us, but Ame's mother had unrepentantly called a "family night." Worried about the lasting psychological effects of the week, she wanted to grasp the opportunity for parent/child communication.

Such were the hazards of being the daughter of a psychologist, Amelia often lamented. Truth be told, I envied that her parents at least wanted to have a close relationship. So Ame stayed home like a good girl, and I snuck out like a bad one. I already longed for a good book and my quilt.

I'd sought Haden in the throng of people since we'd arrived, but wasn't sure he was even coming until I felt the frost of his glare. My gaze darted up to the balcony to find his eyes trained on me, his expression pinched in anger. He wore all black, perfectly tailored. Perfectly dangerous.

And angry. He looked very, very angry. The chill of his stare, like jagged ice rubbing on my spine, made me shudder.

I'd wondered what it would be like to see him again after our brief respite of fun before he'd gotten cold again. I didn't know why he was so mad, but for some reason I liked it. Like I had some precarious power over him. Even if it was a bad idea to use it.

There were no "oh, shit" handles nearby, so I grasped Donny's hand and squeezed.

"What's wrong?" she asked.

Nothing came out when I tried to speak. He hadn't broken eye contact with me. My body responded to his anger in a tangle of desire, making me aware of the erogenous zones Donny often spoke of even when I begged her to shut up.

Donny leaned down and spoke into my ear. "Star-belly Gabe is here. Oh, boy." She tried to sound droll, but I wasn't stupid and I knew her too well. "Great, he's coming this way. God, why can't he just take a hint and leave me the hell alone?"

Gabe threaded through the crowd with purpose, but when he reached us, he grabbed my hand and ignored Donny. "Theia, you look amazing. If you don't dance with me, you'll break my heart."

Donny gasped and then recovered, though none of us were impressed with her charade anymore. "Your kind doesn't have hearts."

He shot back, "You don't know anything about what *kind* I am. When you're ready to find out, look me up." He squeezed my fingers lightly. "Please?"

The dancing looked far less complicated than the macabre waltz I'd accompanied Haden to. The kids just swayed and bobbed their heads to the music. Some were grinding against one another, like sex to music—but not everyone felt the need to molest one another.

I glanced up. Haden still gripped the balcony rail intensely. Spellbound by his dark gaze, I struggled to fight the alarm that fisted around my heart. Panic was not the sole emotion I dealt with. He excited me too.

Part of me, the most wicked part, sang to provoke him further.

I accepted Gabe's invitation while directing my smile to Haden. As we moved towards the floor, I justified my little rebellion. Haden had no claim to me. He ignored me when it suited him and paid attention to me only when it served his purpose . . . whatever that purpose was.

Maybe I needed to force his hand.

The acoustics were actually much better on the dance floor, though Gabe tried talking and I couldn't hear him.

"Huh?" I yelled.

He rested his hands on my arms and spoke low into my ear. "She looks like she's about to spit nails."

He wasn't wrong about that. Donny circled the edge of the floor like a lion preying on a gazelle. And Lord, she looked sexy. I wished I had that kind of power. It wasn't just her clothes, not that they didn't help her cause, but she oozed a sexual confidence as molten as lava. It occurred to me that she would have been a better match for Haden than I ever was.

The spear of jealousy found its mark. And it hurt.

Gabe and I watched Donny slide her body between a random dancing couple. As the guy enjoyed the new short-skirted distraction, the other girl left in a huff. Donny pulled him closer, but it was Gabe she watched.

Gabe she wanted.

Gabe's jaw ticked and the veins on his temples became visible. A glance to the balcony showed Haden with a similar rigidity in posture. The naked fury in his gaze flushed my veins with ice water. He was suddenly much more like the dangerous scoundrel from my dreams than the easygoing boy with the truck.

When Donny turned in her dance partner's arms and slid provocatively against him like he was a stripper pole, I knew things were about to get very out of control.

I grabbed Gabe's chin, forcing his eyes to mine.

"If you lose it right now, you'll lose her," I yelled.

He nodded, closing his eyes briefly to put himself back in

place. "Why does she have to be like that? I've tried to show her . . . I care. It's more than just a hookup. I don't want to be a hookup."

"Gabe, go cut in."

He shook his head. "I just want to go home."

As Gabe deflated in front of me, I realized I'd lost track of Haden. He'd left his perch, making me nervous. Taking care of all the testosterone in the club was getting exhausting.

"Go cut in." I stepped back, giving Gabe the out he needed to stop dancing with me and claim what he really wanted.

Gabe took one look at her, smiling at him, daring him. He stalked over to Donny, physically snatching her away from the other guy and molded her to his body. She didn't object and wound her arms around his neck, forgetting about the boy she'd been relieved of. And most likely me for the night as well.

I eyed the balcony. Next on my agenda was finding Haden.

He hadn't returned to the rail, but he could still be upstairs. I shouldn't have played the game. I didn't understand the rules. At first I'd felt that momentary flicker of power, but now I felt at odds. Distraught, unfinished.

Flashes of skin and the occasional random touch of strangers as I passed eased me into what felt like another world. The dancing bodies slowed my pace as I swam through the crowd. The smell of sweat and perfume, the disorienting lights, and the thrum of the music felt primal. Waves of sexual energy washed over me, seeping into my own skin.

And I hungered for something elusive, yet the air was thick with the promise of it.

It surprised me, this new potent feeling. And it was the

surprise that frightened me more than the actual rush of hormones. I couldn't control feelings that came out of nowhere.

The stairs were treacherous in the unfeasible heels Donny had put me into, and by the time I made it to the vista where I'd last seen Haden, I knew he was gone.

A long sigh escaped my lungs. What was I even doing here? I shouldn't have let Donny talk me into coming. Though my father might be too severe at times, this experience wasn't worth the cost of rebellion.

I leaned against the rail and my heart stopped.

Haden watched me from below as he led a nimble blonde onto the floor of gyrating teenagers. She stared at him, awestruck like he was some kind of rock star. God, I thought she might be right. He murmured something into her ear, but he smiled at me—the kind of smile that signals the demise of the canary to the whims of the cat.

He hooked one arm around her waist and raised a brow to me. I wanted to hate him; the burn seared my heart. When he turned her to face me, my breath caught in my throat. She had no idea he was using her as a pawn to assert his control over me, but I'm not sure she would have minded even if she had known. I doubt, had the tables been turned, I would have cared. To be enveloped in his arms, surrounded by his scent, guided through a dance by his steady hands . . . No, I would gladly have played marionette to his puppet master too.

She ground against him, not unlike Donny but without Donny's finesse. Or charm, for that matter. But I suppose charm wasn't what that kind of dancing was really about. I tightened my grip on the rail if not my emotions, but nothing could make me look away. He'd trapped me in his sinful gaze designed to weaken my will, to raise the stakes in the battle for my heart. Maybe my soul. He wanted me to know what I was missing even as he made it clear I couldn't have it. And I was depraved enough to let him.

The music changed tempo and they cut all the lights but the strobes. The effect heightened the feeling of displacement and made their dancing look like slow motion and out of sync with my perception. Haden gripped the blonde's hips, holding her firmly against his pelvis. She let her head fall to the side, exposing the long white column of her neck. He sent me one more evil grin and kissed her neck.

My knees buckled. I felt the sensation of his lips on my skin. The kiss felt like a shock that started on my neck and traveled on my nerve endings all the way down to my toes. His hand skimmed slowly from her hip to her stomach . . . my stomach. As the sensation crept slowly towards my breasts, my breath hitched. I wanted to drop my head back, but I couldn't. I was standing in the middle of a crowd by myself. He wasn't touching me—I knew that logically, but not physically. The fangs of lust were sharp and without pity.

Finally I was able to break the spell and look away. I glanced once more, met his eyes, and pushed off the rail and back through the swarm of bodies. He'd hollowed me completely. All I could think of was getting out of there. I needed fresh air and silence.

CHAPTER NINE

The girl in his arms writhed against him becomingly. Pity that she couldn't satisfy the dark need inside him. The ache that grew and licked at him like flames. There was only one who could fill that void. And Theia would want nothing to do with him now; he'd made sure of that.

It was better this way. Better for her that she hated him. Safer for them both.

He'd barely begun the familiar argument with himself when he found himself following her to the door. He knew all the reasons he should leave her be—he knew it would end badly. If he touched her . . . God help them all if he touched her.

There wasn't enough room in my heart for all the feelings Haden was trying to put into it. The longing warred with the anger in a violent battle for supremacy. How much easier it would have been if I could have just hated him.

I burst through the doors and the cold shock of air spurred a crop of goose bumps across my bare skin instantly. Curse Donny and her makeover that left me in a dark parking lot looking like a hooker while she seduced the only nice boy I'd ever spent any time with. Curse Gabe for not being the one who interested me. Curse Haden for being the one who did.

"This is a new look for you."

I whipped around, a mistake on ridiculous heels. Attempting to regain my balance and dignity, I dropped my purse.

Haden strolled towards me, stooping to retrieve the purse. Straightening, he offered the strap, dangling it from his finger while his eyes roamed my body dangerously. I wondered which Haden I was dealing with—the one from my dreams or the one from school. His gaze suggested sinful things wherever it landed on my skin and I wondered if maybe there was a third Haden after all.

I snatched the purse and shrugged, trying to remember I was angry with him. "Don't get used to it. I turn back into a mouse at midnight."

"You're no mouse, Theia." He paused. "I also didn't say I liked your new look. I don't care for it much at all."

I shrugged once again. How kind of him to grind me into the ground before he scraped me off his shoe.

"What are you doing out here alone?" he asked. "It's really not safe."

Unable to come up with a coherent answer to that, I stared at him like he was out of his mind. Why on earth did he even pretend to care?

"There is a lot of drug activity here," he explained, as if the scariest thing in my world was drug dealers.

"I don't feel especially safe anywhere lately. Not even my own bed," I taunted. I wasn't trying to be sexual, though I'm sure it sounded that way. I was hoping he'd say something to prove he was aware of the dreams.

He didn't take the bait, but did arch a brow. "Perhaps you need a better security system."

"Shouldn't you be getting back to your date?"

"I didn't bring a date." That didn't mean he wasn't leaving with one.

The wind picked up and I shivered. I was going to have to go back into the club and I really, really didn't want to. Haden was right, though, I wasn't safe alone in the parking lot, even if there weren't roaming drug dealers and other "purveyors of dark" around. I'd let my frustration push me into irrational behavior.

"I should go." I made an effort to step around him on his right, but he moved the same way and blocked me. Thinking it was a mistake, I went the other way and he blocked me again.

"Sorry," he said, with no trace of regret.

"Are you going to pull my pigtails next?"

He laughed, the good kind. "Probably. I don't know what it is about you, Theia. It seems to bring out the bad boy in me."

"Is there another kind of boy in you, Haden?"

He stared into my eyes while he shook his head no. The scrutiny made me self-conscious. I tried to swallow, but my mouth was so dry. Without thinking, I licked my lower lip.

It was as if the action pushed a button and opened a gate. He took a heavy step towards me, wild and unbound.

I shivered with equal parts fear and excitement. And then he stopped short of putting his hands on me.

Someone had started a car, and the headlights shone on us like a spotlight. I saw the same battle in his eyes that I fought within myself. He didn't want to want me—but he did. Without thinking, I reached for a lock of his jet-black hair. I thought only to brush it away from his eyes, but he backed away quickly. "Don't touch me," he growled. "Never touch me."

My hand was still suspended in a futile pose where his face had been a moment before. I snatched it back, and the familiar burning near my heart signaled that another crushing blow to my esteem had been delivered. I willed the stinging tears to wait. Just wait. Not now, not in front of him.

"Why do you hate me so much?" I couldn't keep the words in, though I wished I could. All I was doing was providing him more ammunition.

"I don't hate you."

"I just don't understand why you find it so amusing to be nice to me one minute and mock me the next. The way you stared at me from the balcony . . . Why were you so angry? What could I possibly have done to you to make you so mad?"

Haden's hands pressed against his temples like he was trying to hold back a headache. "Truthfully, I didn't like the way you were flaunting yourself in front of everyone. Your dress . . . the way you look tonight—it's shameless."

I exhaled a very unladylike snort that would have forced my father's temple to throb with displeasure. But that was fine. For once, my own displeasure was more important to me. "What I wear is none of your business, Haden."

"No, I don't suppose it is."

"I was dressed no differently than any other girl in that club," I argued, even though he'd just agreed with me.

"But you are different from all those other girls." His pupils enlarged, darkening his eyes eerily.

"Yes, I know. You don't need to keep reminding me." I crossed my arms instinctively. "If you'll excuse me, I can remove my distasteful person from your sight."

"Distasteful?" he scoffed. "You still don't get it." He took a step away from me. "Is that what you think? That I'm not tempted? That I don't find you more delectable than the sweetest fruit?"

"Is that what the blonde was on the dance floor? The sweetest fruit? What kind of teenager talks like that, Haden? What are you?"

He didn't answer. Of course.

"Does she know you touched her for my benefit?"

Haden looked away. "No. I don't think she does."

I was inhaling in gasps too big to consume. "You're a user. You play games with people for fun. Me, the girl in the club, Brittany, Noelle—all of us are like pawns to you. I don't know who you really are, Haden, or where you really come from, but I think you're the devil."

"You're absolutely right." I hadn't imagined it—his eyes were changing. There was very little white left in them at all. "I've tried to stay away from you, Theia. I don't think I can, but God knows I've tried."

His expression, wild and unrestrained, put a cold terror in my heart. I stepped back. He began to move towards me and then stopped himself. He drew in a ragged breath and it sounded like the word "no" escaped his lips before the windows of every vehicle in the parking lot shattered.

The sound of the blast made me lose my footing on the stupid stiletto heels and I fell to the ground. Glass sprayed, raining glittery shards on us—me on my knees and Haden lording over me with the look of the devil in his eyes.

I didn't understand what was happening. There were more explosions as the bulbs in streetlights and neon signs burst from their casings.

"Haden?" I cried. Lightning gashed open the sky and the wind whipped the dust and glass around me. I covered my face with one hand and tried to reach for him with the other. "Haden, help me up, please."

I looked up through my fingers, but he'd gone. I covered my head with my arms as the sky rumbled as loudly as if Earth had collided with another planet. Hail the size of peas poured out of the sky.

He'd left me on my knees while begging him for help. Alone.

Donny and Gabe found me a few minutes later, curled into a ball and shivering. Gabe coaxed his coat onto me. I should have said thank you, but I don't think I did.

They took me home before the authorities arrived, cleaned me up, and made me tea without asking me to talk or answer a single question. One of my shoulders had taken a fair amount of glass, but the cuts were superficial. I caught their worried glances at each other, but pretended not to notice and let numbness shape itself over me like a second skin.

I stared at the violent storm outside the window, drinking

my tea and pushing their murmured voices from my mind until I realized Donny was telling Gabe to go, that she'd stay with me through the night.

"No," I interrupted. "I'm fine. You should both go."

"Theia, I'm not leaving you like this. Something happened to you out there—"

I shrugged farther into the soft blanket she'd put around my shoulders. "Yes, the weather happened to me out there. It was a frightening storm to be caught in. But I'm fine now." I needed to be alone. My mind couldn't process anything while they hovered over me.

"Thei—" she began.

"I need to sleep, Donny. Please, I'll be fine."

A few more minutes of arguing convinced her, though she was still reluctant to go. Gabe checked all the doors and windows while Donny and I walked to the door.

"How did I end up with Sir Fucking Galahad, Thei?" She hadn't lost her panache for language, but already Donny's face seemed softer to me.

"He seems like a really nice bloke." Usually her club pickups convinced her to leave her friends behind. Gabe had insisted on seeing me home and checking locks.

She rolled her eyes. "You know, he told me he wouldn't sleep with me? While we were dancing, for God's sake. He just announced that there would be no sex until he was satisfied that I wasn't using him for his body."

The first smile of the night swept my face. "But you are using him for his body, aren't you?" I played along.

"Of course. Now it's just going to take me longer." Donny grabbed my shoulders gently and looked soulfully into my eyes, searching for cracks in my facade, I was sure. "Are you sure you're okay? We can stay. The sky is still pissing rain and I don't think we'll get the end of the thunder anytime soon. It's a bad night to be alone in this huge house." She didn't mention all the broken windshields at the club. Hers only had a long, jagged crack. Gabe's car wasn't as lucky. I already knew the newspaper would blame the storm.

"I'll sleep through it. Go on, will you? Maybe you can at least get to second base tonight still."

"Honey, we got to second base on the dance floor."

My turn to roll my eyes at her, and then good-byes were said. I locked the door behind them, then slid down it slowly as exhaustion, physical and emotional, rolled over me in waves. As tired as I was, I knew I wouldn't sleep.

The wind howled, vicious and malevolent. Shrubs scratched and rattled against the windows. Odd bumps and creaks rumbled and scraped across the roof. The power flickered twice, then cut out, leaving me in the dark until lightning strobed the room and flashed strange, long shadows on the wall.

Though our Victorian wasn't old, only built to look that way, it still felt haunted, filled with something . . . *other*. I felt my way across the room, stumbling and grazing the wall. The house should have been familiar, but the ominous darkness changed even my perception of my home. As I reached into the drawer for the flashlight, the kitchen storm door slammed on its hinges. *Bang! Bang! Bang!* I whimpered and then chastised my foolishness.

I had two choices: secure the door or listen to it crash into the frame at random all night. I turned on the flashlight and slowly crept across my own kitchen like a burglar. My hand hesitated on the doorknob, and I took a deep breath to steady my nerves. *It's just a slamming door in the wind.* But still, I said a little prayer, one from my childhood, the only one I could remember at the moment.

I pray the Lord my soul to keep.

I flung the door open and reached for the screen door handle. The wind moaned in agony, but I grasped the handle, heaved it closed, and turned the lock. Working quickly, I did the same with the kitchen door and then sobbed with relief when I had accomplished my goal.

Bolstered by my victory, and the beam from the flashlight, I crossed the kitchen normally and my heart slowed to a standard rhythm. Until I got to the living room and the hair on my nape rose like it had been rubbed the wrong way.

I froze, letting the rest of my senses figure out what was wrong. *It's all in your head, Thei.* Sure it was. Like everything that had happened all week. I tightened my grip on the flashlight, knowing full well that it would be of little use as a weapon. I suspected that whatever I needed to battle wouldn't respond to any kind of force I could provide.

I swallowed the fear and resumed moving. I kept going, up the stairs and then, on a whim, past my room to the end of the hall and the staircase that led to the next floor. Varnie had said I would need a talisman. I wasn't sure exactly what that meant. I assumed it was some kind of amulet, something personal to me, and instinct lured me to the third floor.

I eyed the staircase, pausing for a moment of trepidation

before I climbed the short flight. The attic wasn't scary like some. It wasn't dark—well, except now, with no electricity. There were no cobwebs or strange windows. It was just an ordinary bonus room with the same carpeting as my own room. And yet it had always felt soulless and cold to me, perhaps because it was never used, never lived in. If houses had feelings, all of our neglect was stored in this room. The room that held my dead mother's things.

The howling wind seemed worse on the third floor. The storm, the dark, and my own fears combined like a haunted force field I was pushing myself to go through. Unfortunately, Varnie's words of something attaching to me and wanting me very badly weren't going to soothe me. The sensible thing would have been to curl up downstairs and try to sleep through the storm. My sensible gene was on a business trip, though, so instead I chose to brave the attic in the dark to find something I shouldn't need.

Shaking from too much adrenaline and not enough clothing, I hurried across the room without shining the light into the corners. If something was lurking there, I decided, I'd rather not know about it. I found the box I was after quickly—nobody ever moved anything in the attic—so I sat in front of it and loosened the lid.

From the corner of my eye, I glimpsed a shadow darting across the wall and my heart slammed against my rib cage. I sat very still, unmoving and reluctant to breathe. There—it happened again. Too fast to track, the shadow skittered blithely, though nothing in the room was moving and there was no light by which to create a shadow, much less see one.

My blood chilled with dread, yet my shaky hands finished removing the box lid and I searched for the jewelry box, clutching it to my breast when I found it. I ran across the room to the door. I had to bite my lip not to squeal, because as I closed the door, fingers of cold tried to pull me back in.

I flew down the stairs and into my room, taking great gulps of air. I dropped to the floor and dumped out the contents of the wooden box. I don't know why I was in such a hurry and so careless with my mother's jewelry; I just knew I needed to find the pendant I was looking for. It was a simple black stone set in silver on a chain. My fingers shook with the clasp, but I managed to get it closed around my neck finally.

I wondered when she'd worn it last. I didn't even know what kind of stone it was or if it meant anything special to her. Maybe it was just a cheap necklace she'd gotten at a street fair. It hardly looked like anything my father would have purchased for her. I'd seen her wearing it in a few pictures, but it never appeared to be a favorite.

The weight of the stone on my chest reassured me. For better or worse, I'd found my talisman.

Surrounded by heat, I opened my eyes and was blinded by the bright, hot sun. I squinted and let my eyes adjust to the radiant light.

Beneath my feet, hot sand burned my skin and it became apparent that I was alone in a vast, desolate desert. Not knowing what else to do, I sat.

As the sun baked my body like a roast in an oven, I won-

dered where Haden was. There was nowhere for me to go—
the flat sand stretched for miles on all sides. Nothing broke
the view and no prints in the sand hinted at any other life
nearby.

Vacant, hot, barren. *Damn it, Haden.*

He appeared as if he had always been there, charming in
his coattails and top hat. As if we were to take tea in the oppressive heat. The flash of his white teeth, all the better to bite
me with, unnerved me.

Not content to let him hover over me while I remained on
the ground again, I rolled my knees under me to stand.

"You're still dressed like a trollop," he remarked. "And
you're pouting."

I was certainly not pouting. Why hadn't I changed clothes?
I guess I'd assumed I wouldn't fall asleep. I remember sitting
in the rocking chair in my bedroom to rest a minute before I
got ready for bed. And then I woke up in the desert.

I looked at Haden, remembering coolly how he'd left
me in the storm after he'd worked me into a jealous fit. And
now, to add insult, he called me a trollop. "How old are you,
Haden?"

"Seventeen. That's an odd question, Theia."

"You're not seventeen."

"I'm almost eighteen."

"You use words like 'trollop.' How old are you really?"

"You speak very formally also, little lamb. Should I call
your age into question too?"

My father let me read only classic literature. As much as
I loved Jane Austen, I knew the constant immersion in the

nineteenth century caused another language barrier between my peers and me. I didn't feel I owed Haden an explanation, though, and I gifted him with a blank gaze.

I wanted answers. I needed them, and Haden owed me that much. "What are you?"

He met my eyes and in them I recognized his loneliness. He wanted to tell me; he wanted to open himself.

Instead he told me to wake up.

CHAPTER TEN

Father's voice on the other end of the phone line was brittle and tired. Apparently, the delay in his business trip was less about the airlines and more about "the bloody idjits who won't listen to reason" at his meetings. At any rate, Father would not be home anytime on Sunday either. He hoped the Monday-morning conference call would put this to bed, whatever *this* was.

I hung up and sighed. The power had been restored sometime during the night, and the yard was full of debris and tree branches that must have flown like missiles in the wind. The sky was free of turmoil that morning, though. The sun shone brightly and there was no hint of fog; in fact the air had that balmy poststorm feel. It should have made me feel better, but it didn't.

The fury that rampaged through our town last night wasn't a meteorological event. My unease didn't dissipate—I had a feeling it wasn't over. There was a desperate frustration in that wind, in the bolts of electricity that ripped seams in the sky. The sky may have been clear now, but the leftover emotion still felt strong.

I wanted to talk to Ame about the necklace, the talisman I'd put on last night. Varnie had said she would know what to do. He'd also said I would need it but it wouldn't protect me and, frankly, I had no idea what that meant. Ame always wore crystals for different things, like better concentration or anti-exhaustion—but I thought a talisman was supposed to be more of a ward than a good health supplement.

I wandered the house, full of restlessness and eager for . . . something. I needed a good distraction. And . . . I had an idea. Of sorts. I just hoped my friends wouldn't kill me for it.

I scrolled through the short contact list on my iPhone, finding the number Gabe had used to call me from yesterday. I paced another moment or two, my finger hovering over the CALL button. I'd never called a boy before. Ever.

I was being ridiculous. A product of my father's overprotective upbringing. It was no different calling Gabe than it was Donny or Ame. I pressed my finger to the touch screen and listened to the music while my party was being reached.

"Yo," he answered.

"Gabe? It's Theia."

An edge lined his voice. "You okay? I can be there in five minutes."

I smiled with relief. "I'm fine, really. Thank you for . . . last night. I need your help, sort of. If that's okay."

"That depends. If this is moving-heavy-things help, I'm your guy."

I laughed, wondering again why it was so easy to talk to Gabe and why Donny tried so hard to resist him. "I need to invite Mike Matheny to my house, but I don't know his number."

"Matheny, huh? You already getting over the new guy? Good. He seems like a jerk."

It felt strange to think of Haden as "the new guy." He was so indefinable to me that such an easy explanation seemed wrong. "I'm not interested in Mike that way. He's in my trig class with Amelia. I'd like to invite him over to study— well, I mean, I already did the other day. But then the whole school ended up in the emergency room, so it didn't happen. I mean, I like Mike. I just don't like Mike that way." I paused my nervous rambling and went ahead and took a breath. "So, anyway . . . I thought he might like to study with us. With *Amelia*." I stressed her name, drawing out the syllables hoping he'd understand. "He and *Amelia* would probably get along well, don't you think?"

"Uh-huh," he answered, which must have been guy talk for something. The sound should have been noncommittal, but there were layers in it.

"Donny isn't in trig this year," I mentioned. "But I have a feeling she'll be coming by anyway."

"Uh-huh."

"I mean, unless the two of you made plans for today."

"Nope. She's being . . . herself." He sounded resigned.

I took that to mean she gave him the brush-off already, despite last night. "If you wanted to come by and make sure I'm still doing okay alone in the big house, this afternoon would be a good time to do that."

"I'll keep that in mind." I heard him open a can of soda. It wasn't even noon yet. "So have you always been a matchmaker or is this a new thing for you?"

"New, obviously. I'm not very good at it, am I?"

"I would sound like a real jerk if I told you I got a lot further with your friend last night than I would have if you hadn't gotten involved, so I'll just shut up about it and give you Matheny's number."

I blushed with the same old fear. "Gabe, um, I don't know if I can call two boys in one day now."

"You really are an odd girl. I'll just bring him by. We'll see what happens."

"What if he's busy?"

"He won't be. There's a protocol."

"What kind of protocol?"

"I can't give up trade secrets, English." I smiled at his use of Donny's nickname for me. I heard a drawer open. Was he getting dressed? I blushed hotter. "If Matheny thinks I need him as an excuse to be at your house, since I'm not in your trig class, he'll assist for the score. It's what we do."

I paused. Assist for the score? Then I realized it was a sports metaphor. Not a very flattering one, but I was proud of myself for understanding guy talk.

We ended the call, and I rang the girls next. I didn't tell Ame that the boys would be there, and I *forgot* to mention that Gabe would likely be with Mike when I asked Donny to come by. It must have slipped my mind.

Donny borrowed her mother's car, since her windshield was cracked, and brought both Ame and a huge bag of snacks. Amelia eyed us both suspiciously in the kitchen.

"What's with the pork rinds?" she asked Donny as she unloaded the grocery bag.

"I know it's been a long time since you've eaten anything that's not salad, but pork rinds are what we like to call a *snack food*. And why are you wearing so many watches?"

Amelia had four on one arm, each brightly colored with cartoons. "I couldn't decide which one I felt like wearing today. Since when do you eat pork rinds? And don't even tell me they're for Theia."

I wasn't exactly sure what a pork rind was myself, so I read the package while they argued and then wished I hadn't. I grimaced in a less than ladylike manner that would have raised my father's blood pressure. "Why *did* you buy these?"

Donny mimed the cut sign at her throat and I shrugged. The doorbell rang and Amelia narrowed her eyes at us.

"I'll get it," Donny offered.

That was not a good idea. I didn't need her shooting Gabe down before he had a chance to come into the house. I jumped in front of her. "No, I will."

"Maybe I should get the door," Amelia said, clearly realizing now that something was up.

"Noooo," Donny and I answered, because that would have been disastrous.

And then it was on.

The three of us raced to the front door, giggling, pushing, and pulling one another out of the way. I went down first, but I took Ame with me—well, after I grabbed her shoe. Donny shook her hips in victory and threw open the door, out of breath and laughing.

The laughter died quickly. "Haden? What are you doing here?"

Haden? I stood up quickly, wiping my eyes and clearing my throat, embarrassed and completely out of sorts. What *was* he doing here?

Haden held up a pink bakery box like an offering and looked over Donny's shoulder at me before he answered her. "I was hoping Theia was home. We have a history project. I thought we could work on it today."

"Did you call first?" Donny wanted to know.

"No," he answered sheepishly.

She leaned on the doorframe, crossing her arms. "You just showed up at her house thinking she'd drop everything to study with you?" Wow, Haden didn't stand a chance. She was veering towards level-two bitchery already.

"I brought pastries," he answered, using a humble tone I'd never heard from him before. "I should have called."

"Did you bring enough for all of us?" Okay, he had half a chance here.

His practiced grin slid across his face. "There are a dozen red velvet cupcakes in this box."

Donny nodded. "By all means," she said, gesturing towards the room. "Come in. Let me take the box for you."

Donny snagged Ame's sleeve on her way to the kitchen and left me alone with him. Awkwardly alone.

He seemed out of place in my house. He even seemed out of place in the jeans and tee he wore. He moved differently, uncomfortably. He looked right at me then, and I swallowed hard. Haden was blushing.

I couldn't believe it.

Apparently blushing is contagious, because my face heated to my hairline too. We didn't say anything for a very long moment, and then tried to speak at the same time. After a couple of false starts, I held my hand over my mouth and pointed to him to begin.

"I'm sorry I was sort of a jerk last night."

I didn't know how to respond to that. I really didn't. When hadn't he been a jerk to me? And why apologize now? There was real sincerity in his voice, though. He seemed so different today, almost sad.

"Sort of?" I asked.

"Right." If there had been a hole, Haden would have crawled into it. "I'm sorry I was a big jerk last night. You're a nice girl and I'm not a nice guy." He didn't look at me while he spoke. "I find myself not knowing how to act around you, I guess. You're not like . . . you're not like I thought it would be."

I felt the pinch of my brow. "Like what would be?"

The doorbell rang again and Haden blew his breath out in relief. "You better get that." He finally looked me in the eye, revealing a soft smirk. "Before one of the girls tackles you to get there first."

"You heard all that?"

"It sounded like a stampede from the other side of the door."

I covered my face briefly. It was embarrassing—but not humiliating. It was . . . kind of nice. "There are snacks in the kitchen."

I hurried to the door and let Gabe and Mike in.

From behind, I heard Donny. "Thei, we moved the snacks to the sunroom. It's the only room that doesn't feel like a museum display—" She paused. "What the hell are *you* doing here?"

"Hey, Donny." Gabe took off his coat and stuffed it in the crook of her arm. "We're here to study."

She let the coat fall to the floor and turned around in a huff.

"Christ," Gabe muttered while smiling, "did she paint those jeans on?"

I made the world's most pained introductions to the three boys, though I'm sure they already knew one another. I caught sight of Ame flashing in and out of the room as soon as she saw Mike. I tried to usher them back to the sunroom, but Haden flinched when I got too close and stared at Mike and Gabe with unfriendly eyes.

He noticed me watching him and smiled, covering his distress. "Theia, you have company. I should have called."

"Stay, man," Gabe said easily. "Only half of us have a trig test anyway."

Mike looked confused. I felt bad for him. He was the only one in the house who really had no idea what all the strange currents were about, but once we made it into the sunroom, he made a beeline for the snacks. "I love pork rinds," he said, and that seemed to make him happy enough.

Donny smiled with satisfaction that her covert intelligence had been credible. Still, Mike and his snack happiness aside, the rest of the room crackled with tension. Ame was flushed and I couldn't tell if she was glad or upset that we'd invited Mike. I knew Donny was only pretending to be angry at Gabe's presence, but that didn't mean I wouldn't pay for it later. Haden was wary of both the boys, and Gabe just wanted Donny to look at him, which she refused to do.

"So, Theia, how can we help?" Gabe sat on the wicker couch and pulled me next to him. "Make flashcards or something?"

Donny scowled when he put his arm around me. We all knew it was friendly and designed to irritate her. Well, most of us knew. Mike was still crunching on his pigskin things and didn't appear to notice, but Haden looked distinctly unsettled.

Donny pulled Ame to the love seat and sat Mike next to her. Haden took the chair. When the wicker creaked as he sat down, I remembered my violin smoking when I played in that chair. And then I thought of the black rose in my drawer and the burning man falling from the sky. And then the school bell and the tarot cards. And last night's storm. Despite the warmth of Gabe next to me, I was chilled from head to toe. I'll admit he smelled nice, though.

Donny didn't sit down. It was either too much coffee or too much weirdness in the room. Nobody said anything. Except for Mike's crunching and the rattling of the pork rind bag, the room was unnaturally quiet. It seemed like someone should have at least brought up the school bell that deafened us, but in Serendipity Falls denial would prevail. Amelia was the only one who made any attempt to pull out schoolwork.

"Where's yours?" Donny asked Haden.

"Excuse me?"

"Your books. You said you were here to work on your project, but you didn't bring any books or papers." She executed a perfectly arched brow, and I vowed to learn to do that someday.

Haden leaned back in his chair. His grin was dark. "I lied."

He had all our attention then. He aimed his at Amelia. Something stole over his face like a shadow, like it had that morning in the courtyard. A sort of static electricity hummed around him and I caught a whiff of sulfur. I shivered, but no one else seemed to notice. Except maybe Amelia, though instead of exhibiting dread, she sat up straighter and cocked her head at Haden.

Her eyes got glassy and her breathing changed, deepened. I looked back at Haden and he seemed so ugly to me just then, though I couldn't explain why. He was just . . . wrong.

"Stop it." My voice was small, but firm.

The charge in the air evaporated instantly. Haden's face returned to, well, too handsome for words, and Amelia blinked a few times. Everyone else looked at me like they wondered what I was trying to stop exactly.

"Stop interrogating Haden, Don," I said quickly, covering.

Haden looked at me, really looked at me then. In his face I recognized the sheepish boy and the dangerous man all blended together. I knew, in my soul, that he was indeed the Haden from both worlds. He was far from innocent and at the same time somehow as naïve as I was.

"May I speak with you in the kitchen, Haden?" I stood, my legs a little wobbly.

"Of course," he answered, unfolding himself from the chair with the kind of grace normal people just didn't have.

When we got to the kitchen, I turned to him to begin a likely stilted conversation because I had no idea what I wanted to say, but I stopped before a word escaped my lips. He was right there, so close, with just a breath between our bodies.

He blinked slowly and inhaled deeply, like he was smelling a flower.

I ached to press my lips against his eyelids, to feel the soft thicket of his lashes on my skin. When he opened his eyes, the moment stood still, trapping us both in a strange tenderness that we hadn't yet experienced together. I reached into the pocket of my khaki pants and pulled out a black petal I'd saved from the other morning. It rested gently in the palm of my hand, perfectly preserved yet not made of silk, and I brought it up between us, forcing him to see it.

He stared at the tear-shaped petal. "Not today, Theia." He released another sigh. He lowered the timbre of his voice until it tugged my heart with its pleading tone. "Just for a few hours, can we forget? I know it's a lot to ask, but please. Please, can we just have *one* afternoon?" Haden's voice shook. "It would be a gift, and I would treat it as such, if you'd just allow me to be . . . me . . . for a little longer."

"I don't understand. You want one afternoon of what exactly?"

"Just to be normal. Just to be here. With you. Your friends. I can't explain how much it would mean to me if you could find it in your heart to forget about everything else for just one afternoon."

I searched his eyes for something to explain his request. "You have to promise not to do that . . . whatever you were doing to Amelia."

He nodded his assent, looking hopeful.

"Will you answer me one question?"

"I suppose it will depend entirely upon what you ask."

Tell me again he was seventeen because he certainly didn't

speak like it. "Why won't you touch me? You avoid it like I'd burned you."

"Will you believe me if I say it's for your safety?"

My expression must have said no.

Haden leaned towards my hair, his breath warming my ear and setting off a trail of warm, tumbling sensation throughout my whole body. He whispered, "I can't touch you because I *want* to touch you more than anything in the world."

I swallowed around my heart, which had edged its way into my throat.

"If I give in to that," he continued, "all will be lost."

Learning to listen to your intuition is an important life skill that will keep you out of danger, save your life, and win you a huge mound of cupcakes.

Either that or Amelia was cheating at poker.

After an hour or so of failing to get any studying done, Gabe came up with the idea of poker. Donny suggested we play for clothes, but Haden thought perhaps cupcakes and cookies could suffice as the chips. I'd never played poker before. Also, as evidenced by my small stack of cookies, I wasn't what one would call a natural.

All I had left were animal cookies, which I liked, especially the pink ones, but I was coveting the chocolate chip cookies that everyone else had. Looking at my cards, it was obvious I wasn't going to win one in this hand either.

"Don't even think about it, Theia," Haden said. His voice, still full of mischief, also sounded relaxed.

"Think about what?"

"I see you eyeing my chocolate chip stack."

"I am not," I protested. Weakly.

He shared a small smile with me and it spilled over my soul like sunshine poking through the clouds.

Donny pushed two cookies into the middle of the kitchen table. "I told you we should have played for clothes, Theia. Just think, you could be eating cupcakes right now. Of course, you'd be completely *naked* and eating cupcakes, but at least there would be sugar involved."

Haden blushed again and tried to hide it behind his cards. I was used to Donny's brassy comments and they normally didn't bother me. When I stuck out my tongue at her, I realized they didn't bother me in front of the company either. She inferred nakedness—*my nakedness*—in front of three boys, one of them Haden, and I didn't really care. I was having too much fun.

The kitchen seemed homier, pleasant and well lit. I brought my iPhone dock downstairs and we put Donny's phone on it for music. The table was small for six of us, but we all crowded around it amiably. Mike and Ame were the quietest of the bunch, although part of me thought it was because Ame was putting all her energies into being a cardsharp. Gabe was really good at putting everyone at ease and keeping us joking, and he excelled at keeping Donny in line. And Haden sat next to me.

I felt . . . happy.

"So, Mike," Donny began, "if you weren't here being fleeced by Amelia, what would you be doing tonight?"

Amelia and I leaned forward. It was an interesting question. He'd been so quiet, not really coming to life at all unless food was mentioned. He understood the trig, so he had functioning brain cells, but I couldn't help but feel that personality-wise he was sort of like a block of tofu. He didn't have one of his own; instead, he absorbed everyone else's.

Mike shrugged for an answer, and I sat back in my chair and exchanged an exasperated look with Donny. Ame, on the other hand, pinned her with a "shut up now" look, but Donny pretended not to notice.

"What do you like to do?" Donny tried again. "Besides eat." Because Lord knew he'd done enough of that to qualify for an Olympic event.

"I like video games."

Donny waited for more words that didn't come and then answered, "Ame can kick everybody's ass at *Call of Duty*."

"Really?" All three boys answered, suddenly very interested in the blushing Ame. It was another of her contradictions. She was very concerned with world peace—yet she excelled at first-person shooter games.

"I guess I picked the wrong girl," Gabe muttered. I couldn't see Donny's hand, but judging from his harsh curse, she pinched him under the table.

Mike looked at Amelia a little longer than usual, the skin above his nose creasing like maybe he was surprised to see her or something. She looked over her cards at him and smiled shyly.

I wondered if that was all it would take.

Another deal. Another bad deal for me. I folded. Again. And after Haden put his last cupcake in, he leaned towards me with a chocolate chip cookie between his fingers.

I leaned towards him too, as if we were alone in a room full of people. "Are you teasing me?"

Our faces were very close and he smiled, completely un-guarded and without a whiff of his sardonic attitude. "I feel sorry for you is all."

I took the cookie, and even though we didn't touch each other, a brush of our hands couldn't have felt more electric.

"Dude, you can't give her your cookies," complained Mike.

I took a quick bite before anyone made me give it back.

"Cheater," Mike teased.

"You're going to ruin it for the rest of us, man," said Gabe, looking directly at Donny. "Now they're *all* going to expect to be coddled."

Donny rolled her eyes and raised him another cookie.

By the end of the hand, everyone conceded that Amelia was by far the best of us. With our admission of not be-ing worthy, she granted each of us a cupcake, since she'd won them all.

I couldn't remember having a better time while I lis-tened to Gabe and Haden discuss baseball as they cleaned the kitchen. Mike, still a little clueless if you asked me, and Amelia had sunroom duty, and Donny came with me to put the music away.

"The sneetches are growing on me," Donny said, flopping on my bed. "I feel so dirty."

"How do you think Ame and Mike are getting on?" I asked.

"He's a little . . . slow on the uptake. I'm not sure I under-stand the draw."

I had to agree, unfortunately. "What do you think of Haden?"

"Honestly?" She stood and walked to the door.

I held my breath.

"He's out of my league. I can't get a handle on the guy. Sometimes he seems so into you, and other times he's . . . sort of the Antichrist."

"That about sums him up," I agreed, joining her.

We got to the stairs and she stopped me. "How do *you* feel about him? That's the important thing."

I shrugged. "Up is down. Down is up."

"And that means . . . ?"

"I'm probably half in love with a boy I don't really like."

Donny nodded. I had a feeling she understood exactly what I was saying.

CHAPTER ELEVEN

It shouldn't have been surprising to wake up someplace other than my bed, but it always surprised me nonetheless.

"I have to admit, the trollop dress was becoming, but I find your virginal nightgown pushes the blood through my veins with greater force."

I rewarded Haden with a sidelong glance. No longer dressed in his jeans, he seemed older again in his Regency-era finery. And he definitely didn't have the shy-boy look in his eyes anymore. He was back to his devious self, yet a sadness tinged him.

"Thank you," I replied, as though it was a compliment and not a poke at my always apparent bashfulness. If I was completely honest with myself, I'd worn the gown a little bit on purpose. I could have gone to sleep in sweatpants and combat boots—but I chose to continue wearing the nightgown.

I took in my surroundings. The riverbank again, I decided, though instead of sunshine, twilight cast a bluish lens to the scenery. "The river is beautiful."

"Is it?" He raked a hand through his thick hair. He was at odds again. "It's called Fleuve des Larmes. It's a river of tears, lamb, the tears of mothers. You'll notice it never recedes from the banks, as there is always plenty of misery to feed it. A never-ending bounty of pain has always been bestowed upon mothers."

I inhaled sharply at his description.

"My world is no place for you, Theia."

Straightening my spine, I put aside the anguished look on his face and persevered. "Tell me about the night you fell from the sky."

Haden's dark eyes flashed. "I wish you'd never seen that." He closed his eyes against the unwanted memory, but we both knew he still saw it. We both did.

"I gave you the afternoon, Haden. It's past time that you explained everything to me. I deserve to know what is going on. I know there are billions of things I don't understand about where I am right now as opposed to where we were this afternoon. And I know, for you and me, it started with you falling from the sky."

As if to show I had all the time in the world, I eased onto my side, bending my elbow and propping my head on my hand.

Resigned but not defeated, he lowered himself to the ground in front of me. "It was a penance of sorts. For coming to your realm. The first time a person goes through the veil that separates our worlds, they burn. And now there will be another kind of penance, only I fear it's you who will pay the price."

A shiver coursed down my spine. "What is my price?"

Haden shook his head. "I don't know. That's why I hoped you'd stay away."

"Why didn't I burn the first time I came here?"

"You're not really here. You know that."

I shook my head. "The roses . . . my stained nightgown . . . if I'm not here . . ."

"You're going to have to suspend your disbelief enough to accept that your body is not here, but *you* are. It doesn't fit the parameters of the science you know and understand from your world—it barely fits the parameters of what I understand from mine. We're not supposed to be able to be here together, but we are. Sometimes the lines that separate our realms must bleed a little to allow for it. I guess that's why you can keep the roses."

I sighed. "All right. I'll try to understand that I'll never fully understand that. But why . . . Why do you . . . Why are you so . . . whenever we get close . . . ?"

He interrupted me. "I thought if I pushed you far enough, perhaps you'd be safe."

Pushed me far enough. Is that what he did when he kissed that girl's neck so that I felt the sensation of his lips without the reward of his affection? "Haden, you pushed me away only after you drew me to you—time and again."

"I never claimed to be very good at staying away," he agreed. "I need to get better at it, though."

"Why?"

"My original purpose, the errand that brought me into your universe, is of very dark origins. The closer we become, the more embroiled in my future I fear you are. I won't have that."

The sound of the rolling river filled the silence while I gathered courage to ask what he seemed unwilling to divulge, knowing that at the heart of it he'd just told me he didn't want me in his future. On a shaky exhale, I asked, "What is your errand?"

He squeezed his eyes and his face tightened. "I'm to fetch a bride. A human bride."

My heart clutched. A bride. That's how all gothic fairy tales end, with a girl in white. And of course he didn't want me.

"You should take greater care with your thoughts. One can read them easily just by watching your face. I have already told you that I want you, lamb. Not abducting you to the underworld as my kidnapped bride is not a rejection, though I can see you take it as one."

My mind stopped trying to process and just halted all thought. "This is the underworld?"

"Part of it, yes."

"And you are going to abduct a human . . . bride?"

"Again, yes."

"What does that make you, then, Haden?"

"Why, I suppose that makes me a monster, Theia." He paused. "I came to your realm to take you."

It should have been no surprise. Either he was from a world I didn't understand or my mental health was in jeopardy.

In either case, no good would come of the night I watched the burning man fall from the sky.

He wished he could show her the memory of the very first time he'd laid eyes upon her. A random moment, his window to her world, and yet it had pierced his excuse for a soul as if it were destiny. As if she were his destiny. A thousand times he'd looked through the realms, but one glimpse had forever changed their paths.

And now, she reclined on the grass before him, pure and heavenly. Like a treat, a present to open, an offering, while his blood hummed with unspeakable urges.

But beneath his appetite, a yearning for more than just slaking his thirst thrived despite all reason. He would give his life for her. To ensure her safety, her happiness, her soul.

God only knew which compulsion would be stronger in the end.

His eyes darkened and his gaze intensified, causing an answering flutter deep in my belly. My thoughts scattered just when I needed to be most vigilant. Closing my eyes against the onslaught of his stare, I hoped to regain the balance I would need to get some answers, tangible ones.

With my eyes still closed, Haden told me, "My father was human, but my mother is . . . not." He took a breath. "She's a demon."

My eyes opened like a snapped shade. "Demon?"

He looked away sheepishly, embarrassed by his heritage.

"What does that mean?"

"It means I'm half demon. And I live in the underworld.

And you're smack-dab in the middle of it. How does waking up sound now?"

I shook my head numbly. "No, tell me what it really *means.*"

"I don't know what it means." He reached to pull a blade of grass from my hair. "I belong to neither world, yet I'm pulled to both. Demons by nature don't have a large range of emotions. We're impulsive and egocentric. Some have stronger . . . issues than others. My human capacity for human emotion coupled with my demon capacity for . . . Let's just say demons aren't known for controlling their urges. It's a bad combination. Very, very bad."

"The school bell."

"Aye, the school bell. I didn't even know I was doing it at first." He looked to the clouds for answers. "You gave Mike your number and I saw red, Theia. I didn't consciously set the hell noise into motion; it just erupted from my fury." Haden hung his head in shame. "So many people hurt because of me."

Before he could stop me, I touched his arm. The feel of his skin on my fingertips was electric. He flinched, but I grabbed his forearm and held. We stared at the place where our skin met and his chest heaved.

"I wish you hadn't done that," he said simply, and yet the world hadn't come crashing down around us. "My feelings for you, lamb . . . I swear I never want to hurt you, but I don't know how to rein myself in. The jealousy, the joy, the lust . . . one second of heedlessness and I could ruin us both, destroying everything and everyone around us."

He was obviously shaken, and I knew he wanted me to understand and to agree with him. Of course, finding out he was part demon should have sent me scurrying for the nearest exit. Whatever he was or wasn't, underneath, at his core, he was a scared boy. A human boy. One who didn't understand his own emotions any better than I understood mine.

"Do you have . . . a tail?"

He chuckled. "No."

"Horns?" I winced, but he shook his head. "Scales?"

He pressed his fingers to my lips, the first time he'd willingly touched me. "No cloven feet, no discolored skin, or strange appendages of any sort."

"Fangs, then?"

"No," he said on a laugh.

"Then what makes you demon . . . ish?"

"Aside from the fact that I live in a realm of hell, you mean?"

"Yes, aside from that." I rolled my eyes. He was trying my patience, and it wasn't nice. After all, I wasn't the one who dropped the demon bomb into the conversation; the least he could have done was give me a reasonable explanation. "I obviously knew you were different, Haden. Prior to today, the word 'demon' meant something else to me."

"My demonic attributes are all on the inside, love. I employ the Lure to draw others to me."

He didn't need to explain what the Lure was. His intoxicating, spicy scent, the promise of sin in his chocolate eyes, the sculpted muscular shape of his frame—he was the embodiment of enticement. The way he incited a maelstrom of reckless need throughout my body. So, I was a plaything, like the other girls.

"The Lure is our weapon of choice. Humans cannot resist

the temptation, you see. My kind don't resort to violence or bloodshed. We get what we need by offering ourselves."

"What do your kind need, Haden?" The air was so thick, like it was humid with meaning instead of moisture.

Haden stroked my cheek lightly, his gentleness contrasting with his dangerous words. "Our power is fed by your kind. Your energy . . . your essence . . . eventually, your soul."

His magic, what he called the Lure, ribboned around me, smooth as satin yet taut and strong. I rested my cheek in his hand and breathed in the temptation he offered, my essence no longer my concern. When Haden touched me, I felt a peace I'd never known before. I suppose there were worse ways to go, yet it rankled that I was neither the first nor the last for him. That I was simply one of the masses and not special.

Soup du jour.

Though I was clearly drowning, words formed and were spoken. "How do you feed?"

He spoke softly, leaning into me and murmuring into my hair. As if we were ordinary lovers, stealing a moment along the bank of a river, and not a demon stealing the soul of an innocent on a grassy knoll in hell. "We take what's offered through touch—intimate caresses and kissing, but mostly—" He faltered and then his hand stroked my arm. "My mother is a type of succubus. Do you know what that is?"

"No," I whispered. Being so close to him was intoxicating.

"She's a sex demon. She . . ."

"I get it." I didn't want to hear about sex demons. I wished he would lie down next to me and pull me into his arms. I wanted to be surrounded, with no escape. "Are you going to . . . ?"

Picking up my hand, he kissed my knuckles, his features full of mischief. "No, lamb. No, I'm not going feed from you."

So, I wasn't the same as all the other girls after all. I was found lacking.

"Your eyes are burning holes into my flesh, Theia. You would rather I let loose the demon and devour you?" His words were menacing, yet his tone was teasing and playful.

No.

Yes.

His face changed. A mask of Haden briefly took its place and I shrank away. Uncomfortable static buzzed between us, a precursor to imminent high voltage. Like yesterday, when he looked at Amelia, and the other day in the courtyard with Noelle and Brittany. Not like the electrical charge I usually felt around him. Instead, it grated on my nerves, making me nauseated. I edged away from him. Then just as quickly, it was gone. Haden smiled brightly, himself again.

He collapsed suddenly onto his back, laughing like a madman. He stretched his arms to the side and drew in deep breaths. "You are glorious, Theia." He popped back up, imitating my pose on one elbow. "You've no idea how wonderful you are."

"What are you talking about?" Jekyll or Hyde? Who was this boy next to me?

"Don't you see?" He stroked my face again. "You are immune to the Lure. You're repulsed by it," he added emphatically and with a joy I didn't understand.

"What are you talking about?" I asked again. Clearly, according to every single hormone in my body, I was not immune to Haden's allure.

"I can't put you in a thrall." He ignored my incredulous expression and smiled as bright as sunshine, pleased with himself. "You don't like it."

"Haden, I'm not experienced in a lot of . . . ways, so maybe I don't react like other girls you are used to. But, honestly, I'm not repulsed by you. I'm not sure what I'm doing to make you think that I am. I mean, I do everything but drool on you."

The heat of my cheeks reminded me how foolish I sounded and I looked away quickly, only to have him cup my chin tenderly and bring my focus back to him.

"You are the most precious of gifts. I would burn a thousand times to see you if my presence in your world weren't dangerous to you and those around you." He lay all the way down onto his back again and stared at the clouds. I followed his gaze, and as he watched them, the shapes changed, morphing into fluffy hearts of varying sizes. "The Lure is something I produce. No, that's not it. I wear it, like an aura. When I use it in your presence, you freeze up. In fact you make this cute little face, like you just smelled an onion in your rose garden."

"When *your* face changes, you mean? That's when you're using the Lure?"

"Aye. Though most don't see a physical change. Most women feel compelled to be near me, but you recoil."

"Compelled. Like Brittany and Noelle?" My eyes narrowed. "And Amelia?"

He laughed at my jealous tone. "And the secretaries, and the teachers, and the girls in band, and the—"

"That's enough, Romeo. I get the picture."

Surprising us both, I scooted closer to him and rested my head on his chest. The steady beats of his heart were the best kind of music, and I considered myself a pretty good ear. Haden held my hand to his lips, and the rhythm of our hearts slowed until the measure could be matched. In that aching moment of clarity, awareness crept across my soul like a shadow. I was in love with a demon, and it would end badly.

His arms tightened around me. "So you understand what I'm saying, don't you, Theia? Your feelings for me are not manufactured by evil. What you see when you look at me is what you really see, what you really *feel*. I never dared to wish for such a freedom. You can't know what that has meant to me, what it's been worth."

A moment passed while I absorbed his words, while I luxuriated in the perfect feeling of being in his arms. He felt hopeless for our future. The doubt radiated from him in waves, even while he held me.

He held my hand to the center of his chest, his other rubbed circles into my back. The intimacy, the immediacy of his heart and his hands, shocked my senses, as I had no memory of ever being cuddled. My father's hugs were functional but awkward. The only other people who touched me were Donny and Amelia, and while they were free with affection, it was quite different being held by another person as if I were precious.

He kissed the top of my head, maybe sensing my unease. "I used to watch your world from a looking glass, ever since I was a child. The things I've seen change in the last one hundred and seventy years . . . the things I've seen were wonderful and terrible. I longed to be able to live as a human, to understand the things I felt that nobody else in my realm understood.

Why I felt sad or happy, why I needed things no one around me seemed to need in order to feel good about myself."

"I thought you said you were seventeen."

"I am, mostly. Time moves differently in this realm. Ten years or so to every human year. I'm not immortal, but my life span is quite long."

I tried to fathom aging so slowly. I couldn't imagine being in high school for forty years. Surely that was a curse.

"What of your father?" I asked. I didn't add "the human," but we both knew that's what I meant.

Haden sighed. "My father tried, but he was even more lost in Under, my realm, than I was. He was never happy there; death seemed to finally put him at ease. I think my mother tried, in her capacity, to make him comfortable. But he was her prisoner—he was spiritless for most of his captivity."

His words came back to haunt me. *I'm to fetch a bride. A human bride.* Like his father had been fetched?

I shoved the thought away to deal with later. The moment I had in his arms was the one I wanted to cherish. I knew this perfect twilight would be gone soon enough, and that I'd have plenty of time to think the unthinkable thoughts when I lost the light.

"So I watched your world like it was my cinema," he continued. "I watched weddings and wars with equal fascination. And one day, I watched you." He kissed my head again, lingering there as I stiffened in confusion. "You were lost in your music, playing for no one but for the joy of playing. You set your soul free into your music. Most people don't have that talent. Or maybe don't want it. But you captured my heart that day."

"I'm not sure how I feel about you watching me when I wasn't aware I was being watched."

"I never claimed I was good for you, love. I do find it humorous where you finally choose to draw the line. You barely batted an eye when I told you I was a demon."

"Every girl dreams about having her very own demon, but a stalker is another story."

"Oh, she makes a joke." He laughed. "I hardly stalked you. I may have peeked in on you from time to time." He sounded indignant. "I tried not to intrude on any private moments anyway."

Private moments? I cringed. "You tried? Does that mean you weren't always successful?"

"I never intruded on you when you were completely alone. I swear it."

"Can you see me blushing right now?"

"No."

I exhaled the breath I hadn't realized I was holding. "Then tell me more about the looking glass."

Haden chuckled. "Very well. My window, as it were, showed me humans laughing and fighting . . . falling in love, holding each other. I longed to reach into that window, to have contact with someone who had feelings. Who could love and be loved without deception. It showed me all the things I wanted but could never have. And then it showed me you."

He lifted our hands and we splayed them together, palm to palm, mine so much smaller than his. An ache spread across my chest.

"Then what happened, Haden?"

"And then I became a miserable excuse for a human or

demon. I moped and sulked and was surly to anyone unfortunate enough to pass by me."

"Aren't most demons, um, surly?"

"Many, yes. Most sex demons don't have much to complain about, truthfully. Though we're not safe by any means, we tend to be a fairly congenial lot so long as we're getting our way."

"But you were unhappy."

"Do you know what it's like to only be half of yourself all of the time? To never express what seems dying to get out?"

I thought of my constant battle to live up to Father's impossible standards. To be his daughter and forget that my mother's blood also runs through my veins. To tamp down my spirit when it yearns to fly. Yes, I understood.

I sat up, though reluctant to break the enchanting spell. The air was changing, and our time would be over soon. The temperature cooled, but my ardor did not. I rose, pulling Haden with me.

"I'd like my first kiss now." I held my hand to his lips when he tried to argue. I moved my hand to his cheek, searching his eyes for understanding. "I know you must have dreamt what that kiss would be like—to kiss a girl who saw you as a whole, not as just what you showed."

He shook his head. "No. I never dreamt of kissing *a girl*—I only ever dreamt of kissing you."

My breath caught in my throat, and I smiled, feeling the heat of my ever-returning blush. Then a prickle of cold followed the heat. "Our time is growing short, isn't it?"

He gripped my hand on his cheek, pulling me to him even as he spoke. "I should leave you be."

I closed my eyes and waited, pursing my lips.

A chaste touch of lips dotted my forehead. I tried to memorize everything. The way he smelled, the touch of his lips, soft and warm on my skin, the sound of the river gurgling contentedly behind us. The next brush was softer yet, but his hand pushed into my hair. His lips traced a light path to my temple. Then my cheek. Still softly, they roamed like whispers. He paused and my eyelids fluttered open. His eyes were dark promises, trained on me.

"Kiss me, Haden."

"Aye."

Both hands moved to cup my jaw, and he leaned down. His lips met mine, a light brush. I could taste his nervousness. I hoped he could taste my delight. For a sweeter kiss had never been bestowed upon a girl. Not in storybooks or real life.

Not in heaven or hell.

Gently, he plied from me every dream I'd ever had with light sweeps of his mouth. He retreated briefly, then dipped again, deepening the caress, parting my lips sweetly. Delight bloomed inside me, its roots strong and sure. Haden drew me tightly into an embrace, his kisses less tentative, and my answering mouth growing bolder.

He stole nothing of my essence, but instead gave to me his own.

"Good morning, Theia," he murmured.

And I awoke to a new day.

CHAPTER TWELVE

Spring whispered to the streets of Serendipity Falls as I walked to school Monday morning. The air seemed richer and sweeter to me, the sun brighter. I wore a pink blouse I used to hate, just last week in fact, but it mirrored exactly how I perceived the world that day—girlish and darling, like the blossoming cherry trees. I declined Donny's offer of a ride to school so I could enjoy a little more time to myself.

There was a heady promise on the breeze, but it was also razor-edged with potential for catastrophe. While Haden's kisses engaged my heart and soul, he still threatened to break me open. He was a demon, and he was here to take a bride. Danger lurked in the one place I longed to bestow my trust.

When I reached our bench in front of the Main, I realized that I was the only one lost in the clouds. Students passed on their way to class, talking as usual, but their tones weren't light and casual. Though everyone was trying to act normal, they each betrayed the ruse with a hesitant glance at the bell above the doors leading into the school. It was covered in a brown bag to hide the bullet holes. A sharpshooter on Friday had finally taken each bell out with a high-caliber rifle because that was the only way to stop the noise. Some bells had required more than two or three shots. Or so said the hushed rumors.

Amelia came out of those doors instead of from the direction of the parking lot where Donny and I had been watching for her. She hurried to our spot. "Wow, it is *really* weird in there."

Plopping on the bench next to me, Ame grabbed Donny's mocha for a quick drink before she started talking. "They called my mom in. We've been here for about an hour already."

"They called your mom in? Why?" Donny asked.

Ame handed Donny back the drink. "They called *every* counselor and psychologist in the area to come in. And audiologists from all over the state are setting up in the gym to retest our hearing. I think the school is tweaked about liability issues."

"Great." Donny slumped in her seat. "That means a dorky assembly and touchy-feely emotion lectures all day. Why don't they just fix their stupid equipment and leave us alone?"

I hated talking about emotions as much as Donny did, but judging from the wary expressions of our fellow students every time they walked under a school bell, I could see why the administration might need to do some damage control on our psyches. I was just glad my father was a barrister and not a psychologist like Amelia's mom. I couldn't imagine him dealing with my instability, much less an entire school of it.

"How is Mike?" Donny asked Amelia.

Ame shrugged. "Fine, I guess. I passed him in the hall and

he said hey." Amelia turned her eyes to me. "How's Haden? You two seemed pretty cozy yesterday."

I thought of our perfect kiss last night and looked at my shoe, trying to come up with an answer that wouldn't embarrass me completely or begin with *By the way, he's a demon.* "He's . . . he's . . ."

"He's getting out of Noelle's car," Donny finished for me.

Of course he was.

Humiliation felt like a pebble in my throat that wouldn't go down. I didn't look up. I didn't need to. I had been an interesting diversion, but that was all. What made me think he was going to be any different today? I couldn't believe I had let a demon kiss me. What was I thinking? That I had some sort of magic to tame the forces of evil? I let him use me. . . . I let him . . . *play with his food.*

Since expressing emotion was undervalued in my upbringing, it had been a long time since I let myself feel much of anything. Well, no, that was a lie. I felt things, but I let them pass through me without attention whenever possible. At that very moment, though, I was angry. And disappointed. And jealous.

As the tempest of emotion gathered inside of me, I thought of my mother. She was reckless and wild, the way I felt. She was everything my father taught me not to be. Her unchecked enthusiasm was the reason she was dead. How many times had I been warned?

And then her necklace warmed the skin near my heart.

My life had been lived driving away her influence, pushing down what came naturally, and turning away from excess of emotion. She'd been quick to laugh and found everything and everyone interesting.

But she was also stubborn. By all accounts, my father, though he never spoke of it to me, had been caught up in her enthusiasm from the very minute he laid eyes on her. She steamrolled over all his rules and expectations and forced him to love her despite his better judgment.

What did she possess that allowed her to stay spirited in the gloom of my father's temperance? Fingering my wild curls, I had only an inkling of her fortitude.

It would have to do.

I tried to imagine what my mother would do if faced with a boy who ran so hot and cold. It was difficult to know, since I'd never met her—but I thought of all the times in my life I'd held back my first impulse and instead behaved the way I knew Father expected. I never saw a banister that didn't trigger a wish to slide down it—though I had never allowed myself the fun. The things I'd refrained from saying, the dreams I'd tried to keep from forming—it was exhausting sometimes to be the opposite of what felt so natural.

A vision of the world whirling around me as I danced with Haden spun through my mind. Sometimes, when I was with him, I felt like I was finally allowing myself to be *me*. It suddenly didn't matter so much what my mother would do or what my father would expect.

I pushed off the bench and stalked down the sidewalk towards Haden and Noelle, determined to find out once and for all where my worlds, my dream one and my waking one, met up.

No more tamping down my impulses. I could be a steamroller too.

Haden stopped walking, watching me warily. I, however,

didn't stop. I didn't even slow. Like that first day in the hall, it seemed that the world stood still. When I reached him, I pulled him into the grass and cupped his surprised face in my hands. "I missed you," I said, and before he could respond, I kissed him with all the unpracticed ardor I possessed.

"What the hell?" I heard Noelle say, but by then Haden was smiling into my kiss and returning it. He placed his hand behind my head and pulled me closer. Noelle left in a huff.

"You're a minx," he said when I allowed him up for air. "And you're going to get us both detention for PDA *and* walking on the grass."

"I had to make sure you weren't another dream, that you recognize me in both worlds." Though it was much more than that. I needed to know I affected him the way he did me, and I needed to stop being what everyone expected and start being true to myself.

"I'm not a dream. And yes." His eyes searched the skyline. "I recognize you; I remember every second. I am aware of you constantly, to my peril, both here and . . . there."

"Then please stop using other girls to make me jealous. It's very trying." I kissed him quickly one more time. "See you in class."

I left him there and returned to Donny and Amelia, who stared at me openmouthed while I hiked my bag onto my shoulder and pretended not to notice their confusion. "I guess we should go to class," I said.

Donny recovered herself. "Dude, that was the seventh sign of the apocalypse. I'm so not going to class on the last day of the world."

"Ha-ha."

Ame agreed with Donny. "Seriously, if my mom weren't in there, I would totally skip. You just slipped the hot new guy the tongue. Who wants to spend their last precious hours on earth taking a trig test?"

We all glanced at the bell that didn't ring, creeped out and unsettled. A touch of unease crawled over us.

Ame mumbled, "When I got here with my mom, they were covering all the bells with brown paper. And everyone was super quiet. It was eerie."

Haden caught up to us then and noticed what we were looking at. A darkness shadowed his features, and he turned away from me. Tension, like a coil, twisted his hands into a fist and squared his jaw in a clench.

I reached for his hand. He uncurled his fingers and twined them through mine. He didn't look at me, but he squeezed my hand.

I eased his burden.

Theia surprised him.

Her quiet strength that championed him when he least deserved it. Her boldness when he least expected it.

In the sun, her curls whipped around her like caramel ribbons. The light danced off her, dazzling him. He'd stood in her path, mesmerized by the paleness of her skin and her rosebud lips. He'd forgotten his resolve to push her away, his grand plan to sever the cord that bound her to him.

He'd done what he could to harness his attraction. At times, he just wasn't strong enough to drive her away. Especially when he realized that it wasn't the Lure that drew her to him.

That, in truth, the Lure actually repelled her.

He didn't deserve her trust, though. And she didn't deserve the heap of destruction that would accompany any relationship they tried to forge.

And yet, her small soft hand quieted him now.

They were doomed.

If he were smart, or at least strong, he would finish this tonight. Once his dark deed was accomplished, at least one of them could rest easy.

He vowed to find the strength to end this. Tonight would be the night he'd forget about Theia Alderson and follow the path he'd been born to. Tonight would be about taking what didn't belong to him in order to claim what did. His inheritance, as it were.

But if this was to be his last night on earth, if he must sacrifice everything—shouldn't he at least get a taste of what he must leave behind forever? Did he not deserve one moment to call his own before he damned himself to hell for an eternity?

The day trudged along. We did indeed have a touchy-feely assembly after homeroom. And each student was given an appointment in the gym for hearing tests and an appointment in the library to speak to a counselor. Therefore, all classes were truncated and there was no trig test. There was also no Haden in history. I'd endured the sly looks and hushed whispers from our classmates alone.

The story of the infamous kiss on the school lawn traveled quickly and, like most juicy morsels of gossip, had been embellished so much that even I started enjoying it. His disappearance from campus only added flavor to the dish. Apparently we'd been secretly in love for years, living on covert e-mails and texts. We tried to pretend we didn't know each other, but it was obvious to anyone who had paid attention to us in class or in the library that we were like Romeo and Juliet.

Or so the story went.

It was why I never talked to boys, the school had decided—because I was already spoken for. That morning in front of the school, I'd had some kind of breakdown and couldn't stay away from him one moment longer.

Romeo and Juliet . . . That wasn't very comforting, considering how that all worked out for the two of them.

I had no way to get in touch with Haden. I didn't even know where he lived or what his phone number was. Donny sent me strange looks all day after I'd told her that. After school, she handed me a photocopy of his registration card from the admin office.

"This is highly immoral," Ame said, eyeing the flagrant invasion of privacy in my hand. Not one to let that get in our way, she added, "So, where does he live?"

"Park Place," answered Donny. "Get in the car, girls. We're doing a drive-by."

There really wasn't a Park Place in Serendipity Falls. However, there was a Parkerhouse Hotel. His floor number indicated penthouse.

"He lives in a hotel? That's kind of weird." Ame looked at me pointedly, the glitter from her mascara shimmering in the sun.

"Maybe his parents are building a house," Donny answered for me.

"Maybe," I mused. Or maybe demons have a hard time getting mortgages. I shrugged. "Like I said earlier, we never talked about where he lived." I didn't want to drive by his hotel.

It seemed obsessive. Which I was, but I didn't want to appear that way. "I'll get in the car if we can go someplace else."

"Beach?" Donny and Ame answered simultaneously.

I nodded quickly. "Yes, please."

We loved our beach. When it was the three of us alone, the sand and rocks pulled secrets from us. We planned our lives and spilled our fears on the jagged coast. We also drank a beer there once, before Donny had her license. Her father had dropped us off for three hours, and it had taken that long for the three of us to share the one can. It seemed like another three hours before I could get the taste out of my mouth.

We settled on a log, and I could tell by the way they stared at me that they were waiting for me to begin spilling the details I'd been holding in all day. They had been patient during school, enduring the rumors with a pretty good sense of humor considering they didn't really know the true story either. The fact that I had kissed Haden in front of everyone at school and yet had no idea how to call him was more than odd. Stranger still, the last time they'd seen us together, we were smiling shyly over cookies—not even close to kissing. They weren't aware of the trips I'd made to Haden's Under, especially last night's when everything changed. It was probably time to trust them. But would they believe me?

"Haden isn't exactly a normal boy."

Ame and Donny shot knowing glances at each other, but didn't interrupt me.

"Remember the stuff . . . the . . . bad juju that Varnie told us about?"

Ame leaned closer and Donny leaned back, crossing her arms over her chest and visibly closing down.

"Haden is from someplace else, someplace darker. Varnie was right—the things happening, the cards, the weird things . . . he was right."

Donny didn't believe me, but she didn't say it out loud. I could tell just from the expression on her face. Ame looked at me like I had just read five winning numbers of the six on her lottery ticket and she was waiting eagerly for the last.

I tried again. "Remember the dream I had about Haden before I saw him? That was really him. We sort of meet up in his realm, he called it Under, when I'm asleep. It's like Oz or Wonderland or even Narnia—only it's the other side of dreams, I guess, and he comes to this realm when I'm awake."

"Sweetie"—Donny covered my hand with her own—"Oz, Wonderland, and Narnia are fiction. You get that part, right?"

It was okay. I expected her to be difficult to convince—the whole story sounded ridiculous even to me. "And we sort of made out last night in his world. It's all very complicated and I don't really understand much more than that. Except that . . . well, he is supposed to abduct a human girl for a wife." I kept going quickly, so they wouldn't have a chance to launch hard questions yet. "I tried to visit Varnie—"

"Oh, God," Donny muttered.

"But he'd already moved on. He left me a note, though. He said I needed a talisman and that you would help me with it, Ame."

Instead of being excited about the talisman, Ame surprised me with, "Did you say 'abduct a human girl'?"

"I don't think he really will. We haven't had a chance to discuss it."

"Are you even listening to yourself?" Donny, no longer

able to contain her . . . Donniness, exploded off the log. "Some creepy stalker is threatening to kidnap you!"

"No," I answered. "I'm pretty sure he doesn't want me."

"Theia, he's dangerous. As in not-quite-right-in-the-head, psycho dangerous. I don't believe this realm stuff, but if he's threatening to abduct someone, you need to tell the cops."

"Well, since he told me in a *dream* that you insist isn't real, maybe I'm the psycho here."

"This isn't like you. I mean, I'm glad you finally found a guy that greases your wheels, but this seems like a really unhealthy way to start a relationship." Donny wasn't the type to talk about healthy relationships. "I mean, I get that he's really hot and has that building-a-mystery vibe about him. But all this talk about—"

"He's a demon," I interrupted. "Well, half demon. His father was a human. And he's one hundred and seventy years old, give or take."

Ame inhaled sharply. "His father is one hundred and seventy?"

"No, Haden is. They age slower there. He says he's seventeen, but he was born one hundred and seventy years ago—in our years, I guess."

"Are you listening to yourself? Thei, you've totally gone one French fry short of a Happy Meal here."

"Did he fang you?" Ame asked.

"Stop encouraging her," Donny demanded.

"He's not a vampire." It just seemed wrong to bring up the sex demon stuff right then. It was a lot to process, and Donny would latch on to the sex part and not listen to another word. "I understand that this all seems very convoluted right now—"

"You think?"

"Haden doesn't want to hurt anyone. He wanted to experience being human."

In a falsetto Donny cried out, "He wants to be a *real* boy."

I shot her a look I learned at my father's knee and continued. "He doesn't want to bring me to his world."

"So, who's he going to bring? And by 'bring,' we're talking 'abduct,' right?"

"I don't know." The breeze felt a lot colder then.

"Why did Varnie leave you a note?" Amelia asked.

"Because he knew I was coming over."

"So he really is a psychic?"

Nobody spoke for a minute, letting the waves provide a calming sound track.

"He really is, Ame."

She watched the water for another minute. "Did you find a talisman?"

I tugged the pendant out of my shirt. "It was my mother's. Do you know what to do?"

The wind lifted some loose wisps of hair around Amelia's face. "I've read about talismans. They store supernatural energy—sometimes protection. We should say a blessing over it. For protection." Her normal exuberance relaxed into something that felt wise—reassuring. "Why did you pick this piece?"

Why had I? "My mother . . . she was very strong. She . . . she trusted her heart."

Amelia nodded. "I'm not like a real witch, you know—I barely even dabble. I mean, I read a lot of metaphysical books, so I'm not . . . I just, sometimes I feel like I just *know* things. But that might be wishful thinking—"

"Ame." I stopped her. "I trust you."

She nodded. "Okay, I know some words—kind of like a spell—that I read recently, but you have to believe the words have power or it won't be worth anything."

Donny snorted, but I said, "Okay."

I took the pendant off and tried to hand it to Amelia, but she shook her head. "Only you should touch it right now."

I squinted at her. "Why?"

"It will concentrate your energy to it."

I held it in the palms of my hands in front of me, and Amelia put one hand on my shoulder and one on Donny's. Donny rolled her eyes, but closed the circle. Amelia closed her eyes and this really peaceful look crossed her face. The wind picked up her dark hair, and I realized that if I believed in all the crazy things that had happened to me lately, I also believed in that moment that my friend was transformed by something really powerful. Ame opened her eyes and told us to repeat after her:

> *Though in the shadow, darkness hides,*
> *This spell protects and thrice provides.*
> *For whom I trust the dark divides,*
> *But whom I love my will decides.*

We did it three times. Donny may not have believed it, but I felt the pulsing of the amulet in my hand. Varnie warned it wouldn't protect me—but I surely felt stronger.

CHAPTER THIRTEEN

Dinner with Father had been as if nothing had ever happened. I tried to introduce conversation; he tried to deflect. Oddly, in its own way, it was comforting. He didn't suspect I'd gone out Saturday night, nor did he seem to have an inkling I'd had a houseful of people over the day before. We certainly didn't discuss anything about Friday other than that my hearing test came back fine.

He went into his study to catch up on work he'd had to put off because of his impromptu business trip, and I went to my room with the idea of practicing.

Don't be scared. There is a boy in your room.

The slightly ominous text stopped me short in the hall outside my bedroom door. I didn't recognize the number or I'd have reasoned it was Donny playing one of her games. There had never been a boy in my room before, so it would be just the thing she'd like to tease me about. Except that now it wouldn't be funny anymore. Donny hadn't yet decided whether I was crazy and Haden was a perfectly harmless crush or I was sane and in terrible jeopardy.

I opened the door cautiously, deciding that if there indeed was someone in my room, which I doubted, why would he warn me before I entered? I flipped the light as I closed the door.

"You really have no self-preservation skills at all, do you?"

My heart expanded in my chest, filling the cavity to over-flowing, as Haden turned around slowly from the window, the devil in his eye and a naughty grin on his lips.

"None at all." I crossed the room as if I were floating to him, as if finding boys in my room were a common occur-rence. "I'm a damsel forever in need of a saving. I suppose you'll have to do."

Haden chuckled and hooked his arm around my waist, bringing me up against his solid form. "I'm a wicked sort, lamb."

"I missed you today," I answered as he dove for a kiss.

His lips fit perfectly to mine. I don't know how I'd made it seventeen years without kissing. It was the finest thing I'd ever known. Like stumbling into heaven. He framed my face in his hands and treasured me with soft yet firm caresses with his mouth. I sighed, the pleasure of this new dance swept over me, and I pushed myself farther into him, a silent entreaty for more. His body was so different from mine, all hard planes where I was soft, and it made me feel safe and endangered at the same time.

Haden groaned, the sound filling me with awe that I was

able to elicit it. But he pushed me away and inhaled deep, raspy breaths. "We need to talk," he said finally and sat me on my bed, switching on some music to cover our voices before he sat next to me.

"Where were you today? I thought ..."

"I had to think. I needed to find a way to keep you safe."

"Safe from what? You? You keep telling me about this danger, but I don't see it. You told me never to touch you, but I did and I'm fine. You're fine."

"You are certainly not fine. I was afraid if I touched you, I wouldn't be able to stop myself from partaking of your essence."

"And you didn't, did you?"

"My hold on my demon side is tenuous at best. You're still in very real danger."

"I don't understand you, Haden."

"I hope you never do. This is the last time I'm going to visit you, Theia. I'm leaving." He reached for my cheek, then snaked his hand away. "I'm trying to save your life."

"Where are you going?" I had just found him. Loneliness clawed inside me as I thought of him gone. Just gone. Because I knew if he left, it would be like he had never been here.

"You can't know what it's like. I've wished I could walk away from you—even stop thinking of you for an hour, a minute. But I can't. I've tried. I need you with a longing that will surely kill me if I don't give in to it—but it will kill you if I do."

That got my attention. Fear pulsed through me at his words.

His jaw ticked. "Finally you're afraid. Let's hope it's not too late, shall we?"

"Why do you want me to be afraid of you?"

"To save you. To save us both, because if you aren't, we are both damned."

"I don't want you to go."

As if we were bound to the same string, something pulled us closer together. He had never looked so vulnerable, so lost. "You need to let me."

I angled my chin, willing him to kiss me. I didn't think he would, so I whispered, "Please."

Haden groaned and thrust his fingers into my hair, pulling me to him, as if I'd have fought him. I went willingly, throwing my arms around his neck, desperate to touch him and feel him against my skin. His mouth sought mine and my soul caught on fire.

This kiss was so different from our others, fueled by desperation. As if he'd struck a match to me, I was ablaze in a sweet heat that seared me from the inside. We clutched each other tighter and my lips opened to his insistent tongue. I slipped further into the flames, knowing I dragged him with me, but all I cared about was being close to him, keeping him. I wanted so badly to keep him.

As hungrily as he'd begun, he pushed me away with equal power. There was anger in his features, and it hurt to look at him.

"You don't have the sense to protect yourself. Everyone around you could tell you I'm no good for you. The danger is very real. I'll hurt you and doing so will be my undoing too."

I groaned. "Why are you saying these things to me?" I felt like a yo-yo.

He held my face in his hands, forcing me to look into his

eyes while his voice rose and shook. "What I feel for you could boil the ocean if I let it. I push you away because I'm evil." He shook his head to stop me from interrupting. "I am evil, trust me. I'm afraid I can't stop it. The closer I get to you, the more control I lose."

"I don't understand." Except, truthfully, I just didn't want to understand.

Pain shadowed across his face. "Darkness lives in me, Theia. Inside of me. Like a sickness. And right next to it, intertwined with it, are my feelings for you. If I act on one, I'll act on the other. The darkness in me wants you the way a black hole eats stars. I dream of tasting you, devouring you." His eyes darkened terribly.

"Haden, stop trying to frighten me."

He carried on as if he hadn't heard me. "This isn't a crush; it's an obsession. You are never *not* in my thoughts. Your scent carries across a room and paralyzes me with longing. I don't want to hold your hand. Part of me wants to set you on fire and hold you while the flame consumes us both, to eat your heart so I know that only I possess it entirely. Are you scared now? Does your human mind comprehend the danger at last? I'm not like you. I'm not human, not completely anyway."

He let go of my face, and I shrank away from him. His words hit their mark with stunning precision. Every part of my body that had been so hot only a few minutes ago was now ice-cold. Yet, despite his threats, I thought of all the times he could have done me harm but hadn't.

"I'm a demon, Theia. You have to stop pretending I'm not. If I ever did anything to hurt you, it would kill me. But I can't control it."

"You're lying so I will let you go. You think if you scare me enough, I'll believe you want to murder me or take me, and I'll wish you gone. Because making me hate you by coming on to the other girls didn't work, you think this will."

He closed his eyes, but he didn't deny it. "I'm going back Under. For good."

"You've chosen your bride, then?" Jealousy blew a stinging kiss down my spine. Did I want to know whom he would choose if he couldn't have me? *Wouldn't* have me?

He stood. "Theia, we both knew we weren't going to find a way to be together. I won't have you suffer any longer. You take foolish risks with your body and your heart already. I won't have you jeopardize your soul. Not for me."

"And your absence will stop my suffering? Knowing you are making a life with someone who isn't me is supposed to make me feel better? Knowing you *kidnapped* another girl will keep me carefree?"

He raked his hands through his hair. "You're like an open vein to me, Theia."

"Who are you taking?" A thread connecting me to him snapped. I hoped the rest would go all at once or I would go mad with each little loss, one at a time. "One of the cheerleaders? Are you going to pick someone I hate? Do you honestly think that will make it easier on me?"

"No."

"Then who?"

"I'm not taking a bride."

That was a choice? "This whole time you've been tormenting me and you could have chosen not to take anyone? Why didn't you just tell . . . me . . . ?" The shadow that crossed his face spoke volumes of sadness. "What *aren't* you telling me right now?"

"My mother will not be . . . pleased."

Crossing a demon, even one that gave you life, must be quite an undertaking. I rose to my knees on the bed. "What will she do?"

"She'll . . . I don't know. Which is why I have to break all ties with you. Tonight. Now."

"Can't you stay here?"

"She would find me, and it would be worse. She wants me to inherit her domain. She'd never just let me go. She allowed me to come here only to choose my victim. I assumed it would be you, given my unholy obsession with you. Because that's who I am. I thought that since I wanted you, I should have you. But the first night, when I burned—"

He paused and I choked on a cry.

"You were so compassionate. You were like a balm to me. I decided I didn't want to hurt you, so I thought I could just pick someone else, but still be near you while I was here. But the more I'm near you, the more I want to be what I'm not. But my mother—she won't understand."

I reached for his shoulders. "You can't just give up. She's your mother. . . . She loves you. We just need to convince her that you're happier here."

He pressed his forehead to mine. "She's a demon, Theia. She doesn't reason and she certainly doesn't love." He tried to push my hands off him. "And there is no 'we.' You will never get anywhere near my mother. Never."

"So you go Under, never to return. How does that help anything at all?"

So far away he went, behind his eyes, his expression so very grim. "Nobody else will pay for my heritage—isn't that enough?" He sat back down on the bed. "I won't ruin your life or any other. Bringing a young girl to hell is a mistake."

"And not bringing one to your mother will bring the wrath of hell onto you, won't it?"

"I can handle my mother."

"Take me," I whispered.

"No." His voice cracked.

"Please. I've been Under half a dozen times already. It's no hardship. We can be together."

"No."

"You won't even listen? Haden, there must be some reason that I've been able to go back and forth between our realms, why I don't succumb to the Lure." I held his face and forced him to look at me. "It might be my destiny, don't you see? Maybe I'm *supposed* to go with you. Your mother will be happy, and we'll be happy together. Why not?"

He gazed into my eyes, his eyes like deep pools I'd have drowned in if he let me. "How can you ask me why not? Theia, what about your future? Your friends and your family?"

I shucked my pride and climbed into his lap. "What if you are my future, Haden? How can you think I'd ever find happiness if I knew you were miserable? If I knew you were alone?"

His fingers glided through my curls, my cursed curls of all things. He seemed to like them; he touched them often enough. In all, it appeared to me that Haden enjoyed the very things about myself that I was most uncertain about. He stroked my hair longingly while he spoke, "The idea of you withering away hurts me more than anything my mother could dream of doing in retaliation. And you would wither there, just like my father did. If you want to please me, promise me you will live . . . really live."

"Haden, give us some more time. We could come up with a solution. We don't have to give up so soon. Please."

"I can't control my urges. When I feel things as a human, it inflames my demon side. What if I hurt you or someone else? You remember the day I turned the entire school deaf, don't you?"

I closed my eyes against the memory. He was going to leave, and I couldn't stop him. My heart was aching so badly that it hurt to breathe, but I needed him to understand. I needed to say it right. Haden should know, before he left, that his time in my life meant something. "Before you came, I was different. You've changed me. I'm learning to stand up for myself—and not to be so shy." I blushed a little. "I'm still working on that."

Haden stroked my face. "I'm different too. Before I met you, I would never have walked away from something I wanted so badly. I thought I deserved to take whatever I desired. I didn't know what it was like to care more about someone else's happiness than my own. I never thought I would know what it was like to fall."

His words burst something inside me. The unfairness of his sacrifice—that the only way he could show his humanity was by giving up being human—made me want to scream. He deserved so much more. I kissed him then. It was a promise of heartache. Something tugged at me from the inside, loosening the knot of desire I'd kept hidden, and unleashing dark, mysterious tendrils of yearning. Haden's breathing changed, causing a flare of white-hot awareness to my core. I needed him, needed to be closer, to touch his skin.

I pulled us back towards the bed, ignoring his protests, and we tumbled onto the bride-white quilt.

"Theia, slow down."

"No." I dragged him back for another kiss. Though he resisted initially, I arched into him, eliciting a groan of pleasure and perhaps defeat.

His hands roamed my torso, and I tried to get mine under his shirt. He stopped then, and grasped my wrists to hold them together in one hand above my head. "We can't do this. I'll never forgive myself." He drew in ragged breaths against my neck, his body on top of mine and sandwiched between my bent knees.

He inhaled deeply one last time at my neck and pushed away to stand next to my bed. I immediately sat up, hugging my knees and waiting. Waiting for the barbed thorns of his words to push into my flesh. Because they were coming.

He pressed a kiss to my forehead. "Be well, Theia."

"Wait." The words wouldn't come, all the reasons I needed him to stay, not to leave me. I'd just found him, how could I say good-bye forever? I wanted to tell him all the secrets of my heart, but only one mattered. "Haden . . . I think I love you." Maybe I shouldn't have said *think*, but it seemed too soon, so rushed. But he was leaving and he might never know.

He squeezed my shoulder tightly and disappeared. Just evaporated.

My heart returned to its own beat.

Broken and useless.

CHAPTER FOURTEEN

I don't remember falling asleep, though I remember trying very hard, hoping that in my dreams I could find Haden again. Instead, I drowned my pillow in tears and ached in the hollow where my heart used to be before he took it with him.

I remember dreaming that I was trapped in my room. Every time I managed to get out of it, I woke up with a start. All night, I drifted in and out of restless sleep, trying to leave my room and always failing. When I awoke the last time, I realized that it was Haden's doing. He was keeping me from traveling somehow. He'd succeeded in shutting me out.

I heard Father's car pulling out onto the street, and I rolled over towards the window. The day was thick with fog, ceaseless in its gray shroud. A mirror of how I felt. Though I should have begun getting ready for school, instead I threw off the covers and began searching under my bed for the box of photos of my mother. I wasn't sure Father even knew that I had them. My aunt gave them to me. They were from before they got married.

As a child, I would paw through the photos whenever loneliness squeezed my heart too hard. I used to talk to my mother while I looked at the pictures, thinking that the box held her soul in it; I'm not sure when I stopped doing that.

I opened the box slowly, not knowing what I expected. Comfort, likely; the ghost of my mother to save me, possibly. Instead, it was just a box of three-by-five prints. The photographs captured a woman I didn't know, who died giving me life. She looked so small when everything around her was big. Big hair, big earrings, big shoulder pads. My mother loved acid-washed denim and long-haired rock bands. And animals—she adored animals, dogs the most.

She'd been waiting tables to put herself through veterinary school when she spilled a plate of chips—fries—in my father's lap. My aunt said he was smitten instantly, though I can't imagine it. I'm sure he fumed and chastised her clumsiness. Told her she should be more careful. But instead, somehow, they'd fallen in love.

By all accounts, my father had loved my mother very much, and she him. In all his heeds of caution and *dire* this and *dismal* that, he'd been reluctant to ever speak of her as his wife, my mother. She was a poster model of hazard, not the woman he loved.

My aunt told me the story, once, of the girl my mother had been. Jennifer Hadley, smart, beautiful, funny, and fearless. As a child, she'd come close to losing a fight with sickness, losing a kidney instead. When she went into remission, she bloomed into health and vowed to live—really live. She held nothing back and faced each day with a passion that must have blinded my father.

She also wasn't supposed to have children.

What would my mother have done if she were me? I wondered. What advice would she give me about saving a boy from the demon that lived inside him? Would she caution me against the danger or tell me that nothing was more important than what I felt in my heart?

It didn't matter. Jennifer Hadley was dead. She wasn't coming back to help me figure out my life. She was never going to fix my father's heart either.

I didn't want to live his life. I didn't want to be careful anymore.

I found myself in Father's room. It was particularly menacing to me, the immense, masculine furniture full of sharp angles, and the scent of my father's soap a subconscious signal to me to be cautious. I crept across his thick carpet as if I weren't alone in the house because I knew invading his suite was wrong. Perhaps I was hiding from my own judgment.

The bottle of my father's sleeping pills from the top drawer of his nightstand shook in my hand as I tried to open it. Backing down was out of the question. I needed to go Under again. Haden would not be able to get rid of me so quickly now.

I texted the girls to let them know I was coming down with something and wouldn't be at school. And then I went back to bed to wait.

When I opened my eyes, I was in someone else's bed.

I sat up, startled, throwing the sheets off me and rolling to my feet.

The room smelled like Haden, felt like him. It was almost the normal room of a teenaged boy. A very spoiled teenaged boy. I walked around on wobbly legs, touching the corners of his furniture, hoping it would make me feel closer to him. It sort of made me feel like an intruder. Or maybe a ghost.

His bed was unmade, the sheets rumpled into a red and black lump. Perhaps when we met in my dreams, they were his dreams too. I'd never thought to ask; there were always so many other questions.

I don't know why, but I began smoothing the sheets. It seemed so intimate to make his bed. The ache started in my belly and moved to my heart. I found his duvet on the floor, and, as I shook it, his scent carried gently on the breeze I'd made. I plumped his pillows, imagining that I was going insane. Why was I making his bed? Surely there were far more important things to do. My head was filled with cotton, though, so I righted the corners on the blanket.

If things were different, if we got married in the future, we would make the bed together in the morning, I imagined. I would probably blush, like I was doing now just thinking about "our bed." Our tousled sheets.

I couldn't quite capture my own thoughts. The sleeping pills, I guessed. Forcing my gaze away from the bed, I looked at the rest of his room. He had a large flat-screen TV on the wall opposite his bed, with shelves and shelves of movies below it. They were double-parked—two rows to each shelf. The titles were current as well as older films I hadn't heard of, but that wasn't unusual, since Father and I didn't watch much television or view many movies. Haden apparently did, and he really liked space movies. One row held everything from *E.T.* to *Mars Attacks!*

A different shelf system held several video game consoles and hundreds of games. Again, space themes seemed to dominate. Not a speck of dust covered any surface. Either the servants cleaned regularly but skipped making his bed or Haden himself liked things neat.

The room was almost eerie and it broke my heart. All Haden wanted was to be a regular lad. Yet he'd barely been allowed to participate in the world he longed for. This bedroom seemed a sham, a bandage to cover the scrape but never heal the wound.

There were no dirty clothes on the floor. Even if he cleaned his own room, he probably needed a valet to take care of his clothes with all the cravats and starchy collars. And while I will freely admit to finding his tight jeans and tees sexy, his formal wear did something special to my insides. Knowing that beneath the refined, old-fashioned clothes was a young man of desire and passion—passion for me—made his distinguished and respectable appearance even more rakish.

"What are you doing here? Wake up."

Haden stood in his doorway, looking pale and unkempt. So unusual for him.

"Hello, Haden." The word stuck in my mouth strangely. More cotton. "I don't feel so good."

Everything shifted into waves and shapes, like the room was underwater. My legs turned to noodles, and I started going down.

"I've got you." Haden's voice sounded so far away, but I

realized he was carrying me. "What have you done?" he asked. He sounded so worried.

"I'm fine," I sighed. "I just wanted a little visit." No matter how hard I tried to form the words, they came out slurred. I opened my eyes and blinked at my Prince Charming. "Hello, Haden."

Despite the concern lining his brow, he laughed. "Hello, Theia."

"Your bed is very nice."

"Why, thank you. How kind of you to notice."

"Oh, I notice lots of things. You have dimples. Did you know that?" Oh, my head was so heavy.

"Yes, I knew that." He opened a terrace door and took me outside. "Are you drunk?"

"Noooo." The fresh air was so lovely. "I'm just very well marinated."

"Marinated?"

"Wait, no, that's not right. It's an 'm' word, though."

"Try to take a few deep breaths, lamb."

"Medicated! That's the word." I bet we were so pretty, standing on the terrace. I would have liked to open my eyes to make sure, but it was really hard suddenly. I kept trying until I finally got a blurry vision. Haden was wearing all black and was carrying me like I weighed nothing at all. He was so hot. I think we were on a mountain. It looked very rocky around us. "We're very high up here, aren't we?"

"Well, you certainly are. Theia, I need you to wake up."

"Did you know that I have never seen a penis?"

He laughed again. "When you wake up, you are going to hate yourself."

Something wet plopped onto my nose. First I thought Haden was crying, but then I realized it was rain. Each drop that touched me brought with it a little more consciousness. "You know how to make rain?" I asked him.

"No, love, it's not me."

My vision cleared a little more and I realized he looked stricken. I traced his lips with my fingers. "You should kiss me," I said.

"I should never have kissed you," he replied, but did so anyway.

Raindrops began falling harder, plopping on us like tears from heaven. As it fell steadily, we lost ourselves further into the exploration of a perfect kiss. The water soaked our clothes to our skin, and we dripped and sloshed as we held on tighter, sinking like stones into abandon. It grew colder and I shivered in his arms. I didn't care. There was no place I'd rather have been.

And then I felt him fading. I clutched at him, trying to grasp his shirt but unable to grip anything but air. "Haden?"

His lips moved, but his voice was gone from me. We were slipping away from each other, no matter what I did. The pain in his eyes pierced me.

"Haden, what's happening?"

He mouthed the word "good-bye," and I knew he meant forever.

Something held me firmly, though nothing I could see or fight as it yanked me farther away from him, my heart. I pushed and pulled to free myself as everything turned white but the rain continued dumping on me relentlessly.

"Theia!" A voice cried out from somewhere—behind me, inside me, below me; I couldn't tell.

Water clogged my nose and mouth and clogged my vision.

"Theia!" The voice grew more insistent, louder.

With fresh energy, I made a last push and gasped for breath. My hands finally locked onto something and I sobbed when I couldn't move it.

"Theia!"

"Father?" I opened my eyes.

"Thank God." He was weeping. "I couldn't wake you up."

The rain pounded on me still, but then I realized it fell cold from a showerhead and I was lying in the tub in my nightgown. My father's face, etched with worry, loomed over me as the cold water soaked me.

"What were you thinking? How many did you take?"

I followed his gaze to the bottle of sleeping pills on the counter. The ones I'd taken from his bedroom so that Haden wouldn't be able to wake me up.

"Answer me! How many pills, Theia?"

I tried to sit up but kept sliding. I gripped the edge of the tub and vomited on the Italian slate floor.

CHAPTER FIFTEEN

I was to rest.

Set up in the sunroom with an afghan and a pile of books, I drank the PG tips Muriel brought to me regularly and stared out the window. My skin felt foreign, like an ill-fitting coat. I hadn't been allowed to leave the house in three days.

I was exhausted, physically and emotionally. Sleep didn't provide me any rest. I'd hoped to return to Haden, but my dreams didn't come. Instead, it felt like a wall of static separated me from the deep sleep I used to lose myself to in Under.

I missed him dreadfully. To be ripped away from him left an open wound, and not knowing what had become of him poured salt into it. Questions, questions, questions, and no answers. Limbo felt like swimming in gelatin.

Father, my dutiful jailer, entered the room. "I just spoke with the doctor."

"I told you I was fine," I answered, my voice as monotone as I felt.

"Fine people don't overdose on sleeping pills."

I closed my eyes, wishing to shut him out but unable to. "I didn't overdose, Father. I told you that."

"If I hadn't come home early . . ."

"Then I would have slept through the afternoon and awoken later a little groggy but otherwise fine." My tone shocked him. It shocked me as well. "I didn't overdose on pills."

"You wouldn't wake up, Theia. I had to throw you into a cold shower."

I shrugged. It was all he would get from me. I wanted to go to school, to get out of the house. The oppression was stagnating.

"I found this in your room." He pulled wrinkled red fabric from behind his back. "Care to explain?"

I turned back to the window. "It's a dress." I'd hidden Donny's dress in the back of my closet after the disastrous night at Chasm.

"This scrap of material is not a dress. Are you telling me you wore this? Where the hell would you wear something like this, young lady?"

Technically, I suppose I did wear it to hell briefly, but that wasn't the best answer if I hoped to avoid another visit with the doctor. "I wore it to a club."

I could barely dredge up enough energy to look away from the window so he could have his moment of rage. My lethargy crippled me, and I'm sure my lack of participation in his manic explosion made it worse. Imagine, my father being overexcited.

"A club? I left town for a few days and you threw everything we believe in out the window?"

The numbness cushioned me from caring. "I suppose that since you don't believe in me having my own life and making my own choices even though I'm seventeen, I guess I did throw it all away. You're absolutely right." Father wouldn't understand sarcasm, and when did I acquire it? "I went dancing. With my friends. I didn't break any laws."

He threw the dress across the room, though the material was too light to accomplish his goal and it fluttered to the floor only a few feet away from him. "I raised you better than this." His face reddened and the veins in his temples throbbed.

"What is so wrong with having fun, Father? It's not a crime."

"You sound like your mother," he bellowed.

"Good."

One word squeezed his anger completely out, leaving him thinner, gaunter, and much, much older than the minute before. "Theia."

"I should apologize, but I won't. I'm tired of pretending I was never born."

He collapsed into a chair. "What are you talking about?"

"Who do you hate more, Father? My mother or me?" The walls of good sense had fallen. The losing battle with sleep had apparently let loose the thoughts I would normally have kept to myself.

"Where is this nonsense coming from? I'm not a man who shows affection freely, but you know I love you." He lowered his voice. "You know I loved her."

"Of course." I returned my gaze to the window.

"What is the meaning of this rebellion?" Father asked me. "We've worked so hard to make you reasonable. What happened?"

"Maybe I was meant to be unreasonable."

"I don't believe that. Your mother . . . she didn't understand the real world. She saw only what she wanted to see. Nothing bad could happen to her—until it did. But you're not like her, Theia. You're pragmatic. You understand consequences. You know that it's better to be careful than to—"

"I don't know that at all." And I didn't. Being careful hadn't brought me any measure of joy—but then again, neither had being reckless.

"This pointless rebellion stops now." Father stood with renewed energy for the argument. "If you don't learn from her mistakes, then her death will have been for nothing."

"And what was her death for, Father? What grand thing did it serve? Perhaps we should be more concerned that I learn from her successes instead of her mistakes, so that her *life* will have not been for nothing." Tears spiked my lashes. "Her death wasn't for nothing, though, was it? It was for me. Because I killed her."

He didn't rush to fill the silence.

"It's true, then. That's what you believe. That I killed her. It's my fault she's dead."

"No—"

"No? If I hadn't been born, she would have lived."

Father paced, filled with an unusual energy instead of sedately in control. "You know it's far more complicated than that. She made her choices, God rest her soul, and left us to live with them. If I were a different man, perhaps I could have handled this better. Perhaps I should never have brought you back to this country."

"It's not the country's fault that I want to have a life, Father. Or wear my hair loose or go dancing with friends. You can't forbid me forever. What will I do when you aren't around? Some choices need to be mine."

He crouched to my level, deep grooves of his face that I'd never noticed before telling of a life of pain. I scarcely knew the man before me. "She dazzled me. I don't talk about her much, Theia, because the pain is still so fresh. Every morning, I awake as normal and then the pain comes to remind me she's not there. It hasn't lessened in seventeen years. I knew absolutely nothing of love before her, and she was gone so quickly I hadn't an opportunity to learn all I needed to carry on, much less raise a child."

I squeezed the end of the afghan. "Tell me about her?" I needed to hear, in his words, from his heart.

His countenance held firm, but the light in his eyes changed. "She was beautiful." He closed his eyes to savor the moment. "I was in the States on business and had been talked into visiting a dingy diner that boasted the best pancakes in America. It was horrid, bad lighting, bad food. She wasn't our waitress; she'd been taking care of the table behind me when she stumbled and spilled greasy hot chips into my lap. I was livid, as you can imagine." Even though I'd heard it before, the undignified encounter seemed impossible to imagine. Father was not a person upon whom things were spilled. "She apologized and rambled on while picking up the potatoes one by one off my pants. They were hot, burning her fingers, and I was angry, and of course the location of the mess was embarrassing to us both." And yet he was smiling. "I kept trying to push her hands away, to no avail, of course. She used to joke about that night—that she didn't know what came over her that she couldn't keep her hands off my pants at first sight."

I scrunched my eyes tightly. "Father, please."

"Too much?"

I nodded, and he chuckled. "Jenny's light was so bright, Theia. She rushed headlong into everything she did. Falling in love was no exception. Of course, I resisted. It wasn't practical. I was only visiting; I lived in another country, for God's sake. We had different tastes in music, politics, entertainment . . . but when she smiled at me . . . your mother was an angel."

My stomach clenched at the unfairness. An angel. And she fell in order that I might live. Why must everyone fall in order to love me?

"I don't hate you." Father reached for me, patting my hair awkwardly. "I could never hate you. I'm sure I've done everything wrong, Theia. But I swear I don't hate you. Try to understand. If she hadn't died, I wouldn't have you—but if I didn't have you, she wouldn't have died. The anguish of her death is matched only by the joy of your birth. I've never known what to do with either, I suppose."

The anguish I saw plainly. He lived it day to day and thrust it upon me most of mine. The joy was what I'd never seen, therefore never believed. I yearned for it, to be loved completely and joyously by my father, but I knew this afternoon's respite from his dour nature was temporary. A step, surely, but not the whole mile.

Just like loving Haden brought little joy for either of us.

Perhaps no love did. Maybe my mother was wrong to believe it could alter anything, make anything better.

Mother had been told by the doctors that a pregnancy would put too much strain on her kidney. It was weak and the other had been taken during her childhood illness. Her other organs were never as strong as they should have been either, though her spirit kept them running well most of the time.

"Why did you allow her to have me, Father?"

He eased away and into a chair. "There was no such thing as *allow* when it came to my Jenny. She made that clear to me from the first. But I won't claim I didn't try." His eyes pierced my heart. "Oh, Theia, it shames me to say that, but I ordered her, pleaded, cried. . . . You were an accident to me, but a miracle to her."

My father ordered her to abort me. Even expecting it, knowing it, couldn't have prepared me for hearing it. This conversation may have been my idea, but it poked holes at my insides.

"You have to understand. We took precautions. I had an operation when I realized how serious her medical situation was. I didn't want to put all the responsibility for birth control on her, but the surgery didn't take. At least not soon enough." Father paused, closing his eyes to retreat to his own painful world. "She said that you needed to be born. That if you got through two forms of birth control, you were meant to be here and she was having you. She threatened to leave me if I ever brought up abortion again."

I shouldn't have been born. I'd been displaced from the moment I was conceived. And now I was a walking, talking exercise in heartache. If my father loved me, he betrayed the love he had for his wife. If he didn't, he betrayed her love for him.

And poor Haden, forced to make a decision with no right answers. Love me and be miserable—that was my legacy so far. And yet I knew that if I ever saw him again, I would rush into his arms without thought of consequences.

"She was never happier than when she carried you."

The sharp turn of his words took me from the road my own thoughts were traveling on and surprised me. I dared not speak and waited for him to continue.

"She never held you in her arms, but she loved to cradle her rounded belly. You were everything to her. It was as if she lived her whole life for those nine months." Father reached tentatively to stroke my cheek. "She'd be so proud of you. Especially your music—but really, everything. She'd have my head for all my transgressions against you."

"You wanted to protect me," I answered.

"I want to love you as well. It's just . . . difficult. I knew before falling for her that love was rash and unkind. I'd avoided it as long as I could, but then I met your mother, and something made me want to try. But I failed, Theia. Love bested me. My consolation was that perhaps I could protect you from heartache." Unguarded, my formidable father reminded me of a boy my own age. "Instead, I fear I broke your heart several times over. For that, I'm sorry."

"You were right to try, Father. Love is impossible."

"I wish fairy tales were real." He patted my hand. "The doctor says you can return to school tomorrow." He paused. "I'll be in my study if you need anything."

After he left, I sighed heavily. So much had changed, yet nothing really had.

I wondered if I would ever cease wishing I was ten years

older. As a young girl I thought, with fervent hope, that ten years was some kind of magic formula. That if I were seventeen instead of seven, I would know how to handle myself better in a situation. That a passing decade would fill in all the cracks where I ached, by adding wisdom or, at the very least, understanding. But seventeen had come, and there I sat, no more used to heartache than when I started. And more confused by it.

I'd thought I would be glad to get out of the house, to return to school—to normal life. I was wrong. Everyone knows high school is the opposite of balm for the soul, but apparently I had to figure it out for myself.

The last time I'd been on campus, the whispers and stares had been almost humorous. I'd been newly in love with a boy who felt the same, and possibility bloomed like flowers everywhere I looked. The obstacles had seemed trivial that day, a few weeds in my garden of hope.

Everything was different now.

I stepped out of Donny's car, and exhaustion set into my bones immediately.

"You okay?" she asked.

"No."

Each step seemed to take energy that I just didn't have.

"Theia, maybe you're still too sick. Do you want me to take you home?"

I shook my head but couldn't look at her. My absence from my life had been explained by the flu, though I don't think Donny or Amelia believed it. I wasn't ready to talk about it. Not yet. They didn't know about Haden returning to Under, or the sleeping pills I took, or that my father had asked my mother to terminate me before I was born.

My insides were too raw for the discussion just now.

The fact that Haden had stopped coming to school about the same time I got the flu was too coincidental for the school rumor factory, which manufactured story after story, each more lurid than the last. As I wound through the busy hall to the admin office with my sick note, the whispers and stares were no longer humorous. They must have known I could hear them, but the students carried on as if it didn't matter.

I heard she got mono.

No, it's cancer. And Haden was so heartbroken he ran away.

No, her dad ran him off. He found out about their affair.

I heard she got in trouble and her dad made her go to the city and, well—you know—get rid of it.

That whisper plunged into my heart like a dagger, so fresh on the wound of finding out my father had tried to convince my mother to get rid of me.

I bet Haden couldn't deal. I bet he won't come back to town ever again.

Maybe he's a demon.

I stopped, and all my blood turned slushy cold, and my skin prickled at the word. The whisper had been only a breath away from my ear, and yet no one was there.

I must have misheard anyway, I lied to myself. I hugged my arms closer to my chest and looked at the students around me a little bit more closely. The whisper, though, still seemed to be caressing my ear, a trace of it left behind. I shivered and continued to the admin office.

The day was going to be a long one.

At lunch Amelia peered at me with an unwavering look. It unnerved me, and the fuse of my temper was already short. "What?" I finally asked, exasperated. I set my Tater Tot back on the tray. "What?" I tried again, with a touch of civility.

She pulled an orange juice out of her lunch bag. "You shouldn't eat so much junk food if you've been sick. Drink this."

"I'm fine," I answered mulishly, closing my eyes. "I'm sorry. I shouldn't have snapped at you." I said the words—I even meant them—but my fingers still clenched the fabric of my pants under the table.

I felt like a teakettle just about to whistle. Emotions rolled inside me in a slow boil, building steam and getting ready for the big show. I didn't know how to stop them. They just gyrated and spun, bringing me closer to a loss of control every minute. I wanted to shout out—scream, really.

I missed Haden. And I wanted my mother.

Amelia pushed the juice at me when I didn't take it from her hand. "It's okay. I know you don't feel well."

"It's not an excuse to become a bitter, hissing crone around my best friends. I'm sorry."

Ame patted my head, and then she craned her neck sharply to look at the door behind us. I turned to see what drew her attention. About ten seconds after I looked, Mike entered the cafeteria door looking the same as he always did. Jeans, tee, letter jacket, boring.

What was wrong with me? That was rude. Mike was a nice lad. Just because I didn't find him all-consuming didn't mean he was boring. Better for Amelia that he was a touch bland than a demon who wanted to eat her heart, after all.

That's when I realized something about the timing of his entrance was off. "You don't think that's strange?" I asked her.

"What's strange?"

"That you knew Mike was coming before he got to the door?"

The pink began in the apples of her cheeks until her whole face flushed. "I didn't."

"Yes, you did. Your neck nearly snapped, you turned so fast, and he didn't come in until *after* I tried to see what you were looking at. Are you turning into a psychic? Like Varnie said?"

She shook her head. "I don't think so. I mean, maybe sometimes, but I still can't do readings." She pressed her lips together in a firm line. "Every now and then, though, I feel something really strongly." She shrugged. "It's weird. I can't control or direct it, and it isn't a vision—just a feeling."

Mike didn't stop at our table, but he waved and said, "Hey," as he walked by.

Ame's shoulders slumped after he passed. I wished Donny wasn't late for lunch. I was in no mood to cheer Amelia up, but that's what friends did, so I kicked her foot under the table. "I'll drink your bloody orange juice if you eat some of these Tater Tots."

We smiled at each other.

Neither one of us meant it, though.

About a week after I had gotten over my "flu," I was going through my daily routine and, as usual, my hair wouldn't co-operate. It occurred to me to just leave it down—and so I did.

Nobody remarked on it at school, but Donny's forehead

creased when she first saw me. Father didn't even mention it at supper, though I could tell he wanted to. He'd been measurably more careful with his comments since our discussion about my mother.

And so the next day and every day after, my curls were free. No more headaches from bands too tight, no more escaping tendrils—just loose and slightly demented curls.

Just to see what would happen, one morning I dug through my closet until I found a pair of jeans Donny had given me last year because she had accidentally bought ones labeled "short." I wore them to school. Donny and Amelia raised their eyebrows at each other, but didn't say anything to me.

It was like that now.

The three of us tiptoed over eggshells around one another. Since Haden had left, I'd kept all but the most superficial thoughts and feelings to myself. They seemed to understand I needed space, but at the same time, they telegraphed what they wanted to say to each other as if I couldn't understand them.

A few days later, I stopped doing my homework.

It all seemed so pointless. I stopped playing the violin too. I just didn't care about pleasing anyone at all anymore. If they didn't like it, they could bugger off.

One night, Father was running late, so Muriel stayed to eat supper with me. I conned her into ordering Chinese. We were getting ready to eat in the kitchen, as we always did when Father was gone.

While she got the plates out, I began pulling the takeout containers from the bag. As I opened one, a movement caught my eye. I peered back into the white box and found a writhing mass of white worms looping around one another trying to get to the top.

I shrieked and clapped one hand over my mouth while I dropped the worms with the other hand. Muriel ran to me as I staggered backwards.

"What is it, Theia?" she cried.

I choked back my gagging noises and simply pointed to the mess, just knowing they'd be crawling towards my shoes.

"Pumpkin, what is wrong?" she asked again.

Couldn't she see? I looked at the floor. Nothing moved. There were no worms, only noodles.

"That's impossible." I stooped lower. "They were moving. They were . . . worms or something and they were alive."

Muriel's hand stroked my back. "Someone has been watching too many late-night movies."

"No," I protested. "I swear. They weren't . . . noodles. I *saw* them."

"Just a trick of the mind, Thei. I'll get this cleaned up. Why don't you go splash a little cool water on your face? You've had quite a scare."

I nodded, but I couldn't take my eyes off the still noodles on the floor. I waited for them to move again, to prove that I wasn't insane. The hair on the back of my neck rose and I felt like I was being watched. Then, just as suddenly, the feeling was gone.

After the night with the noodles, I was hypervigilant. Everything made me wary. Out of the corner of my eye I kept seeing things move. Things that weren't there. Many times, the songs on my iPhone would sound scratchy and I would almost be able to pick out voices—like when radio reception loses strength and you get two channels at once. I couldn't hear what the voices were saying, but they gave me the chills all the same.

I'd taken to sleeping with the light on, but sometimes that was worse. Now and again, shadows seemed to move in ways they weren't meant to. Every day I became more paranoid and withdrawn.

One day at school, Amelia touched my arm and we both recoiled from the electric shock it produced.

"Sorry," she said. "God, I've been doing that all the time lately. I can't figure out what is going on. It's like I'm a lightning rod or something. Everything I touch shocks me."

"Did your mom switch shampoo?" Donny asked. Donny placed a lot of importance on shampoo.

"Um, no." Ame said with a laugh.

We'd decided to eat outside that day. The weather had been strange—alternating between showers and a warm sun—but it was sunny at lunch and we all craved the vitamin D therapy, as Donny called it.

I wasn't eating, though I stared at my lunch very hard, something I found myself doing often.

"Where's Gabe?" Amelia asked Donny.

She shrugged. "How should I know?"

It wasn't until Donny looked at me quizzically that I realized I was staring at her. No—I was glaring at her. I replaced my angry face with a pleasant one quickly and looked back down at my lunch again. It's just that it was hard, sometimes, not to be upset with her. Gabe treated her so well, and everyone knew she had feelings for him. It seemed so wasteful to me that she kept denying something that made her happy—or would make her happy if she'd stop being so stubborn about it. I missed Haden. One thousand times a day, I wished for him to come back. Gabe was right here, and she kept pushing him away.

Mike strolled by, surprising us all when he actually stopped at our bench.

"Hey," he said. Like he always seemed to say.

"Hey," Amelia answered.

I nodded a small greeting and Donny sort of waved, not looking up from texting. She was probably texting Gabe to find out where he was. Even though she didn't care.

"Ame, I wondered if you wanted to go over last night's trig."

Mike didn't include me; everyone in class knew my trig grade was falling because I'd stopped turning in the assignments. I needed to get it together. While a part of me was enjoying not living up to everyone's preconceived notions of me, I really didn't want to be the girl whose life fell apart because of a boy. It was so . . . cliché.

It was also really, really easy to let happen.

"Sure," Ame replied. Her smile lit up her entire face, and I felt a guilty stab of envy.

Then Mike looked at my burger. "Are you going to eat that?" he asked.

I shook my head and handed him the whole tray, making excuses to everyone about needing to go do something. I didn't stick around to explain—I just got up and walked away from my friends, something I was getting very good at doing.

I should have seen it coming.

"Where are we going?" I asked as Donny drove past the turn to my house.

"We're nabbing you," answered Amelia.

I rolled my eyes. I'd barely made it through the entire school day. I didn't want to be nabbed; I wanted nothing more than to crawl under my covers and sleep. Just like I had every day lately. It seemed safer to sleep during daylight hours.

She'd *said* she would give me a ride home.

Not for the first time did I curse my father for not letting me get my license. Too dangerous, of course. And what did I need one for? Serendipity High was within walking distance of our house and the fresh air was "good for my constitution." Donny's parents actually bought her a car—an older Honda Accord—but she also had to taxi her little brother to and from practice every day and take over the grocery shopping. It seemed fair to me. Everything about her parents seemed rational and fair. Their rules, though she often broke them, made sense. And her privileges, when she earned them, were more than just.

If I wanted money for something, I had to ask and explain why. What did I need it for? Muriel packed my lunch in the evenings, Father's shopper purchased all my clothes, and his decorator made small variances to my room two or three times a year to keep me from being bored with the design.

He didn't understand that I might like to have a bit of spending money that I didn't need to account to him for. I'd have gladly done chores or even gotten a job—if he had let me.

Ame also had her license, but no car. Which gave Donny a lot of power in our relationship. Which she certainly took advantage of, but didn't usually abuse.

"Look, you've been all Emo Barbie and we're tired of it.

We're taking you to the beach." Donny met my gaze in her rearview mirror. "And before you whine and say, 'I don't want to go to the beach,' you should know I'm past caring."

"That's very nice, Donnatella." I sneered and folded my arms. "I'm glad you've found a way to make this all about you."

"You can be a bitch if you want to, but we're still going to the fucking beach."

Amelia turned around to look at me from the passenger seat. "Please don't fight, you guys. We're just worried about you, Thei. You won't talk to us anymore. Not since the day Haden stopped coming to school. We miss you."

I hugged myself and stared out the window. "Well, he's gone. Talking about it won't make him come back."

The trip to the coast took only ten minutes, but it seemed longer. Amelia peppered Donny with inane conversation to keep her off my back. I should have been more grateful. Instead, I just wished longingly for my bed.

I don't know why I pushed them away so hard, or why I actively sought out an argument with Donny. My heart ached, and it colored everything around me black. I wanted nothing because I couldn't have the only thing I really wanted. And I guess part of me wanted nobody else to get what they wanted if I couldn't.

Some friend, right?

"Get out of the car," Donny told me.

"I'm fine here. You guys go," I answered.

"Get. Out. Of. The. Car."

I drew my mouth into a grim line that hurt my jaw with its frozen force. I pushed out of her car and stomped ahead of them in the sand, not even closing the door behind me. The bitter spring wind whipped around me as I trudged to the line where the ocean met the land, and there I stood, wishing the water would just claim me and get this over with. What did drowning feel like? It couldn't hurt more than my decimated heart did, could it? Would it hurt more than burning to ash like Haden did that first night?

Donny and Amelia joined me at the water's edge, book-ending me between them. The tumultuous waves crashed over themselves; the tumbling repetition should have been ineffective, and yet that was how the coast was formed, how it was transformed. It was how I felt standing there—like I'd been battered endlessly by waves and it was changing me in nearly imperceptible ways. Though judging by the way I'd been treating my best friends, the imperceptibleness was questionable.

Winter hadn't completely let go yet, despite the earlier sunshine. The beach was still cold and unforgiving. I inhaled the briny air deeply, suddenly very glad to be there. The ocean always unlocked something in me, a fact Donny knew well. "I'm sorry. Both of you. I haven't been myself and I'm ashamed of the way I've treated our friendship lately."

"We're just so worried about you. You've been so un-Theiable lately."

I nodded. "Haden is gone for good. I know that I'll never see him again, but I really love him and it hurts . . . it hurts to breathe."

They were on me in a second. There-thereing and it's-not-so-badding, holding me up and keeping me strong. Better yet, being strong for me.

Ame pulled a lock of windblown hair from her mouth.

"Theia, we didn't get to know him very well, but he must love you too, right? I mean, he didn't take anyone, did he?"

I shook my head. I explained to them that he could still be in danger for angering his mother. That he seemed truly adamant that she would not be understanding. "I don't know if he's okay. I mean, if I knew he was happy or okay, I could get through this."

"Oh, God, I think you guys are starting to make me believe in all this crap," Donny said. And we laughed.

Huddled together, the three of us, it did feel significant. Our little circle against the world.

I told them about my father. How we'd finally spoken about my mother, how it had hurt but felt good at the same time. I told them that the last time I went Under, I had to take my father's sleeping pills.

"That is so not cool," Donny said as she pinched me. "We don't let boy problems turn us into druggies—got it?" Her tone was light, but her message was stern beneath it.

"I don't think I can get back that way again. He's done something so that I can't go there anymore. Maybe..." I looked at Ame. She might know a way. She'd been studying so many metaphysical things.

I was about to ask her opinion when a strange wind picked up. It wasn't just bitter cold, it was malevolent and searching. We gasped and instinctively began to break away from our circle in the confusion, but Amelia's face took on a stubborn expression and she squeezed us tighter, so Donny and I held on. The wind carried voices, whispers and hisses of words swirling around us, getting faster and faster. Donny grew pale looking towards the horizon. Amelia and I followed her gaze over the water and watched as the darkest clouds I'd ever seen gathered, turning the sky bruise-purple.

A gale-force wind blew and the mottled clouds raced across the sky and straight towards us. It wasn't just the color or the speed that scared us—there was a smell, a tinge of sulfur that accompanied their tumbling roll. Amelia yelled at us to hang on, and so we did, without thought of consequence.

The wicked wind blew through us, trying to tear us apart, but also at work was another force. The pendant—my talisman—seemed to glow heat against my skin, and as it spread, the warmth buffeted the impact of the gathering storm. Rain fell like bullets from the sky but didn't touch us. I looked up and noticed the black clouds were directly over us then, with a break in the center like a hole in a doughnut.

The wind still stung at us, and lightning bolts landed sporadically around us, but somehow we knew we had to hold on. So we faced the freak storm, and it dissipated as quickly as it had come on. No theatrics. Just gone.

"Well, that was weird," Donny said dryly.

"Thei," Ame began, "I don't think this is over yet. Whatever that was, I think it wanted you."

I shivered. Amelia was shaken, but she looked . . . in control, empowered.

Donny watched Amelia very carefully too. "Ame, what the hell is going on?"

She shrugged. "I'm not sure exactly, but I think it's time I started really paying attention to my Hello Kitty tarot cards."

After returning from the beach, I had to wade through a painful supper in which Father and I both tried to make believe

things were looser between us now. They may have been better, but it was hard to tell given the current climate of "let's
pretend." Let's pretend you didn't want to abort me. Let's pretend it doesn't bother you that I'm wearing blue jeans and my
hair wild. Let's pretend we have a different relationship now
that we understand each other.

Once we'd run out of idle chatter, rehashing the inane details of our day that neither of us cared about, we returned to
an uncomfortable silence. I couldn't stop thinking about that
storm, about Amelia's warning. What had it meant?

"Are you taking a chill?" Father asked. I must have looked
confused, because he clarified his question with, "You just
shivered."

"Oh," I answered. "I'm sure I'm fine. Must have been a
draft."

We went back to silence. What would supper have been
like if my mother had lived? I'd bet we'd eat in the kitchen
more often.

"Father?" A punch of panic wouldn't let me go any further.
I'd simply meant to fill the silence with something, anything.
But as my mouth formed his name, I realized I wanted to talk
about something real.

"Yes?"

"I've been wearing one of my mother's pendants for a
while. I got it from the attic," I confessed.

The fork stopped in midair. He set it atop his plate carefully. "I see."

"Are you angry?"

"No," he assured me. "I should have thought to bring her

jewelry down to you a while ago. She would want you to have it." He cleared his throat. "I want you to have it."

I smiled at him. A real one. I felt . . . closer to him at that moment than I ever had.

After our meal, I tried to play my violin. Father had dismissed my tutor without questioning why I didn't want to play anymore after . . . well, after the night with the pills. But suddenly I wished I wanted to play again. I picked it up, the weight of it foreign and familiar at the same time. I re-haired my neglected bow carefully and then eased into a song. I didn't feel it stir my soul. It was just notes and mechanics. Perfunctory practice. Boring.

I put it down.

I took a bath, long and hot. I tried not to think about anything, but my mind kept circling back to the beach. When Varnie had told me that something dark had attached to me, I assumed it was Haden.

Whatever had been on the beach—it hadn't felt like Haden. It had felt evil.

The bathwater turned icy. How long had I been in it? It had felt so warm only a moment before, it seemed.

I got ready for bed, still shivering from my bath and ignoring that I had a metric ton of schoolwork to catch up on. Then from across my bedroom, I saw it.

A long-stemmed black rose lay on my pillow.

Haden?

I approached the bed slowly, as if the flower were going to flee like a scared animal. My heart picked up an uneven, frenzied rhythm and sent the blood rushing to my head. I snatched the stem and a razor-sharp thorn pricked my finger. Haden had never left me a rose with thorns before. As the bloom fell from my hand, I brought my finger to my mouth, the coppery taste of blood on my tongue while I witnessed my own shadow shifting apart from me on the canvas of the wall.

I jerked from the unnatural sensation of seeing myself disengaged. My shadow turned to look behind her and then ran frantically. I watched her, fascinated as she ran a circle around the room, trapped on the wall yet oddly not attached to me any longer.

I stumbled backwards, searching the room for whatever malevolent force had scared my shadow so much that she was able to flee my person. I felt trapped. An acre of carpet separated me from the safety of my bedroom door and possible escape. All at once, she stopped racing and spun around and upside down like a pinwheel, getting smaller and smaller. Then the other shadows in the room began funneling towards her disappearing shape, and they too whirled like water around a drain. In horror, I watched them all swirl into a pinpoint and disappear.

A room without shadows is an abomination of the laws of our universe, though I'd never much thought of it until I was left in one. It made me itch. The door still seemed so very far away, but I had to try. Girding my nerve, I padded in that direction, only to stop short in front of my mirror.

I wasn't in it.

I had no reflection, though everything behind me was clearly visible. When I heard the creaks and clicks coming, I was well aware of the state of my affairs. I remembered that sound, that detestable, hideous noise, from the bonfire in

Haden's world. Being frightened wasn't even an option anymore. The fear had progressed beyond that into something more primal.

It wasn't Haden who had come for me. I knew that now.

I waited for the skeletons to materialize, my fight-or-flight instinct subdued by an understanding that neither would do me any good. Hell had come looking for me, and I'd rather it found me alone than take someone else in the house along for the ride with me.

Click. Click. Clack. Scrape.

The noise got louder. Then they came through the wall.

Materializing from the pinpoint into which all the shadows had disappeared, four bodies of bones crawled out of my bedroom wall. I whimpered but did not scream, hoping to save the life of my father and Muriel with my last act of bravery, to face the animated corpses alone. One scuffled across my room, reaching his bony finger towards me, though I shrugged into myself to avoid his touch. His joints popped as he wrapped his dry bones around my wrist, startlingly strong. A last effort on my part to pull back from him gained me a slap across my face. The sting and revulsion of his touch battled for supremacy of my senses, but I didn't fight him again when he dragged me towards the wall.

He placed me in front of the pinhole that had sucked in my shadow. As I looked at it, I saw through it and I realized I could see my room, only without me in it. I'd already been taken to the other side. Yet the journey wasn't over for me, not by a long shot.

Trapped in darkness, I lost my bearings. It wasn't just black or the absence of light. I was fixed in shadow. Even more alarming than my previous experience with the laws of the universe being broken in my bedroom, I had been thrown into a vortex made up of stolen shadows from my own world. Shadow was different from dark. It had depth, it felt thick.

My nose stung with the scent of sulfur, so overpowering that I could only guess it was brimstone. It made me choke and clogged my lungs, and the harder I coughed, the more my chest was filled with it. A warmth spread slowly from my toes and worked its way through the rest of me. The heat wasn't unpleasant. Not at first, or maybe I didn't notice it as such because of the retching and gagging from the vile odor of hell's smoke. At some point I realized that the heat had intensified and that I was slowly catching fire.

I panicked. I didn't go gently like the burning man floating past my window. I screamed and clawed at my own skin. Wanting it off me like it was offensive. Vulgar. I lost track of my escorts as well as my surroundings. Perhaps I was moving, maybe I was standing still. Whichever the case, I was burning alive. Though I was in the dark, I could see my bones charring by the light of my ignited flesh. Had there been any justice at all, my eyes should have gone first. Even when I had no skin left, and therefore no nerves to sense pain, I still felt the excruciating effects.

I begged for mercy, for an end to my suffering. My last coherent thoughts were of Haden burning like this just to see me. Parts of my body that should have been gone hurt with agonizing intensity.

And finally, blessed unconsciousness.

CHAPTER SIXTEEN

My skin stretched over my bones too tautly. I'd been put back together wrong.

I suppose the important thing was that I'd been put back together at all. I remembered nothing after I fainted until I awoke on a cold stone floor, my head throbbing and every molecule in my body protesting whatever new arrangement it had been aligned into.

I lifted my heavy head and tried to focus on my surroundings. One would think the damp coolness surrounding me would have been welcome after the heat and flames I'd endured; however, the scene that greeted me was not for my comfort. The floor beneath me was coated in a slimy substance that I dared not try to name. There was little light, enough to elongate shadows and illuminate the remains of two people chained to the wall. They'd been there a long time, if the length of their hair was an indication. I didn't think they would come to life like the bony skeletons who'd taken me from my room—but I couldn't decide if that made me feel better or worse.

Where was I? I didn't remember anything but burning.

Bile churned in my stomach. I had to get out of there. Things were crawling on me already. Things I couldn't see; things I thought were already under my skin. I crawled to the iron gate that imprisoned me with the dead. An unrelieved corridor stretched to both my left and my right. I used the bars on the gate to pull myself up and tried to angle myself for a better look, but none was afforded me. Just a bleak and barely lit hall.

I was in some kind of dungeon. But why? Would I be here as long as the corpses I shared the cell with? I stood there for a long time, waiting for something to happen next. I stayed there for so long that I started to wonder if I had died and was in some sort of purgatory. My stomach rumbled around emptiness, but I couldn't have eaten even if my captors had left me something. The smell of brimstone mixed with decay took care of that—but it was the smell of fear that was the worst. I had never known until then that fear really had a scent attached to it. It was palpable and overwhelming. This place was filled with the smell of it. It lingered in the air and was so potent that I realized it wasn't just my emotion or the emotion of the two behind me who'd long since left this place. Hundreds of people had had the life scared out of them in this dungeon.

I could feel them all.

Why was I here? As the hours crept by, I thought perhaps it was best if I never found out. Maybe my kindest end would

be to be forgotten and left to rot. I had a feeling that was better than some of my predecessors had gotten.

I remembered Haden telling me that the first time he
physically entered my world, he burned. I assumed that meant
I was in Under—but it didn't explain why I was locked in a
cell.

I stood at the bars until I could stand no more. As I slid
slowly into a heap on the slimy floor, I lost what was left of
my dignity and spilled my bladder. It didn't matter anymore. I
began praying for death.

Click. Clack. Click. Scrape.

I didn't open my eyes. I knew *they* were there. The skeletons again.

I'd been dreaming of Haden. Real dreams, not the lucid
traveling I used to have. The dreams were disjointed and unforgiving, but all in all a much better alternative than my current reality.

Two skeletal minions hoisted me up, one under each arm,
and dragged me down the hall. I finally opened my eyes and
was shocked to see there were other cells like mine lining the
corridor, and people in them in various states of lost hope.
Why hadn't I tried to call out? Perhaps we could have bonded
together, if even for a short while.

Just before we turned the corner, I glanced into a cell and
my heart stopped.

Haden.

He jumped to the bars when he saw me, reaching out and
yelling my name. But my jailers didn't stop or slow down, even

as I kicked my legs and flailed to get back to him. He was gaunt and dirty, but otherwise alive.

If I was going to my grave, I would take that thought with me as my last one.

The skeletons were not concerned with the state of my skin as they continued dragging me through the dungeon. They pushed and pulled me, scraping me against walls and sometimes their own rough bones. We moved upwards, each floor a little more luxuriant than the last. Perhaps they were going to torture me with fire again. As soon as the thought crossed my mind, I pushed it away. The shreds of my sanity dictated that I remain in denial as long as possible.

We finally stopped using stairs, and they dragged me down a carpeted hall. The stone walls were lit by tapered candles in shining sconces, the corridor too bright after my time in darkness. They opened a heavy door and threw me in, slamming it behind them.

I landed hard on my knees, the shock jolting through my body. I didn't think I could stand, so I rolled to a sitting position to take in my new surroundings. A new word for "surprise" was needed because that could never adequately explain my astonishment at the lavish room fit for a fairy-tale princess.

To my right, a large hearth burned logs that smelled like cinnamon. To my left, a floor-to-ceiling bookcase climbed the wall. I tried to get up to inspect the rest, but my shins felt brittle and sharp. It was then that I looked at my own arms. They were so raw and mottled that I didn't recognize them as mine.

How long had I been in that dungeon?

The door behind me opened again, and I braced for more rough treatment. Instead of skeletons, I was surrounded by dresses. They pranced around me without speaking, so I finally looked up at the women in them.

Each woman was scarred by black stitching, as if they had been sewn together piecemeal. I gasped to see each of their mouths sewn closed with thick black floss. They each wore the same dress, but in a different color, and their heads wobbled unsteadily on their necks, scars crisscrossing their throats. I flashed on my recollection of waking in my cell, how wrong I felt, and I hoped I didn't look the same as these women. Was I made up of sutures now too?

They gestured to a tub in the middle of the room, and I noticed steam coming from it. Again I tried to get up, for a bath would have been heavenly, despite my situation; it beckoned to me like a desert mirage. But I couldn't rise on my own. The women rallied around me and gently held me up and helped me over to the tub. I was grateful for their treatment of me and tried not to react in disgust when the stitches on the arm of one rubbed my skin.

They took my weight and settled me into the huge bathtub, stripping off my stained clothes. I was past caring about modesty. The hot water stung my scrapes, but it felt so good to rinse off the grime and filth that I blinked away the momentary tingle. A heavenly scent of roses reached my nose and for a moment I wondered if they were steeping me like tea for some unknown evil to partake of. And then I looked up at the wobbly-headed ladies-in-waiting and realized that my errant thought might not be too far from its mark.

They fluttered around me, tossing flower petals into my bath and looking at one another like they were so very pleased with their task. As if they were some kind of Stepford wives.

It was upon closer inspection that I realized the piecemeal of their bodywork reflected a pattern of sorts, a morbid one at that. The scars on one matched the scars on the other two. None had a matching set of eyes, but each was different in the same way. The three of them were a . . . blend of one another.

Someone had hacked three women apart and darned them back together as a mix-and-match.

I shuddered. Had their surgical adventure begun in a rose-scented bath as well? Was I being prepped and sterilized for a date with Dr. Frankenstein?

One of them pushed me under the water and I came up sputtering and panicked, only to have soap massaged into my hair gently. I relaxed for a moment and she dunked me again. The alternate rough-then-tender treatment was more jarring than the actual aggression. I never knew what was coming or who to be on guard from. The heads wobbled loosely and the eyes held the look of madness as they rinsed me and cooed over me, the sound caught strangely in their throats since their mouths were seamed closed.

Two women hauled me from the tub violently, and then the third wrapped me in the softest towel, warm, as if it had just been taken from the dryer. They fawned over me, patting me gently and mewling like kittens, and then I was shoved into a wooden chair, bruising my tailbone. A brush was yanked through my hair while a soothing balm was applied to my skin.

"Why are you doing this?" I asked, knowing they couldn't answer.

A silver file appeared, ominous in its length and the sharpness of its tip. I stopped breathing for a moment, waiting for it to be plunged into my heart. Instead, the woman wearing the pink gown knelt in front of my chair and gave me a pedicure.

There were more powders and lotions to follow. My hair was pulled into an intricate updo with braids and pearls and shimmery gems. As they worked a sort of devilish makeover, I sat in the chair and cried silent tears.

They pulled me out of the chair and dragged me to a large armoire. In it was one dress. They unwrapped me from my towel and shoved a chemise over my head without touching my hair. I stepped into a petticoat and I stared at the dress while they wrapped a corset around my chest. The dress beckoned like sin. I knew it had been made especially for me; it practically called my name. Bloodred satin. Something I would never have chosen for myself, and yet it had chosen me.

Finally, the woman in the blue dress pulled out my gown. It pulsed with vitality and I realized I was bouncing a little on the balls of my feet—and standing without help. The bath's restorative powers or the pull of a really great frock?

I stepped into the gown and they pulled it up my form. It molded to my body flawlessly. This I knew without even looking. My mother's necklace warmed against my skin while they adjusted the gown. As soon as they were done fastening it, one woman pulled me by my wrist to the looking glass, her fingernails drawing blood.

The stranger in the glass startled me. All my wounds had somehow healed already. I had no suture marks or scars, and my face reminded me of my own, and yet it was different. I was different. I felt like I was looking at myself from the wrong side of the mirror.

But I was beautiful.

Skeletons entered the room and hauled out my tub. The woman in the yellow dress pushed me onto a velvet settee and there I was to wait. For what, I didn't know.

I took in the rest of my surroundings for the first time, since I was no longer being poked, prodded, and lavished over. I'd grown up in a beautiful home, but I'd never experienced such opulence. Crimson, plum, and luscious gold fabrics covered the bed and windows. On the walls, tapestries of the same rich colors bathed the room in affluence and luxury. I didn't understand why I'd been thrown in a dungeon and then hurled into sumptuousness.

I didn't dare question my fortune.

All at once, everyone left me alone. I stayed on the settee longer than I care to admit, frightened that it was a trick, that I'd been left unattended only to secure my own misfortune. After a long while, I slowly stood up, waiting a breath before I moved. My heart beat so quickly in my chest it seemed it was going to leap ahead of the rest of my body. I tiptoed across the vast room and rested my ear against the door gently. It was too thick to hear anything, so I shored up my nerve and tried to open it. Locked, of course.

A little braver, I ran to the window, easing back the heavy drapes to find iron bars like those in my dungeon. The view from my new room was a little better, however. Outside the castle, a murky fog obstructed most of the scenery, but what I could see was alarmingly eerie. It seemed the castle perched itself on the tip of a mountain. The craggy kind. Lightning cracked open the sky just then, and the clap of thunder jolted me several feet from the window.

The thought of Haden still locked in that cell agitated me. I would have to wait until they opened the door and try to make a dash then, or sometime thereafter. As I paced, I looked longingly at the bed. The duvet beckoned me. It was a deep red velvet and so ridiculously full and downy that feathers escaped the seams. A nap would certainly be welcome, but I wasn't sure if I should let my guard down. They had trussed me up for some reason; I couldn't afford to dull my senses until I knew what I was facing.

The bookshelf might have served as a distraction, but each tome I opened was written in a language I didn't understand. My stomach growled ferociously, reminding me that it had been some time since my last meal. I just had no idea how much time. Haden had told me time moved differently here.

Pacing once again, I let my mind wander to the first time I'd seen Haden in the labyrinth. How wicked and extraordinary he was in his cravat and tails. Had I known where he'd take me, would I still have embarked on this journey?

Yes.

As soon as I'd made the declaration to myself, the lock on the prison door sounded as the bolt was thrown back. I stood up straight, squaring my shoulders and determining to face my destiny with courage. My newfound pluck faltered a bit when a man with no face and a perfectly tailored tuxedo entered and crossed the room to where I stood. He bowed like a gentleman, and I returned with a curtsy and a whimper. With no eyes, how did he see? Where his facial features should have been, there was nothing but taut skin.

He held his arm out to me, and I rested my hand on it. It

wasn't as if there were many choices available. He was going to take me somewhere; if he couldn't have handled the job by himself they would have sent the skeletons to take me.

My escort's gait was smooth and he led me gracefully through the halls of the castle. The keep was both magnificent and garish. Fine furnishings and tapestries lined the corridors, yet there were macabre touches interlaced with the luxury—a crystal bowl of eyeballs, human joints lacquered into wood, portraits of death, chilling in their intensity, hanging in gilded frames.

I had to stop looking. I kept my gaze on the floor, trusting, I suppose, that my guide would not allow me to falter. Voices grew louder as we walked, accompanied by laughter and the sound of utensils and plates. Suddenly we stopped at an archway, and all the noise diminished at our entrance.

A banquet of splendor covered the long wooden table. Guests lined only one side; on the other there were just two table settings with empty chairs. Candelabra glowed brightly, shining on the heavy china and polished silver. Enormous fruit spilled from baskets, and pitchers of beverages glistened with condensation.

I was led to an empty chair. The faceless man pulled out my seat while the rest of the guests whispered in hushed tones. I'd interrupted their merriment, but judging by the still-moving entrée on a silver platter, the dinner party had just begun. My stomach curled at the sight of an animal I didn't recognize squirming against the ropes that held it to the table. My gut wrenched even more when I met the gazes of my dinner companions. The same hideous dancers I recognized from my earlier trips Under ogled me like I was an iced cupcake in a bakery window.

My pulse raced. I should have tried to run away before I sat down. Every nerve in my body signaled danger. The hairs on my nape rose, urging me to run. I tried to swallow, but fear clogged my throat, gagging me until I nearly choked on it.

"Everyone, please welcome our much-honored guest, the delectable Theia."

I turned to the speaker at the head of the table. She was gorgeous and very, very evil. I had no doubt that under her beautiful facade she was the most dangerous of all predators. And humans were her chosen prey.

Her onyx hair fell straight to her waist and looked shiny enough to see a reflection in. Her dark eyes pierced me while she smiled with no joy from her overly red lips. The resemblance to Haden shimmered beneath the surface. It was there, but fleeting. She was obviously his mother, but she was something quite a bit different from him.

A rustle at the doorway brought our attention to another guest being escorted in roughly by three skeleton guards. He fought fiercely, but they dragged him in anyway.

"Haden, what have I told you about roughhousing at the dinner table?" his mother asked.

He brought his head up sharply, and I gasped his name.

His eyes flashed and he stopped struggling when he saw me. He closed his eyes, as if he were in pain. "Mother, what have you done?"

CHAPTER SEVENTEEN

Haden's mother smiled without joy. "Now that both our guests of honor have arrived, we can begin the festivities." She spoke each word with the confidence of someone whose every whim is catered to.

Haden still fought to shrug off his guards, but stopped short, a new fear in his eyes. I followed his gaze to the head of the table, where his mother had picked up an imposing knife while she looked directly at me with a gleam in her eye.

"Haden, do sit down. I'd hate for a vicious accident to happen to your fiancée." *Fiancée?* When he was slow to move, she added, "She's such a lovely, delicate young thing after all."

Her words, though polite and formal, were as effective as razor wire. The guards brought Haden to the table without further incident. He sat in the chair next to me but didn't look at me, and suddenly I felt more alone than I had in the dungeon. Below the table, he reached for my hand.

His fingers, strong and sure, wrapped around mine briefly, squeezing a short burst of comfort before he pulled back again.

His message was clear. He didn't want his mother to know how he felt about me. She was peril in a long black dress.

"Mother, I do not wish to marry. Locking me in the dungeon didn't change my mind; neither will parading trollops in satin in front of me."

She laughed then, mirthless and cruel. "We all know she's no trollop, my darling boy. The scent of her innocence is quite invigorating. I'm sure I'm not the only one at the table interested in a tidbit of her. But we've saved her for you." Her eyes darkened until no white was visible, just inky black orbs. "If you don't want her, I can assure you she won't go to waste. Not a single drop."

Coldness seeped into my pores, chilling my blood and bones, moving through my body until I choked on my icy breath. I clutched Haden's leg under the table in terror.

"Mother, stop."

At once the chill disappeared and I coughed. "What do you want?" I rasped.

"Only my son's happiness, pussycat." She poured from a pitcher into a tall goblet. The liquid was deep red and thicker than wine. "My son laments his heritage, so his human *feelings*"—she rolled her eyes in distaste—"gobble him up from the inside. He'll never be what he wants. You and I both know that. But I can give him the next best thing. He'll be happy here, if he has you. So you'll both stay."

"I don't want her." My hand was still on his thigh, and I pulled it away shyly as he spoke. "She was a diversion, nothing else. A human bride would be a mistake. She'd end up just like my pitiful father."

The words were ugly and his tone sharp, cutting my heart even as I told myself he was lying. He didn't mean it. He couldn't. He was just trying to throw his mother off track.

I hoped.

His mother scowled at the reminder. "Your father was weak. He could have been a king, but instead he chose to be a martyr."

"My father had very few choices, but that is beside the point. I'm too young for marriage and I don't want a human. They're—" He shuddered. "They're messy. All their emotions sour my stomach."

I blinked back the tears. I was supposed to not want to be wanted by him, but I'm afraid I wasn't putting on a very believable show. Messy was right.

The dark mistress regarded him ruefully while she tapped her bloodred nails on the table. "Your stomach doesn't concern me, Haden. Your lack of accountability to this realm does. You are heir to its entirety. It's past time you stopped wishing on stars and mooning over insignificant matters of your human heart." She sipped her beverage and watched me closely. "Theia, I've been remiss in my manners. You should have taken me to task for not introducing myself to you. My name is Mara. I'm Haden's mother, of course. Since we're to be family, it would please me if you also called me Mother." She paused. "I see from your expression that would make you unhappy. No doubt you miss your own mother very much. Very well, call me Mara."

"Never say her name out loud," Haden warned me.

"Names have power here. You don't want to give up any of yours to her."

Again Mara laughed. Her vulgar enjoyment of my naïveté washed over me. There were no safe places to step in this world. Every footfall provided me another chance to fall flat on my face or worse. I fingered my mother's pendant—my amulet now—as it seemed the only thing I had anchoring me to reality. The stone seemed alive under my hands.

"Tell me again how she means nothing to you, Haden."

"I'm not going to marry her, Mother."

"Then we've had a change of menu, *son*. Tomorrow we'll pick you a new one. And we will continue to *eat your rejects* until you've bred an heir and taken your rightful place as Prince of this realm." Mara's eyes glittered with malice and she licked her lips as she stared at me. "Pussycat, the smell of your fear mixed with innocence makes you the most delectable morsel we've had in long, long time." She snapped her fingers at the skeleton sentry guarding the door.

Haden shot out of his chair. "You won't touch her!"

"Then you'll have to." She nodded to the guards to back off.

"I don't need to feed." Haden's fingers raked through his hair. "I don't *want* to feed. Just put me back in the dungeon and let Theia return home."

"You may not need to take human essence to survive, but you'll always crave it." Mara dabbed the corners of her wide mouth with a napkin. "I see I've spoiled you. Can't you be gracious enough to thank me? I saw what you really wanted, Haden, and I've brought her to you—gift-wrapped, no less. Do you think she looked that good when we plucked her from her world? She may have been appetizing before, but you can't argue she's succulent now." She stood, holding her drink aloft. "Guests, please join me in a toast to the bride and groom." The ghouls raised their glasses, their bulging eyes and misshapen faces more hideous when portraying their elation. "To Haden and Theia. May you always be as happy as you are at this very moment."

The guests cheered, Haden slumped back into his chair, and I burst into tears.

As the revelry faded, footmen brought tureens of soup to the table. My stomach growled at the smell of food, but Haden put a stilling hand on my wrist when I reached for my spoon.

"Haden, I'm starving. I can't remember the last time I ate. You may not need to feed, but I do."

He squeezed my wrist tighter until I dropped the spoon. "Trust me—you don't want to eat that."

He signaled one of the footmen over and whispered something in his ear—well, where his ear should have been if he'd had one. He took our soup and returned to the kitchen.

My tears hadn't stopped, no matter how hard I tried to still them. Every emotion I'd ever had was close to the surface, ready to spill out. I was hungry and tired and had no idea whether I would live to see another day. The boy I loved sat like a stranger next to me, and I wasn't sure yet if we were already considered married just because Mara said so.

The faceless footman reappeared and placed a dome-covered plate between us. He lifted the lid and I began crying anew. A stack of bread and a jar each of jelly and peanut butter were placed artfully on the platter, along with two butter knives.

"Thank you," I said the servant. And then to Haden as well.

"You're in quite a mess because of me, Theia. PB&J won't get us out of it."

I had already slathered peanut butter on a slice of bread and taken a bite by then, so I just nodded. I didn't think anything had ever tasted so good. I swallowed greedily and spoke. "We can make the best of it, can't we?"

"There is no best of it here." He sighed. "Are you going to let me have one of those?"

"Make your own," I answered.

He chuckled at that, and while he made his sandwich, I knew he was wrong. We could make the best of it. I just hoped we could maybe do it someplace else.

When it came time for the main course, I set my gaze on the strange animal that still writhed on the table. All the other guests picked up sharp knives and looked eagerly at the still-breathing entrée. Bile rose and I wished I hadn't eaten the sandwiches. Sensing my distress, Haden asked if we could be excused.

"Eager to begin your honeymoon?" Mara arched a brow. "How sweet. I've prepared the bridal suite." She formed a sinful smile. "You should both enjoy it very much."

Haden blushed. "I'd rather hoped to begin our marriage in my own—rather, our—room."

"Tonight you shall stay in the bridal suite. I want to make sure I get a grandchild soon."

I shuddered. A child? She wants us to have children already? "Are we already married?" I asked.

"Weddings are different here, pussycat. You'll have a bonding ceremony after you're proven fertile."

Without thought, I reached for my amulet again. The stone felt warm against my palm. I let myself imagine, for only a second, that my own mother was there, watching over me.

The familiar sounds of clicking and scraping heralded the arrival of our escorts made of bones. This time they didn't manhandle either of us, so long as we went where we were bidden. Haden held my hand as we slowly made our way back to the room where I'd been bathed. As the lock clicked into place, fine mauve dust fell from the ceiling and turned into a fog that ribboned around us and throughout the room.

"What is that?" I asked.

"My mother's insurance," Haden answered, dropping my hand and stalking to the window. "It's a spell."

"What kind of spell?"

"One she hopes will work better than the Lure. It's an aphrodisiac vapor."

"Oh." Understanding flitted across my addled brain. "*Oh*," I said with more emphasis. "How long before the *spell* begins working?"

He raked both hands through his thick dark hair once again. The locks fell into a disheveled and inviting mess. "Not very long. I'm very sorry that I didn't protect you better, Theia. All of this is my fault."

"Why does she want you to take a human bride so badly?"

Haden looked at me, the weight of the world on his shoulders and reflected in his eyes. "Demons can't reproduce.

We can only create life from your kind. Vampires make other vampires by taking a human—some demons can impregnate humans. Not all, thankfully, or demons would overpopulate."

I ached to ease his burden. He carried so much guilt for simply being born. I knew how that felt.

He continued, "My mother is especially fascinated by human beings, but she's also jealous—all demons are, really."

"Why?"

"Humans are the chosen ones."

I shook my head. "What does that mean . . . chosen ones?"

"You have *souls*," he answered with a reverence in his voice that jolted me. "Demons covet humanity because you have souls," he repeated. His jaw tightened and he pressed his lips together firmly, like he was holding something back. "It makes us yearn for you. It's why we crave humans and take your essence, your blood, your lives . . . but we can never get what we need . . . what we desire most."

His words made the hollows in my heart ache. I'd never given much thought to having a soul before.

"You—your kind, your mother's kind—take souls, don't you? That's what essence is?"

"I don't need to, not for survival, because I'm also human. My mother is more gluttonous than she needs to be, but even draining someone else's soul doesn't give her one. Theia, a human soul is the most beautiful, most desirable, the most . . . everything."

"And you don't think you have a soul?"

His expression softened again. "I doubt very much that I do."

"You are half-human, Haden."

He shook his head, not wanting to discuss it now. "My mother, she pretends to hate humans, yet she spent many men's lives trying to conceive me. This place, the way she runs things, is a testament to her desire to emulate your world."

"This place is nothing like my world."

"Oh, I know. I know better than most." Haden's voice had a bitter edge. "I've spent most of my life focused on the differences between the two. Humans are her playthings. She likes to play with their minds, dig into their psyches and see what she can pull out."

I thought of the sewn-together women and knew she'd done that to them. An experiment. They were her dolls.

"Now you understand why I don't want you here, lamb. Under is the origin, the birthplace, of nightmares. Every night terror a human has experienced was pulled from this place. And my mother is the ringmaster of your bad dreams. Even if I get you back . . . I don't know how or why you were able to freely travel back and forth before, but she'll find a way to keep you if she can. I can block your deepest sleep only so much. You're far too vulnerable."

Even while I focused on his chilling words, I could feel something else happening inside me. My body felt slower. Even blinking became a sultry, languid movement.

A new responsiveness hummed along my nerve endings when his look darkened slightly. My tongue dipped out to wet my lips, and he looked away quickly, stifling a small groan.

The spell was beginning to work. And not just on me.

Taking a few steadying breaths only intensified my awareness of my chest, the way the gown magically pushed my breasts up and out instead of my usual preference to minimize and hide. They felt tight and tingly pressed up against the fabric. Turning away from Haden so he wouldn't see the flush of my skin, I found myself staring at my reflection in a large mirror. Once again, my mirror image startled me with its un-recognizable likeness. The girl staring back at me was no girl at all. She was a woman, with womanly secrets and needs and desires I'd never understood before. My skin took on a rosy glow, my hair had loosened enough from the updo to look as if I'd already tussled on the big bed, and my eyes shimmered with intensity.

Behind me, Haden raised his head and our eyes met in the reflection. The familiar beat of his heart charmed mine into synchronicity. Time coasted, not really standing still but no longer on the same plane as the rest of the world. Haden swallowed hard and his nostrils flared just a touch.

His gaze traveled slowly to my chest, framed like a gift in red satin. He met my eyes again. They pierced me with a look of hunger. His breath unsteady now, he fought the effects of the spell. I could tell by the way he clenched his hands into fists over and over. Clench, release, clench, release.

I imagined what it would feel like if he touched me right now. My skin felt so hot, I suspected it would burn him. But we'd been burning for each other since we'd met, and I craved to succumb to combustion in his arms, under his hands.

The corners of my mind rounded, softening away thoughts that tried to intrude on the lovely, fluid feelings that had taken over. Haden crossed the room in a daze, stopping just behind me. I stood as still as stone, holding my breath, waiting for the electric moment when he would finally touch me. He brought his shaky hands to my shoulder, only an inch from my skin. I expelled my held breath and panted softly.

A faraway voice—my own, I think—warned me away from him. *Move away, put distance between you, fight the dark magic.*

I could have just as easily held off a tidal wave with an umbrella.

"Touch me," I whispered.

"I shouldn't," he ground out. But the very tips of his fingers traced my shoulders. I shivered from the contact. "Theia." His voice had never been richer, as if the word had been spoken directly from his soul.

Softly, while I watched in the looking glass, his lips replaced his fingers. So tenderly, they traveled a slow path from my shoulder to my neck while his hands gripped my arms firmly. I understood that he needed to hold me tightly to keep us both from floating away. I arched my neck, giving him more access, and leaned my shoulders into his frame.

His warm kisses on my neck turned my bones to gelatin. My hands reached behind me and I grasped his formal over-coat to keep from sliding into a puddle on the floor. Even knowing it was my downfall, I wriggled against him. Urging him down a dark path. He bit me then, lightly, covering the sting with his gentle lips. I whimpered then, and the tug of desire careened into frenzy.

Turning me towards him, he took my mouth in a kiss, a ferocious kiss. I was dizzy with the sensations ricocheting through my body. I tried to loosen his cravat, but it tangled in my fingers, and he had to push me away while he undid it himself. As soon as his neck was exposed, I lunged back on him, pulling his shirt open, exploring his neck and shoulders with my own kisses. We stumbled to the bed, Haden whispering words of love as he pulled kisses from me. I had never felt so very much in my own body before. It was as if I was aware of every eyelash, every cell.

"Theia, wait. We need to . . ." He paused. He tried to blink away the fog, tried to be good, but I didn't want him to stop.

I saw it in his eyes. The wonder, the love, the desire. My heart burst with the power of it, bleeding love like blood through my veins.

"We can't do this. I can't do this to you."

I turned my head when movement caught my eye. Though the mirror faced the bed, Haden's reflection, and only Haden's, was visible. Where I should have been was empty space. My heart seized and I felt myself disappearing again. I tried to clutch him to me, but my hand went right through him and I sank into a spinning vortex. Alone.

Again.

CHAPTER EIGHTEEN

The world was a fuzzy place. I was traveling through a downy, nebulous expanse—falling, twisting, turning. It wasn't like when I fell Under. There was no burning, no sulfur, and no pain. Yet there was also no up and no down. Just a whirlwind of twirling into an abyss. Drowning in stars instead of water.

My body seemed to separate from . . . me. I couldn't see anything, but I knew we weren't together anymore as I spun. My body had been a heavy weight; once I'd shed it, the floating became easier.

"Holy shit. I can't believe that worked." *Donny?* The voice sounded far away.

A man responded. "It didn't work yet. She needs to come all the way into her body."

"But she's right there." Donny's voice was forceful. That meant she was scared.

"Theia's body is right there. I don't know where Theia is."
The man's voice again. Did I know him?

The spinning stopped. I continued to surf on waves, indefinite and murky, gliding in the dark. Oddly, it didn't occur to me to be afraid. Peace like I had never known washed over me. Nothing mattered now.

I felt a sharp tug. Something tethered me from floating completely away. I didn't think it was gravity. I began to resent it. Floating through the universe seemed so much nicer.

The tug became a hard yank. A rush of sensation slammed into me. I was falling. Fast. The darkness had been replaced by a kaleidoscope of too much light and a spinning color wheel. Every sound I'd ever heard rushed into my ears instantly, and I hit something with a thud.

Myself. I'd hit myself.

My body felt confining and cumbersome. Gravity physically hurt. Needles of oxygen poked my lungs with each breath, and the taste of bile overwhelmed me.

"Thei? Tell me you're all the way back now," Donny begged.

I groaned in response.

"Oh, thank God." That sounded like Amelia.

With a lot of concentration, I was able to open one eye. Sure enough, Donny was on her knees on the floor next to my prone body. I had to squint at the brightness. Amelia was on my other side, shell-shocked and pale. They both looked to the person sitting behind my head. I turned to assess, but the world got heavy again, and I had to rest. I threw my arm over my eyes. "What's going on? What happened?"

"We totally rescued you," Donny assured me. "Nice dress, by the way."

"Who hit me with a lorry?" I asked.

Amelia stroked my arm. "Oh, she's back. She's even speaking British again. Truck, sweetheart—you want to know who hit you with a truck."

"How did I get here?" And when would it stop hurting?

"We convinced Varnie to help us find you."

"'Convince' is a nice way of putting it, Miss Donny." Ah, that was the voice. Varnie. "Now that I've helped you bring her back, will you call off your goons at the door and let me go?"

Goons?

"I don't think so, *Madame*. Theia might still need more help."

I raised onto my elbows very slowly. I was still wearing the dress from the banquet. "Where's Haden?" I looked at both my friends. "You left him there, didn't you?"

Ame bit her lip. "We didn't know he was with you."

"Well, can you get him now?" We couldn't just leave him there. Mara would be very angry when she found out I'd escaped. She might take it out on him.

"We can't get him the same way we got you. That was a spell used for finding loved ones. *Human* loved ones." Ame was trying to keep things politically correct.

"He's half-human!" I protested.

"Which half?" Donny answered. "I'm just wondering."

I shot her a look of surprise that she could joke at a time like this. "His life is at stake, Donny. This isn't the time for anatomy jokes."

"You're welcome. You can stop gushing anytime about how we saved your life and rescued you from the underworld." Donny sat back on her heels and glared at me.

"I'm sorry." I lay back down. "I'm really, really sorry. I'm just scared." I reached for her hand, and she held mine tightly.

"We were so worried about you." Ame grabbed my other hand. "Varnie said the spell was a long shot. Actually he said something about a rodeo, but it didn't make any sense."

Varnie sighed heavily. "I said it would be like laying down a rodeo flip without a juicy wave."

"Are we talking about surfing?" Donny asked. "Why are we talking about surfing?"

"It's not just surfing. . . . It's the holy grail of surfing." He shook his head. "What it means is that there is no way that a cross-dressing psychic and an enthusiastic novice should have been able to pull Miss Theia out of that off-the-Richter dimension."

"How did you guys do it?" I asked.

"I'd read about aura trails recently. . . . They're like ribbons of leftover light that trace people's spirits." Ame grew more animated as she spoke. "It's really amazing—you know how when someone dies or moves away, but you feel like they're still around?"

"Like ghosts?" I asked.

"Kinda . . . but not really. How can I explain it . . . ? Have you ever touched something that made you *feel* the last person who touched it? It's not like they are haunting you; it's more like just a vibe of them?"

I touched my talisman. "Maybe."

"I have a sweatshirt of Gabe's that I won't give back,"

Donny admitted. "It's been through the wash, but I still feel . . . God, you guys suck. I can't believe I'm telling you this. When I put it on, it's like he's kinda holding me or something."

Ame snorted. "Yeah, okay, tell me again how you don't like him. Anyway, we did a mash-up of some finding spells and a little voodoo. Oh, and some pixie dust."

"Pixie dust?" I asked.

Ame picked up an economy-size bag of glitter. "I got this at Target. Anyway, it was pretty cool. Varnie opened up his channels, I said some words while holding your trig book that I took from your locker, and then I threw the glitter in the air and instead of landing on the floor it hovered in the air and then formed a plume above the book."

"Yeah, and then," Donny interrupted, "Ame got all chanty and weird, like she was half gone herself, and the plume turned into this long ribbon of fog. It was so bizarre—it was like the ribbon went and found you and then you started appearing right in front of us."

"But you don't think it would work on Haden?" I asked.

Ame shook her head. "Haden is a demon. We could invoke him, maybe."

"No way." Varnie crab-walked away from my head. "I am not having anything to do with summoning demons. You guys are on your own. I'll take my chances with the goons."

Donny helped me sit up, and I tried to figure out where we were while Varnie and Amelia stood up and argued.

"Who are these goons he keeps prattling on about?" I asked Donny under my breath.

"We dressed Mike and Gabe up like Dog the Bounty Hunter. They even have mullet wigs," she said. "We tracked

Varnie down. It wasn't hard—he has a Web site. We made an appointment using a fake name, and the guys helped me *convince* him to come back with us."

Wow. "Have I been gone long?" My father. Oh, dear God, this was going to get complicated.

"You didn't come to school today." A day. I'd only been gone a day. It seemed as if weeks had passed. Donny continued, "When you didn't answer your cell, Ame talked to Muriel. Your father is out of town again. Which, by the way, he's been doing a lot of."

"Father will never believe me. How did you know to come looking for me . . ."

"You mean . . . off the grid?" Donny said. "Ame had a feeling. She's kinda freaking me out with all her paranormal activity lately. Well, you both are."

We both looked up to watch Ame argue—*argue*, of all things—with Varnie. Ame hated confrontations. "We can do it without you, Varnie. We know the demon's name and we have something . . ." Ame paused and looked at me with a wry expression on her face. "We have something he's *touched*."

"Invoking a demon is ludicrously dangerous. You have no idea what you're doing. Just because you read about it on somebody's MySpace page doesn't make it safe."

"Well, we can't leave him there. And if you won't help us . . ."

"A person needs to be very skilled to summon a demon. It's an open door for anything at all that might come in with it."

"Again," Ame argued, "if you won't help us . . ."

We were in a cabin. A fairly rough one. Rain hit like pebbles on the tin roof, and the inside seemed functional, though just barely. The walls were irregular timber planks, and Donny and I were sitting on a rug thrown over a plywood floor.

"Where are we?" I asked her. I didn't recognize any of it.

"Gabe's brother's hunting cabin. I guess he and Gabe built it themselves." She shrugged and pointed to an old, worn couch. "We almost did it on that sofa."

I held up my hand. "Really, Donny. Too much information."

"Did you and Haden . . . ?"

I shook my head vehemently. "No." Too vehemently, judging by the look she angled at me. "Well, almost."

Varnie was stalking about the cabin, pacing and arguing. Ame stood still and let him talk himself into a corner he couldn't get out of. She looked so different to me. The last few weeks had changed her. Watching Varnie now, she was serene and so in control, like she had him on a yo-yo string and was just waiting for the right moment to bring him back with a flick of her wrist.

I doubted that her newfound control had anything to do with Mike Matheny finally orbiting her atmosphere. It seemed more like the closer she got to actual mysticism, the more her inner confidence blossomed.

Varnie stopped pacing. "You have no idea what you are asking me to do."

Ame shrugged. "I haven't asked you to do anything."

"But you know I am going to." He raked his hand through his blond hair. He was kind of cute when he wasn't wearing eye shadow. "You know I can't walk out of here and let you do something that could get you all killed. Or worse."

"I'm going to bring the *goons* in. They're probably freezing out there." Donny crossed between Varnie and Ame, who continued playing chicken with their eyes.

I curled up, bringing my knees to my chest, and watched Varnie try to reason with Ame. I missed Haden so much. I was sure that if he were asked, he would agree wholeheartedly with Varnie. Opening a door to demons was probably foolish. Expecting that only the one you invited would enter was naïve. Still, it seemed that demons were already here in Serendipity Falls, so why should it matter?

I had a feeling it did.

The boys came back in with Donny. They were unrecognizable. They wore wigs of long dark hair with shorter layers on the top. Gabe's had a braid. They had on camo pants and tank tops with black leather vests over them. Also Gabe wore a utility belt, but it looked like Mike had on a tool belt, the kind a handyman wears. I supposed a hammer was as good a tool as any when chasing fugitives, but it was a little odd.

Gabe had a lot more muscles than I'd given him credit for, and I could see how the boys might have fooled Varnie into thinking they were menacing. Especially with the big black boots.

Varnie flinched when Gabe passed him, and I noticed a shadow of bruising under his eye. Maybe they didn't fool him; maybe they'd had to convince him.

I shuddered. I didn't want to hurt Varnie.

How much had Donny told the boys, I wondered? It wasn't a good idea to broadcast the fact that my boyfriend wasn't human—but then again, it was comforting that they were on my side. Especially with those big black boots.

Varnie tried to talk reason to Donny next. Bad choice, of course, since reason wasn't a language she spoke.

"Donny, it would be like opening a barn door during a stampede and expecting only the brown cow with the blue collar to enter. You can't control a stampede."

Donny threw up her arms. "Well, I can't. But I bet you have the ability to. I saw what you did to bring Theia back. You're not just a nut job—you're a really talented nut job."

"I could never have done that alone. Without Miss Amelia's strength it would have fizzled." He realized his mistake as soon as the words were out.

"Well, good thing Miss Amelia is still here, then," Ame said.

I tried to get off the floor, but my dress and gravity were dueling for the privilege of humiliating me. Gabe rushed to me and helped me up.

"Cheerios, English," he said.

Despite everything, I smiled. "Cheerios to you too, Gabe."

"I have no idea what's going on," he said. "But you look real pretty."

His eyes twinkled, and I knew he had a better grasp of the situation than he was pretending. Sometimes it was just easier to play dumb.

Mike still stood by the door looking confused. I didn't think he was playing dumb like Gabe was. In fact, Mike had that same dazed look a lot. What on earth did Amelia see in him?

Having six people in the small one-room cabin was beginning to make me claustrophobic. And nobody seemed to be getting any closer to finding a way to save Haden.

"Varnie, if you don't want to invoke Haden here—can you send me back? It was a realm called Under," I said.

Donny and Ame chimed in with a resounding "no," but Varnie just stared at me like I'd sprouted a second head or something.

"I can't let him stay there alone. I just can't."

Mike finally spoke. "Is there anything to eat?"

Donny shot Gabe an exasperated look.

Gabe seemed to understand what that expression meant, and that if he didn't get Mike out of there, Donny was going to blow a fuse. "Well, it looks like the prank went really well," he said. "So I guess I'll drive Mike back home now. Thanks for playing along, Varnie. We totally punk'd you, dude. I can't believe you really thought we were bounty hunters."

Gabe clapped Varnie on the shoulder and Varnie flinched. "Prank?"

"Taking Mike home is a great idea," Donny said. "See you tomorrow. Thanks for your help."

Gabe kissed her hand. "I'll be back in an hour, *honey*."

She snatched her hand away. "No need, *sweetheart*. We're all fine here. See you tomorrow at school. We'll lock up when we leave."

"Sixty minutes, *sugarplum*." He leaned in for a kiss.

"Get your pleather-wearing long-haired paws off me—"

Gabe kissed her soundly, cutting off her protest. When he pulled back, she was quiet. "Don't burn the cabin down." He brushed his thumb across her cheek. "Be careful, okay? I'm coming back."

Donny nodded. Her fingers lingered a touch too long to be considered uncaring as he brushed past her.

The door clicked behind him.

Varnie glared at Donny. "The thug is your boyfriend?"

"Hell, no." She had her hands on her hips. "But, Ame, when this is all over we need to have a serious discussion about Mike. I think he has way too much frosting on his flakes."

"I know, I know," Ame answered, her cheeks a little pink.

Varnie turned to Ame. "The other one is *your* boyfriend?" he asked incredulously.

"No. Not yet," Ame answered.

"You like him?" Varnie looked a little . . . angry.

"The mullet is a just a wig." Ame crossed her arms in front of her. "Besides, who I like has nothing to do with anything right now."

"I don't care if he's bald. He's practically mute."

Donny and I exchanged glances. The kind that said, "Well, isn't this interesting?"

"He's not mute. He's shy. And why do you care who I do or don't date?"

Varnie threw his hands up. "I don't. I just think you could do better."

"At least he isn't a cross-dresser." She clapped her hand over her mouth, ashamed and embarrassed that she'd let that slip out.

He shook his head ruefully. He started to speak, then stopped twice before he finally said, "You have a natural talent, Amelia. And your life is just going to get stranger as it grows. Guys like that won't be able to keep up with you."

Donny sent me another wary glance. "So, guys . . . how about that demon summoning? Ready to get started?"

CHAPTER NINETEEN

*H*aden watched the snow fall outside his window, know-ing the weather portended his mother's state of mind. He wasn't looking forward to whatever came next, as icicles fell like daggers alongside the snowflakes.

At least she'd locked him in his own room this time, rather than the dungeon. And thankfully, Theia had gotten away somehow.

He missed her. He would always miss her. The gaping crater his heart once claimed would forever feel her absence. Something stirred inside him. A strong desire to go somewhere unnamed came upon him and grew until it became an urgent need. He was be-ing called . . . nay, summoned. He clutched the bedpost as a ter-rible searing overtook his internal organs and he choked on air. It wasn't possible. . . . Surely nobody would . . . Again, a seizing pain clawed at him.

He gasped as he saw his flesh become transparent, fading into *a mere whisper. It was true, then. Someone was invoking him. He prayed it wasn't Theia—but he had no business praying, did he?*

He damned himself for not warning her about this. It was too late for damning, though, and she would know that soon enough.

His body disappeared, and the invoking had been accomplished. Unfortunately for whoever had called him, Haden remained in Under.

Anticipation battered us with stinging whips of sensation. Would it work? Did I want it to work? By the look on Varnie's face, I most decidedly did not. The last chant was spoken, the air stilled, the flame of each candle sputtered, and we waited.

The rain outside pummeled the cabin and the wind roared ferociously, whistling through cracks in the not very sturdy walls. Lightning cracked the sky and where there had been nothing, there was now Haden.

"Hello, lamb. Miss me?"

Donny jumped up. "I'll get the lights."

Varnie put a stilling hand on my arm as I instinctively moved towards Haden. "Wait."

An overhead fixture lit the room and my eyes sought Haden. He was so beautiful it hurt to look at him. I swallowed, relief overwhelming me. "Thank God you're okay."

Haden stared into my eyes. "I don't think we have God to thank for this, do we?"

I started towards him, needing to be in his arms, hear his heartbeat, but Varnie pulled me back. Haden didn't avert his gaze; instead he narrowed his eyes, as if he were looking at me for the first time. And then he smiled. The wicked smile.

I straightened my spine despite its reluctance to do so. Something wasn't right.

Haden pushed himself up from the floor and out of our circle. "How fortunate I am that you've rescued me. Thank you all for this *lovely* turn of events."

An uncomfortable static picked up, and a humming din thrummed through the small room. Haden's predatory mask overcame his handsome features, and he picked up Amelia's hand, kissing each knuckle with mischief. My heart plummeted as I realized he was using the Lure on my best friend.

Varnie yanked her away from Haden, putting himself between them, standing up slowly.

Haden tsked. "Ah, she is spoken for, then? Too bad—all that power would be refreshing right now. I could fight you for her, I suppose, but it seems like a lot of work for a snack."

I stood up on shaky legs. "Haden, what's going on?" He let down his mask when he looked at me, so I stepped closer. "Do you know who I am? Do you remember me?"

"Of course I do, my little poppet. You're the one who saved me." He touched my hair carefully, reverently. "You're lovely, really you are . . . but you're rather . . . Well, let's just say your essence isn't as robust as your friends'. I'm sure I'll get to you eventually."

With each ugly word, my heart broke into more pieces. "Haden, I don't understand. I thought . . . I thought you had feelings for me."

He laughed and gazed across the room at Donny like she was a treat in a sweet shop. "I'm a demon. Have you learned nothing? Demons don't love; they especially don't love silly little girls who hide from anything that isn't *careful* or prescribed as safe by Daddy. Your pragmatism bores me to tears. You were a fun diversion, for a while, but that is all you will ever be."

I looked down at the ball gown I still wore, and I felt so intolerably stupid. Had he been playing me this whole time? No, surely not. But his words crushed me and his face no longer resembled the boy I'd kissed.

Maybe he had.

I'd enabled him to come here, to my world, and wreak his havoc. When I thought of what an easy mark I'd been, I felt shamed. All he'd had to do was tell me he found me enchanting and dangle me on a string. I really was his little poppet. And now, the way he eyed Donny, he was going to hurt the people I loved most because I was an idjit with a dangerously foolish heart.

Why had I stopped listening to my father? He was right—about me, about everything. And now I was trapped in a cabin with the devil because I was reckless just like my mother.

"It's possible that this whole thing is my fault," said Varnie, very carefully keeping Ame behind him while he edged towards the door, where an uncharacteristically quiet Donny still stood by the light switch. "Perhaps we should have used some more-specific wording in the evocation chant."

"Ya think?" Donny answered back.

Haden grinned, and my legs turned rubbery with fear. There wasn't a trace of the person I thought he was in that smile. "Perhaps you are right, sir. It seems you brought forth your demon . . . but you forgot something." He waggled his finger as if Varnie were a precocious child.

Varnie rubbed his chin thoughtfully. "Yes, yes. I see my

mistake very clearly now." He'd worked his way across the room so that now he stood in front of both Donny and Amelia, leaving me in the center of the room with Haden. Perhaps there was hope that he could get the two of them out safely.

I had a feeling I was doomed.

Then Varnie, the self-professed coward, looked Haden in the eye and said, "Sit down on that chair." He pointed to a worn wooden dining chair.

Haden complied immediately with a confounded expression.

"I'm new. I'm inexperienced. But did you really think I would call you to my realm without the caveats?" Varnie practically spat the words at Haden.

Haden was stunned into silence. We all were.

"You are here by *my* edict only. You will do nothing unless I command it." Varnie didn't generally project leadership qualities, and yet Haden swallowed whatever he would have replied with. He hadn't been commanded to speak, it seemed, so he would not.

Varnie called me over. I didn't understand the dynamics of what was going on, but at that point I was more than ready to escape. I picked up the hem of my gown, prepared to prance across the room as quickly as I could. Instead, I stopped cold. The shadows of my friends disengaged and fled across the wall.

No, not again.

Not my friends.

I watched the forms race across the wall. Something was coming.

"Get outside!" I called to them all. "Run!"

Donny resisted, but Varnie and Amelia seemed to understand the change in the atmosphere of the cabin. They had to drag her, but they got Donny out the door before it slammed closed like the lid of my coffin.

I flinched at the sound, but I couldn't move my legs to join them. It was as if I'd been bolted to the floor.

Haden hadn't moved from his chair either. I don't think he was able to do anything against Varnie's wishes—a side effect of the summoning that I hadn't understood. He didn't seem worried. It was probably his mother coming to rescue him, after all. He smirked at me, and I wanted to hate him.

But I didn't.

A whisper of brimstone reached my nose, and I waited for the scraping noises. But no skeletons came through a portal in the wall this time; instead, I blinked and found myself instantly back in the empty banquet room of Mara's castle.

Alone.

While the experience of traveling between the realms was much more pleasant this time than incinerating had been, I dared not be relieved to find myself back in Under. Especially without an ally.

The pain of Haden's betrayal stung again as I remembered he had never been an ally. I looked at our empty seats at the long table, remembering how to fool his mother he'd pretended so stoically that I meant nothing to him. What an actor my demon was.

I wondered why he hadn't joined me.

I waited a few minutes for Mara to summon me somewhere. She had brought me here, after all. Every time I blinked, the writhing creature on the platter was projected across my mind's eye, the ghouls masquerading as revelers. I couldn't stay in that room any longer. I took my chances in the corridor.

I tried to find the room where I'd been groomed like a prize pet as a gift for the heir apparent—the room where I'd nearly lost my virtue to a monster. The corridor made many turns, none of them I remembered. For a castle so large, there were very few doors. Just an unending corridor.

After following it for some time, I began to think of it as a labyrinth. Once again, I was the entertainment, it seemed—the rat in a maze. Perhaps Mara was stalking me and would jump out at some point. Perhaps, more likely, she would let me unravel my sanity like a ball of yarn as I passed hour upon unending hour traveling through her game course.

I came upon a door finally. It was left ajar, so I pushed it with my toe. Haden's room. Reason dictated that I not dare enter. A tidal wave of emotion propelled me inside. What had he called me? *A silly little girl. Boring.*

I replayed every moment with him with this new unflattering filter. The deeper into his room I stepped, the harder each punch of every memory became. Every touch, every kiss. I ran my hand along his furniture and ached with regret and . . . longing. I missed him still, the figment of my girlish imagination. A silk shirt hung on the back of a chair. I brought it to my nose and inhaled the scent of my love dying.

Haden watched her heart breaking in front of him. Powerless to dry her tears, he could only ghost around the room in a fruitless rage against his helplessness. Theia held his shirt and sank to the floor. She was giving up hope. She no longer believed in him.

For the first time in his life, Haden was free of his demon side, of all his terrible urges, and yet he would take it back if it meant he could hold her now when she needed him most. His mother would find her soon, of that he was certain. He couldn't protect Theia. He'd never protected her. Not really.

What a mess he'd made of both their lives.

He lowered himself to the floor in front of her. Not that it mattered. He was ethereal now. It was probably better this way, since if he'd kept his body, the demon that they'd invoked on command would have been incorporeal and a lot harder to contain. For the sake of Serendipity Falls, he very much hoped they were trying to contain him.

Haden ached to press a kiss to Theia's cheek. To speak so she would hear him.

He loved her. He'd never said it to her, never said it aloud. He had thought it would be easier for her that way, but now he was filled with regret because she would never know.

Nothing changed in the room, and yet I felt a shift. Something pleasant and warm surrounded me like sunshine, touching all of me at once. I looked around for the source of the heat, but there was nothing. And then I felt it. A feather-light stroke on my cheek. I swallowed hard and waited. Would it happen again?

When I closed my eyes, I saw Haden crouched in front of me. When I opened them in surprise, there was nothing there. I shuttered them closed again and saw him briefly before I flinched and drew back. The corset I still wore made it hard to take a deep breath.

It had been such a long, terrible night. I was scared and

so tired. I still wore the dress that I would likely die in. I missed my father and my friends. Haden had taken all that from me—my entire world, my security. And yet, when I'd glimpsed him just then, I missed him too.

I closed my eyes again, resisting the urge to open them when he appeared before me, gentle and caring. He wore the same clothes as he had during our wedding banquet and he was rumpled—so unlike him. Lines of worry and concern crossed his forehead.

How was he here and why could I see him only with my eyes closed?

He mouthed the words "I love you."

My heart, my foolish, pitiful, stupid heart, raced. I knew better.

"No more games," I whispered back. "You don't love any-one. Demons can't love." I opened my eyes so I didn't have to look at him anymore. Somehow I found my voice. "You make me sick, Haden. The way you use people, the way you used me. You didn't need to put so much effort into it, you know. I think I belonged to you the moment you welcomed me into your hell."

I got up off the floor. I was tired of wallowing.

"How you must have laughed at my humiliation. Wind Theia up and watch her do her stupid dance." My voice got louder. "Watch how her eyes shine with innocence every time she's told she's special. Watch how she crumples whenever Haden touches another girl."

The rage felt kind of nice—a balm for the irritated skin of my humiliation.

"Well, you've stamped out all that's left of that stupid

child, Haden. I'm hollow now—is that what you wanted?" I tossed his silk shirt across the room, angry that it was too soft to fly very far. "God"—my voice broke—"when I think of how I had to beg you for that first kiss."

That kiss had meant everything to me. Everything. My lower lip trembled. I couldn't possibly cry again, could I? "You don't deserve my tears, Haden." And yet they came. "But I . . . I deserve everything you've done to me for being so gullible."

"Be sure to spare some of your tears, child." Mara's chilling voice brought my gaze to the door with a start. "Your suffering has barely begun."

CHAPTER TWENTY

Mara was alone, but I knew instinctively she was more powerful than the guards she usually sent to do her bidding. She was of average height, and slender, but the power she wielded had nothing to do with brute strength. She wore a blue velvet dress that pretended to be proper and Victorian, but was cut so low as to not leave much to the imagination.

I froze in place, but Mara swooped in, a hawk and a field mouse. "I've been pining for some girl talk alone with you, pussycat. I just know we'll be fast friends." She paused and one corner of her mouth lifted in a sardonic smile. "Won't that be fun?"

I cast my eyes to the floor.

"I'm accustomed to people answering me when I speak, child."

Mara grabbed my chin in her viselike grip and forced me to look at her. Her eyes darkened until once again the whites were absorbed into her inky pupils. It almost appeared as if she had no eyes, just gaping holes where they should have been.

"Yes," I whimpered.

She let go with a little thrust and I fell back a step before regaining my feet.

"Much better, my pet."

I winced, remembering how well she didn't care for her pets.

Mara flounced around the room in her gown, inspecting the things on Haden's shelves with animated curiosity. "It may surprise you to know that I've never had girl talk before." She angled her chin and looked up like she was trying to remember. "I tend to think it's because I always have to remove the larynx so early." She picked up one of Haden's video games and appeared to read the back of it. "It's unfortunate, but when humans lose their mind, they tend to scream ceaselessly or ramble incoherently. It's tiresome. I've never had one who could carry on a decent conversation." She turned to me. "What do you think it will be like to lose your mind, Theia?"

The hair on my nape stood on end. I had to answer her. "I don't know."

"You have been a sliver in my flesh for a long time, pussycat. I am very much looking forward to removing you."

My body began freezing again, like it did at the banquet. The blood in my veins and the breath in my lungs crystallized painfully. I knew this was only the beginning. I knew she had every intention of pushing me to the edge of sanity over and over again until I was just like the rest of her ghoulish menagerie. If I were strong, I'd find a way to end her fun soon, while I still had the ability to do so.

As though in response to that thought, I felt the warm sensation again. I closed my eyes and Haden was in front of me, as if he were holding me. Perhaps I'd already lost my wits, because I let him.

His mother couldn't see him, but surely she knew he was there. She stopped the torture and left Theia gasping on frost.

Theia wasn't strong enough to go toe to toe with his mother. No one was. And without form he was as useful as mist.

He was surprised when Theia was able to see him, even more surprised when she felt his touch—ghostlike as it was. He couldn't physically touch her and that cut him like a knife.

Haden recalled the things Theia had said to him and the pain in her voice. So she'd met the demon, then, before she was brought back Under. He wished she hadn't. She was going to need every scrap of faith she had to come through this, and he could see the demon had stolen it from her. He'd certainly killed the love she had for Haden.

And now nobody had anything.

I fell to my knees and shuddered with each new breath. Mara crossed the room and stood before me.

"You understand that I'm not going to kill you for many, many years, don't you? But when I do, your death will be slow."

"Yes, I understand," I responded shakily, remembering she demanded that I answer.

"I'm not an opponent you and your friends should have taken on, pussycat. I have ruled Under since the dawn of man. Every fear your kind has ever had was put in your head by me. Did you really think you could best me?"

"No, ma'am," I croaked.

Mara's eyes were a terrible thing. "I'm sure Haden explained to you that he ages very slowly, that time passes differently here. But, my little rosebud, no human blood runs in my veins. I am immortal." She loomed above me. Her voice changed. The soft, cultured voice grew an edge and a slight echo.

"Do you know how I eat?" I shook my head. "I steal into a man's sleep. I sit on his chest while he dreams of me, and I leach the essence that binds him to your world, Theia. I eat the souls of men while I torment them with anguished pleasure." She paused. "But that is how I survive, how I feed. Survival isn't my only concern, pussycat. It's not even my job. My real calling is to seed your realm with terror while you sleep." She leaned down and spoke directly into my ear. "I am the mare, Theia. I am the origin of every nightmare ever born and I intend to drown you in them all."

She hissed then. A horrible sound that spoke to every primordial fear I possessed.

"Humans are weak and pathetic. My son should have been proud of his blood, but instead he wanted to throw it away on a dying breed. Get up. Get up before I tire of you and decide to play with your friends instead."

I struggled but managed to stand on shaky legs. I couldn't let her drag them into this.

"What, you don't want company? Just think of how you could share everything with them. Wouldn't you like to see the world through Donnatella's eyes, for instance?"

I whimpered. The women who attended me before the banquet saw the world through another's eyes. "Please. Don't hurt them. They didn't know. It's all my fault. . . . Please."

"Weak, weak, weak," she replied.

I tried to appeal to her motherly instinct. "I know you love Haden and you wanted only what's best for him."

"Child—" No longer did her voice even sound female. It rasped like a harsh whisper and creaked like the opening of a door to terror. "Demons do not love. *Haden* does not love. I want what is best for me."

"You must have loved his father. You let him live."

"It was an experiment. I wanted an heir."

"Why?"

"You're very impertinent." A shaft of light coming through the windows did Mara no favors. It fell on her deceptive beauty like a truth serum, illuminating her real appearance beneath the glamours she coated herself with to appease her vanity and mislead those around her.

She noticed my vision had cleared, that I no longer saw what she wanted, but the ugliness of who she really was. Immorality is startlingly wretched.

Her cultured voice returned. "I didn't love Haden's father then and I don't love Haden now." Mara sneered at me, but for a moment she was unguarded. "I'd thought maybe I would," she added softly.

I pretended not to notice her small pinch of weakness; it would only serve to make her defensive. I had a feeling what she meant was that she hoped they would love *her*.

Once again I felt the warmth that signaled Haden was near me. I didn't understand how he'd become invisible or why he remained so. Even harder to fathom was why he chose to comfort me when only a short time ago it was he who put my heart into a wood chipper and smiled at the mess.

What had he meant at the cabin? What had Varnie forgotten in the conjuration?

None of it made sense. Why had Haden spent so much time seducing me only to hurt me before he got what he really wanted? Surely Mara would have been happy for him to roam the halls of Serendipity High leaching essence everywhere he went. So why the subterfuge?

"You're going to help me get Haden back," Mara proclaimed. Covering her moment of weakness, she continued. "You will then bear a child. I will not make the same mistakes with this one. But don't fret, I will allow you to watch as I raise your babe to be a demon worthy of this realm. And don't think Haden will rescue you or your damned child."

I wasn't sure what to think about Haden, not really. He'd shown himself to be as callous as his mother. And yet I couldn't forget how he'd yearned to be human. Perhaps that had been as much of an act as the rest. Would he allow another child to be raised in this place? I didn't know.

But I wouldn't.

"Lamb," Mara said, and I flinched at Haden's endearment coming from her mouth, "you probably think you can turn him against me like you've done in the past. It won't happen. Not this time. The first thing we're going to do together is make sure Haden's human soul is well and truly disposed of before we bring him back. No sense in risking a reunion."

My head jerked up in surprise. "His soul?"

Mara narrowed her eyes. "Are you playing the fool or are you really that stupid?"

I had to answer. "I'm really that stupid, ma'am."

She laughed. Not a pleasant laugh, but rather the kind that

causes goose bumps to rise and hearts to race. "You and your friends invoked a demon, Theia. A human soul can't travel through an invocation spell. He's still here, trapped like you."

Like a quiver to my heart, the realization hit me. Haden was here. The Haden that I loved—the one that loved me. He'd been trying to make me understand.

And he did have a soul.

The warmth of him brushed against my arm, and for a moment I let myself revel in the blush of love. And then, of course, I realized how much I had to lose.

"I was prepared to stay," I ventured.

Mara only raised a brow and gestured for me to continue. "I love him that much. I would have stayed. If we could be together. I still want to."

"You're foolish to admit your weakness to me, Theia."

My mother's necklace felt heavy on the skin over my breastbone. "I have a good many weaknesses, ma'am. Loving Haden isn't one of them."

"Why are you telling me this? Do you think I will pity you? You forget who I am."

I closed my eyes so I could see him. He shook his head at me, concerned that I was putting myself in more danger. What more danger was there?

I couldn't linger with him, though I wanted to, so I opened my eyes to Mara again. "Neither one of us asked to be rescued by my friends. It felt like being ripped in two when they dragged me away from him. I didn't want to leave. I want to be here, with him. You don't have to force me to stay, to marry Haden."

"You should not trifle with me. It matters not what you

want." There—a slight inclination of her head led me to believe part of her did care. Not about me, likely, but Haden.

"I can make him happy . . . here. He'll stay willingly. We'll raise a family and your legacy will come true. He'll take his place, just like you want."

She shrugged. "Well, of course he will. Now that your friends have done the hard part and separated him from his weak human side, he'll be more than willing."

I exhaled. I had to tread very carefully here. "You'll win, no matter what, but wouldn't you rather win on the original terms? Haden, as a demon only, will do your bidding because it costs him nothing. Wouldn't it mean more if there was a choice and he chose you willingly? If he gave up the human realm because he wanted to stay?"

I danced on a very thin layer of ice.

"You amuse me, Theia. Do you think I can't tell if you are lying?"

"I'm not lying. I swear. I love him and I'll do anything to save him. I will stay."

"You swear you'll stay?"

Haden roared in fury, but it did no good. He tried grabbing Theia, but his hand went right through her. She was ignoring him now, caught up in a futile battle for his soul. He couldn't stop her. He was useless. He couldn't warn her. He needed to warn her.

Never make deals with the devil.

Haden tried his mother next. He launched himself onto her, trying to distract her from the conversation before any oaths were cemented. Mara barely batted her eyelashes and he was thrown across the room and into the wall by the force of her will.

She smiled coolly at Theia. "Tell me again, love. Promise me you'll stay. You'll spend the rest of your life in Under? You won't try to escape? Not ever?"

Haden, though he had no body, felt a twinge that began at the base of his spine and shot dancing sparks through his nerves. Something was happening. He crawled back to Theia, fighting the tugging sensation assaulting his body. He had to reach her before it was too late.

Theia brought her hands to her heart. "I swear. Spare Haden's soul and I'll stay. I'll be a dutiful daughter to you." Tears coursed down her cheeks. "I only ask that you don't hurt my friends and family."

"We'll need blood," his mother said, pulling a pushpin from Haden's bulletin board.

God, no.

"It's just a ritual, lamb." She smiled, and Theia trembled. "To bind our promises to each other." She held out her hand for Theia's, poking them each with a gleeful punch of the pin. "I swear I won't harm Haden's soul or any of your friends or family. I promise this to you, Theia. I'll be the mother you never had."

Theia bit her lip and tried to hold back any more tears. Such a brave one, his girl.

Haden watched in horror as his mother touched her bleeding finger to Theia's and they mixed their blood. No matter how loudly he yelled, Theia didn't hear him. His warning was lost forever.

"You, Theia, swear to me that you'll never try to escape. You'll stay here, as my daughter-in-law. Do you swear?"

Whatever was pulling him was strong. He couldn't leave Theia, not now. She didn't know what she was promising; she couldn't understand. But it was like fighting gravity. He called out her name and felt himself disintegrating. He heard her say, "I swear." And then there was nothing.

UP IS DOWN

CHAPTER TWENTY-ONE

Haden

The fuzzy moment between sleep and wakefulness was my worst time. It always felt like I was standing on the edge of the world, like if I could just grasp something familiar to hold on to, I would be me again. But I never was.

I wasn't anyone.

They told me I had a name, Haden. It took a while before they told me the rest.

This time felt different before I even opened my eyes. Surprised by the thicket of thorns surrounding me instead of the boring white walls I'd become accustomed to, I woke up and was kneeling on damp grass on hands and knees instead of lying on the air mattress in Varnie's guest room. It could have been a dream, but it didn't feel like one.

I pushed off the ground, wiping my wet hands on the flannel pants I'd worn to bed. It was still dark, though torches blazed every few feet, lighting what appeared to be a path through the overgrown hedge. I took one from its sconce and turned in a slow circle, trying to light the shadows. I wasn't scared, exactly, but I was wary.

Fog swirled in curls around me, like it had been painted to the air. In the distance I heard the sweetest melody. It was a tinkle of sound at first, but once it got to my ears, it stayed there, caressing the inside of my head with the most pleasant, soothing sounds.

I moved towards the music, thinking briefly of the chapter in my schoolbook about the legends of the sirens that lured men at sea to their death with song. Part of me didn't care. It felt as if I'd been waiting for this. As if I needed it.

The path narrowed as I walked farther into the brambles. Twigs with barbs the size of my thumb poked me with razor-sharp points. I turned to see where I'd been, but the path behind me was no longer lit. Only the black shadows remained, like dark holes punched into the world.

Déjà vu preceded every step I took forward now, but then, that was pretty much how my life had been since I'd woken up in the cabin. Always on the cusp of remembering, but never quite realizing the memory. I continued down the narrowing path, trying to block the briery needles of the hedge. I couldn't do a very good job of it; my arms and chest were bare and vulnerable. I didn't like that feeling.

The closer I drew to the music, the more I wanted to be near it. It wasn't a sweet song now. There was a melancholy mood tangled in it, and all the notes blended together into a symphony of sound designed to break a heart, it seemed. Behind me, the brambles had closed off completely. In front of me, the path had shrunk to a low tunnel. I had to go to my knees and eventually my stomach as I crawled through. I couldn't go back anymore; there was only forward.

Careful of the flame, I inched through the small opening as the sticks caught my clothes and hair and poked my skin. I didn't think I would make it. I was trapped and thought I might die in the bushes.

And then, suddenly, there was sunshine.

I rolled to my feet, surprised to find myself in a world of vibrant color. The bushes I had come from were gone and there were rolling hills of green grass and bright flowers as far as the eye could see.

And the music played on.

I climbed a short hill in front of me. As I crested, the sight of the girl stole my breath.

She sat in a wooden chair overlooking a river that sparkled like it was crusted in diamonds. She didn't notice me as she played her violin. Her eyes were closed and she was in her own world, while mine came crashing down around me.

Theia.

They'd shown me pictures of her, and I'd thought she was pretty. What wasn't to like? The pictures hadn't triggered any memories, though, like everyone had hoped they would. She was just a pretty girl in a photograph to me.

In the flesh, she was so much more than pretty. She looked like a garden nymph—the sense of everything in the world that was fresh and pure. A wreath of daisies encircled her hair, the bouncy curls the color of honey and caramel. She wore a simple sheath of white and slippers like a dancer would wear.

I realized I must be dreaming. Nobody could be that beautiful. It was as though she pulled the light from the sun and it danced on her skin and hair, throwing glints of raw brilliance at me. And her song . . . the music that wrapped around my insides and brought me to her was not sweet. I didn't know now how I could have mistaken it as such. It was so poignantly sad that it made my heart stagger on its own beat.

Her eyes opened. I knew Theia sensed me there. She lowered her instrument and turned her head to look at me. The distance between us pulsed with energy. I didn't move, didn't breathe, didn't dare blink. I was afraid she would disappear.

Even though I didn't remember her, I felt that I would have recognized her in any realm, in any life. Theia had woven herself into me; she was part of me, in my blood. I knew how she would taste, how the rush of her skin would feel under my palm. I knew she could put me back together, the puzzle of the boy who wasn't.

I waited for a sign, for her to do or say something. But she just looked at me. She swallowed hard, drawing my gaze to her lovely, slender throat. God, I knew how she smelled.

"You shouldn't have come," she said finally. Though her words sank into my gut like a fist, the sound of her voice was magic, awakening every cell in my body.

"You're Theia," I said lamely. I wished I could recall some of the previous swagger they'd told me I used to have. I knew I sounded simple. Foolish.

She smiled wryly at my awkwardness. "Aye."

I took a step towards her and she shook her head.

"Please," I said.

"No, Haden. Not another step."

Why? "You should come back with me."

Her voice cracked. "I can't. Please, you have to leave."

"I can't leave you here. I just found you."

"It's not safe," she warned.

I shook my head. "I know that. That's why you need to come with me."

She stood slowly, setting her instrument and bow on the seat of the chair. She turned to face me head-on. I wanted to touch her more than I wanted to breathe.

"I can't leave. But don't worry, I'm perfectly fine here." She smiled with her mouth, but it didn't reach her eyes. "I'm not the one in danger anymore." She licked her lips, her tongue darting out in a suggestion that I felt in my weakening knees. "It's not safe for you, lamb." She tilted her head and regarded me with a hunter's gaze. "After all, the darkness in me wants you the way a black hole eats stars."

When the alarm shrilled loudly, I thought maybe my heart had stopped. I shot off the low bed and tried to catch up. A dream. It had been a dream.

A bad, yet oddly erotic one.

I stumbled into the kitchen where Varnie was pouring coffee, already dressed except for his turban. "You look like shit," he said and handed me a cup of steaming French roast.

This coming from the world's most awkward female impersonator. "Thanks. You're the ugliest girl I've ever seen, by the way," I answered back.

"No, seriously. What the hell happened to you?" He gestured to my bare chest.

I looked down and saw that I was covered in scratches and dried blood from the brambles. My hand fumbled on my cup and I dribbled hot coffee onto my already raw skin. "Christ,"

I yelled and grabbed a towel. I met Varnie's eyes. Not a dream then. "I saw her."

Varnie stared back at me for a few long seconds. His eyes were wild with excitement and a little terror, and they clashed with the blue eye shadow that tried to make him look matronly. "Theia? You went to Under?"

"I think so."

"She's alive, then? Is she okay?"

"She's beautiful," I blurted. God, I hated it when stuff just flew out of my mouth like that. It was almost always something stupid. "She looked healthy. She said she wasn't in danger."

Varnie set down his mug and started pacing. "Did you try to bring her back with you? What happened? The girls are going to be pissed when they find out you saw her and left her there."

"I didn't have much choice. She told me she couldn't leave. I don't think she was quite . . . the same . . . as you guys described her." That was as diplomatic as I could get before my first cup.

"She's been living in a hell realm." Varnie looked at me like I was an idiot. "It's going to affect a person."

I thought of the look in her eye and the way she licked her lips. Theia wasn't the shy ingénue they'd told me about. She was sexy as hell, though. Literally. "Varn, I think something more is going on. She . . . I guess you could say *warned me*. She said I wasn't safe . . . from her."

Varnie put his turban on, completing the disturbing transformation to Madame Varnie. "I need to take this next appointment. Bring the girls here after school. We'll figure out what it all means."

I nodded. "Thanks, man." I meant thank you for everything he'd done for me, was continuing to do for me. I wondered if he knew that.

Varnie had taken me in shortly after I woke up in the circle on the floor and it became apparent that I'd never make it on my own. Not yet. I didn't have the right skills to survive in their world—or any other realm.

On top of the memory loss, I had no money. I was able to get my clothes out of the expensive penthouse suite I'd been living in but could no longer afford. I also had a truck. That was it. I sold it after the first week to help Varnie with rent and expenses.

I think Varnie felt guilty for everything that happened that night. As much as he wanted to get out of Serendipity Falls, he wanted to make amends more. So he moved back into the house he'd just left and put a roof over my head. I owed him more than I could say.

Donny picked me up for school, like she had every day for the last month. Gabe didn't like it. He wasn't exactly my biggest fan.

Varnie blamed himself for losing Theia.

Gabe blamed me.

"Did you remember anything?" she asked as we pulled away from the curb. She asked every day. It was sort of her version of "Good morning, Haden."

"No. I still have amnesia," I answered. I wasn't sure if I should tell her about going to Under last night. It was probably better to tell everyone at once, after school. Donny wasn't exactly levelheaded and telling her now would mean she'd be unreasonable all day. I wasn't technically lying when I told her no, I didn't remember anything.

But it felt like lying.

Ame would be trickier. It would be in my best interest to avoid spending too much time with her. It was spooky, the way she knew things. Varnie called it her "raw talent." Whatever she had, it still wasn't enough for them to get their friend back. They wouldn't stop trying, though. They were nothing if not tenacious.

I escaped to the library at lunch, mostly to avoid Ame. That wasn't the only reason, though. Sometimes they were too nice to me. Not a thing to complain about for most people, but I didn't deserve their kindness. Theia was gone because of me. Until today, nobody even knew if she was still alive.

I knew I was letting them down because I couldn't remember. I had a head full of knowledge—things most seventeen-year-old kids don't know, but no memories that would help. It hurt them that I couldn't remember Theia.

It hurt me too.

Theia had risked everything to save me. They said she loved me. And I repaid her sacrifice by not remembering her.

"There you are." I thought I'd been pretty clever in finding the small table hidden in the stacks of the library, but my fortress of solitude was no challenge for Brittany. She sashayed over. "I've been looking for you everywhere."

"Here I am," I answered, lamely, of course.

All the kids at school knew I had "amnesia," but they still treated me like I was the same Haden as I was before the "accident." Donny told me that was because the sneetches swam in shallow water. She always looked directly at Gabe whenever she made comments like that. To his credit, he ignored her.

There were murmurs up and down the halls that I pretended I couldn't hear. Theia's disappearance and my amnesia fed the gossip mill until it churned out all kinds of torrid tales. Another sore spot with the so-called sneetches was the apparent defection of Gabe and me to the "dark side." They pretended it didn't bother them, but they spent a lot of time trying to lure me back to the in-crowd. I didn't especially want to be part of the in-crowd. I didn't fit in there or anywhere else.

Brittany perched on the corner of the table, her short skirt riding too high for a guy with a pulse not to notice. I swallowed hard and tried not to anyway.

"We should talk about prom, Haden."

"We should?"

She nodded. Her hair didn't move when her head did. It was the oddest thing. Hairspray, I guessed. "It's coming up."

I knew that, of course. Donny spent a lot of time telling Gabe they weren't going together, and Ame spent a lot of time trying to coax an invitation from Mike. I had no intention of going to the dance. It felt like a betrayal to think about having fun or spending time with another girl. A betrayal to the girl I didn't know, couldn't remember, and who was possibly never coming back.

Brittany drew my chin up with her finger. "Ask me."

"Ask you what?"

"To the dance." Brittany's hand coasted along my cheek and into the hair around my ear. "We'll have fun."

She was tender, playful. Nobody had touched me recently. And before recently I couldn't remember anyway—so it was overwhelming how good it felt. Brittany smelled sweet, like cotton candy. I was tempted. God, was I tempted.

I looked into her eyes, and she smiled shyly. It might have been an act, her shyness. The way Donny and Ame went on about the cheerleaders, they were supposedly in the same class as the demon they exorcised from my body that night in the cabin.

Maybe Brittany and Noelle were shallow, but maybe they were just girls who hid behind their popularity the way Donny hid behind her sarcasm. Brittany seemed genuinely nervous about asking me to the dance, but what did I know about genuine feelings? Especially girls' feelings?

I didn't get any of it, and hanging out with Gabe and Varnie had taught me that my ignorance had nothing to do with the amnesia. Girls were just difficult to understand. It was one of the things that made them girls.

Brittany bit her lip. "You're not going to ask me, are you?"

I brought one hand to her hand, the one touching me, and held it gently in mine. "I really can't."

"Before you got amnesia, I thought maybe you and I would . . ." Her voice trailed off.

"I'm really sorry, Brittany."

"It's because of the English girl, isn't it?"

"Theia?" I asked.

She nodded. "The thing is, Haden. She's not here, but I am."

No, the thing of it was that I was here and Theia wasn't,

but Brittany wouldn't understand that. "It's not going to work out. I'm sorry."

We sat like that for a minute, quiet in our mutual regret. She sighed and placed a kiss on top of my head, allowing me a glance down the V of her top. "You'll be even sorrier when you see me in my dress."

She said it good-naturedly, and I had a feeling she was right. It was then I felt the heated stare.

Amelia.

I don't know how long she'd been there. I know it must have looked bad from where she stood. The shock of my betrayal was clear in her expressive eyes.

"Ame," I said.

She set her jaw and glared at me before turning on her heel. I knew better than to follow her. I'd straighten it out later. I hoped.

CHAPTER TWENTY-TWO

"Well," Varnie said, raking a hand through his hair. "This is going well."

I was blistered. From the inside out.

Ame and Donny were taking turns. There was no good cop, bad cop. Just bad cop and worse cop. They railed at me endlessly. It all jumbled together—sneetches, pond scum, no morals, demon ways, betrayer.

Even Gabe tried to step in on my behalf. "Ladies, let the man at least try to defend himself."

"No, it's okay. Let them get it out," I replied. We all needed it. I was all those things, even when I wasn't trying to be, even when I wanted desperately to be something else.

The night I appeared in that cabin, they lost something, someone, very important. The girls were always so careful to make sure I knew they didn't blame me. But they should have. They would tiptoe around my feelings; make excuses for my lack of anything at all helpful. When they finally let go of that anger on me, it felt like the first real human interaction I'd had with them. I think it purged us all.

After the last harsh word, we all stared at one another, the room filling up with silence. Varnie looked at me like he felt sorry for me because he knew we weren't done.

No point in putting it off. "I saw Theia last night."

"What?" Ame clutched Donny's wrist. "Where? How? I thought you said you didn't—"

"Miss Amelia, let the man talk," Varnie interjected.

"I dreamt . . . except it wasn't a dream. I went to Under, the place you told me she talked about, last night. She's still there." I held my hands up to ward off the oncoming barrage of questions. "She wouldn't come back with me. She said she can't."

"We can't just leave her there." Donny stood up and began pacing. "I can't believe you didn't drag her out with you."

"I don't have any special powers anymore, Donny. I don't know how it works—I asked her to come with me. She said no."

She spun and looked at Gabe. "You would have dragged me out, wouldn't you?"

"By your hair," he answered.

She crossed her arms and glared at me again, vindicated by his answer.

"I wanted to bring her back, I swear."

Ame looked at Varnie hopefully. "Can we try? Maybe the cards or the crystal ball?"

"Of course," he answered, taking her hand and leading her into the other room, not looking as optimistic as she did.

Donny and Gabe stayed in the living room with me pretending we were fine, until Donny was strung so tight, I thought she might explode. She was like a rubber band stretched to its very limit, ready to snap.

Gabe's face was tense with worry. "Babe, you need to relax."

"Are you kidding me?" she retorted. "My best friend has been living in hell for a month. A month, Gabe. God, a month ago, I didn't even really believe in all this crap."

I fought for something to say. "She looked well—healthy, I mean. She was beautiful, and she was playing her violin."

Donny stared at me like she was trying to pick out words she understood from what I said. "She looked *well*?"

"She actually seemed . . ." I really didn't know how to say it without making it sound bad. "She sort of fit in there. Like, it agreed with her." Like she was ready to hunt me like prey is what I did *not* say.

"Your mother is a freaking demon and Theia is her prisoner. I don't think she's *well*. We tried to look your mommy up, you know. If she's who Varnie thinks she is, she is like the patron saint of night terrors."

I grimaced. "I know." I had seen the same tome on demonology. If Mara was my mother—and Varnie thought she was—Theia couldn't last long in that place. "But she still looked okay."

Gabe looked at me like I was an idiot. He was right. "You have a lot to learn about girls, amnesia boy."

I agreed and went to the kitchen to grab a Coke so he could calm Donny down in private. I could hear her yelling at Gabe and his calm voice reassuring her. It felt like I was the kryptonite of their group. I made them weaker, broke them apart. And yeah, I could remember what kryptonite was, but not how I met the girl who loved me so much she went to hell in my place.

I was a curse.

After another hour, Ame came out of the other room looking like a kicked puppy. The three of them left without much of a good-bye. I questioned Varnie with my eyes, but he just shook his head solemnly and I followed him back into the kitchen while he got himself a beer.

"I'll take one of those."

"I don't think so." He did, however, hand me another Coke.

"I thought I was one hundred and seventy years old," I argued.

"Your ID says seventeen."

"Your ID says nineteen."

"Nobody cards Madame Varnie." And they didn't. He used that costume shamelessly to fill the fridge with beer. Beer he wouldn't let me drink.

"So, no luck finding Theia?" I asked, even though it was obvious he hadn't found her.

Varnie shook his head. "Neither of us can get a bead on her. It's frustrating. Especially since now we know to focus the energy to Under. Before it was shots in the dark, but this should have worked. I don't understand why we can't bring her out this time." He took a long pull from the bottle. "You doing okay, man? They were pretty rough on you."

"No rougher than I deserve. They're right. It should be me in that hell, not Theia."

"So why were you hitting on that girl?"

I cast him an are-you-kidding-me look. "I wasn't. She wanted me to ask her to prom. I said no." How many times did they need to hear that?

Varnie hiked himself onto the counter. "Is Ame going to prom?"

I choked on my drink. "Wow, that was subtle."

"What do you mean?" asked Mr. Obvious.

"You interested in Amelia?"

"No," he scoffed and peeled the corner off his label. "Why? Has she said anything about me?"

I didn't really want to get into the fact that Ame only had eyes for Mike Matheny, the guy who could barely string three words together for a sentence but ate every meal like it had been a week since his last. So I just said, "I'd be the last person she talked to."

He nodded, realizing I was right. When Amelia saw me in the corner being fondled by Brittany, I lost her trust. Since I wasn't sure how I had gotten her trust in the first place, I was clueless as to how I was going to get it back.

Or if I deserved it.

"Tell me about the night in the cabin," I said, thinking maybe there was something we'd missed. The key to my memories.

"What do you want to know?" he asked.

"You always do that. It's so frustrating. Look, I understand that nobody wanted to overdo it with the intel when I first woke up. I get it—but I've been around for a while now. It doesn't look like I'm going to get my memories back on my own."

Varnie shrugged. "I've told you everything now. We summoned you, but we didn't know only the demon and your body could make the trip, which meant we managed to lose your soul somewhere along the way. Luckily, because I summoned you, the demon was bound to me, though I'm sure he would have figured a way around that eventually. Something happened—we assume now that it was your mother coming—and Theia sent us outside." He paused, remembering the last time they'd seen Theia alive. "When we came back in, she was gone and we were stuck with the demon."

"But you still didn't know where my soul was?"

Varnie shook his head. "No, and you were a real bastard. Well, I mean the demon part of you. Donny made a comment about wishing she'd paid more attention during *The Exorcist*, which made Ame think we should give exorcism a try."

"Okay," I broke in. "So then you exorcised the demon out of the body, and I—well, my soul—came back into it."

"With no memories," he added. He winced and looked off into the distance. "I still can't figure out what went wrong there. A missed word in the chant, one too many eyes of newt? It doesn't make any sense. Where *did* your memories go?"

"I am more concerned with where the demon went, Varnie."

"Out." He drained the bottle and tossed it across the room, missing the recycle bin, and it thunked onto the linoleum.

"Out where?"

"I have no idea. If you recall, which you don't, of course, that was one of my arguments for not exorcising the demon that night. Of course, I hadn't wanted to summon you in the first place, but the Betties had other opinions."

I picked up his bottle and set it on top of the other glass. "So, my demon half is just out there, circling around, waiting for another chance to make himself at home in my body. Which, I suppose is technically half his."

"Well, we threw him out of this realm, so he'd have to be invited back into your body. I think."

"You *think*?"

"Sorry, I'm not proficient at exorcism. Or spell casting. I'm a psychic. It's like asking a podiatrist to perform brain surgery." Varnie rubbed his face in exasperation. "By the way, I hate spells. I'd like to never do another one. I don't mind poking around in my visions—I'm used to those. But I'm not really interested in auditioning for *Charmed*."

"I'll make a note of it."

"Maybe I should update my Facebook page." We laughed, but the lines on his forehead came back. "I don't know where the demon is, dude."

That news wasn't reassuring. "Are you sure I can't have one of those beers?" I asked.

"Go to bed. You have school in the morning."

I nodded and passed him on my way into the guest room. "Yes, Mom."

I took a long, steamy shower. The hot water stung the scrapes, but part of me wanted the burn, the penance. Once in bed, I stared at the ceiling for a long time, willing sleep to come.

CHAPTER TWENTY-THREE

I heard a giggle and saw a flash of red darting between the trees. I blinked hard. What the hell? Where was I?

I was surrounded by trees as wide around as a full-grown man was tall. They stretched to the sky so far that I couldn't see the tops, the boughs providing a canopy of lush, wet green tenting over me and creating a strange, insular world. Moss draped over some branches like tinsel, and in other places it clung like a dense carpet. The air was thick with moisture, but the temperature was moderate, almost cool.

I saw the flash of red again from the corner of my eye. It was a cloaked person darting between the humongous trees. Theia maybe? I hoped it was, so I followed the figure. I had to stop several times, when I lost sight of the red, and listen for snapping twigs. I got a glimpse of the cloak and realized it was a girl for sure, but she reappeared behind trees she couldn't possibly have reached without me seeing her. She just kept popping up here and there, and whenever I would get close, she'd be behind me instead.

I began losing my patience as well as my breath, and stopped to lean on one of the massive trees. As my heart slowed down, the bark changed beneath my fingers. *Strange*, I thought, and looked closer. It morphed into a human face and I snatched my hand away and stumbled backwards.

The entire tree was made up of faces pressed into the bark like masks. Angry, sad, and mean faces glared and snarled and screamed at me with no sound, moving around in a macabre fashion while trapped on the surface of the tree. Fear gripped me and I ran blindly away from the tree, bumping into another, realizing as I hit the trunk that it was the same. All the trees around me were the same.

The bark writhed and pulsated like the faces were moving beneath a blanket. Their pain and anger consumed me. Madness descended over me, drowning everything but the kind of fear that made a man saw off his own leg to flee a trap. Everywhere I looked, the faces haunted me. I'm ashamed to say I curled into a ball on the ground. I didn't want to see what they were going to do to me. I couldn't look at them anymore, and with my eyes open I couldn't see anything else.

I sensed someone else then, in front of me. I peeked and saw black riding boots. I followed the leather up a woman's calf until I got to the hem of a red cloak. I sat up quickly.

"My, Haden, what big eyes you have." Theia removed the hood and crouched down to my level. "You shouldn't have come back."

She looked so cool and collected amidst the horror, and there I was, hyperventilating and dripping in the cold sweat of fear. I could barely breathe. At least the faces were gone. For now.

"This is no place for you. Not anymore."

I swallowed. "This is no place for you either."

"Oh, I don't know about that." She looked around like she was appraising a house she was thinking of moving into. "It has a lot of promise. I kind of like it." Theia stood up. "The neighborhood is a little rough sometimes, but it's got good bones." She laughed at that.

I didn't know why.

"I'd help you up, but it's probably best that I don't touch you." While I was getting up, she walked over to a tree and touched the bark lightly, reverently. "They were human once. All of them. She drove them mad and collected them like bugs in a jar." Theia glanced at me. "I'm speaking of your mother. You don't remember her, do you?"

I shook my head.

"You don't remember me either?" She looked away before I could shake my head again. "It's for the best, I suppose."

"I don't remember you, Theia, but I still have feelings for you. Feelings I can't explain, I just know they are there."

"Get rid of them." Her answer stunned me. "Feelings like that won't help you. Not now. It's best if you just move forward from here."

"I can't move forward knowing you're trapped here. Tell me how to get you out."

Theia clucked her tongue. "I chose to stay."

"Why would you do that?" And then, just by looking at her face, I knew. "It's because of me."

She shrugged. "I made a bargain."

"For me."

She sat down on a log, wrapped in that hooded red cloak from a fairy tale. Only I wasn't the wolf. Not anymore. I think maybe she might have been, though.

"Mara, your mother, was going to do something to your soul. I don't know what. It didn't sound good. We made a blood oath—I thought it meant you and I would be together. I thought it was the only way. And then while I was swearing my life to her and she was giving me the blood of demons"— Theia scrunched her eyes tightly at the memory—"they found a way to bring you back. But I have to stay."

I joined her on the log, looking first for trapped souls in the wood. "They exorcised the demon. Varnie and Amelia. And when it was out of my body, my soul came crashing back into it. I woke up and didn't remember anything. I mean, I know some things . . . I know I hate rap music and I remember what the world was like during World War II. But I have no personal memories. Like the slate was wiped clean."

"How are they—my friends?" Her voice was so small. I wanted to pull her into my arms and never let anyone hurt her again. How I was going to do that, I didn't know. But the feeling that settled in my heart wouldn't accept any other outcome.

"They miss you. They miss you like crazy."

"Mara told me I could watch the world, like you used to, through the looking glass you had. But I just can't. It would hurt too much."

I reached an arm around her, but she jumped away. "Please," she begged. "Please don't touch me."

"Why?"

"You had decades of practice being a demon and a human, and it was still hard for you to control your urges. I don't have the benefit of time. I could hurt you. . . . I could kill you even if I didn't want to."

"Theia, what are you saying?"

"I took a blood oath with a demon." She sent me a look like I should have understood, like I was missing a big piece of the puzzle. "What do you think happens to someone with the blood of such a powerful demon inside her, Haden?"

She raised her brows, and it hit me. What I hadn't wanted to accept, but had suspected since she first warned me away from her. Blood drained from my cheeks. "Oh, no. Theia, no."

"It happened so fast. At first I thought it was just the blood ritual that made me feel strange . . . foreign. I promised her I'd never escape." She held up her hand and stared at it. "But I can feel it inside me, separate but one. It's always there, waiting for me to be weak."

I closed my eyes. "I'm sorry. I wish I'd never darkened your door."

"You see now why I can't leave." She leaned away, to put more distance between us. "The demon is inside me. It wants unspeakable things. It makes *me* want unspeakable things."

"We'll get it out of you. Just come back with me. We'll find a way." I rubbed my face to keep myself from reaching out to her, but I wanted to touch her so very badly to reassure her, reassure myself. "Please, Theia, let me hold you. You won't hurt me."

An exasperated gasp left her lungs. "I wish that were true." She laughed, the way people do when something is the opposite of funny. "You don't remember, but we've had this conversation before. Only it was you telling me to stay away and me thinking that love could conquer all."

"You don't believe that anymore?"

Her gaze snapped to mine with a ferocious intensity. "I would do it again. To save you. I don't regret that you have a chance now. Go away. Go be the bloke you've spent your whole life wishing you could be."

"Not without you." I let her roll her eyes before I asked. "Has she hurt you . . . Mara?"

"Surprisingly, no." Theia began walking away from me onto the trail, so I jumped up to join her. The woods were peaceful again, now that she was with me. "She's actually been quite accommodating. She misses you, I think, though she'd never admit it. She knows I can't leave, but I think she wants me to *want* to stay. I mean, we're not exactly friends, but we have fallen into a strange kind of coexistence. She thinks it's only a matter of time until I am just like her."

"Don't trust her." She looked at me questioningly. It also surprised me that I said it. "I don't even recall what she looks like. But just . . . don't trust her."

She inclined her head slightly. "Don't trust me either."

I gulped. There was something very hot about being a little afraid of a girl.

"I'll never trust Mara," Theia went on. "Don't worry. Even when she's being accommodating, she's not exactly pleasant. Besides, I don't think she's given up on getting you back here for good. We can't ever let that happen, Haden."

She began walking again, and I stumbled on my feet a little to catch up. "Nobody has given up on you," I said when

I reached her. She needed to understand that we all wanted her back. "Every day we try to find a way. We've met some really interesting . . . people . . . during some of the séances and locating spells. It's just never you."

"Tell me about them. My friends . . . not the people you meet during the séances."

"All right. Donny still won't admit that Gabe is her boyfriend."

"Has she hooked up with anyone else?"

"No, though she threatens to all the time."

She considered that carefully. "Well, that's good. He's good for her. What about Ame?"

"I think Amelia would surprise you. Varnie calls her a raw talent."

Theia stopped walking. "Varnie is still around, then."

"Yeah. He's making sure I don't fall on my ass. I'm sort of like a newborn these days, only I have to go to high school and act normal. Anyway, he put a roof over my head. And he works with Ame, developing her psychic abilities."

Theia wrapped her arms around herself, but smiled. "God, all her Hello Kitty readings were horrible. I'm glad she's coming into her own." She paused. "Mike?"

I blew out my breath. "Still hungry."

"Are they dating?"

"Not really. It's hard for her. She can't really include him in the stuff we do. He doesn't get it."

She nodded. "But Gabe knows."

"Yeah, he's pretty open-minded. More than Donny. They all help me. You'd think they would hate me, but they all try to help me adjust. The school, everyone else, thinks I was in an accident and that I have amnesia." I waited for her to ask, but she didn't. "They think you ran away."

She looked down quickly. "My father?"

"He's distraught."

"He believes I ran away."

"Yes. He calls Donny and Amelia every day to see if you've called them. He doesn't know about me. . . ." My voice trailed off. "You shouldn't be here, Theia. It's all my fault."

She began walking again. "I found your truck."

"My truck?"

"You have one here. It's pretty beat up. If I had seen what you'd done to it before you asked me to go stumping with you, I might have said no."

I'd taken her stumping?

A tear rolled down her cheek in a slow trail that made me feel fierce and weak at the same time.

She wiped her eye and pressed her lips together. "I sleep in your room. I'm fairly pathetic about it, really. I wear your T-shirts to bed and watch your movies." She paused. "And you don't even remember me."

This time I stopped walking. "Do you think it's easy for me?" She had gotten a few steps ahead and turned to look back at me. "No, I don't remember you. I don't remember holding you or talking to you or falling in love with you—but I walk around with a giant hole in my heart all the time. I feel your absence every second of the day. It aches and nothing soothes it. Losing you is bad enough, but I don't even get the comfort of remembering that I had you once."

I thought she understood, for a second. And then something crossed her face, an expression I couldn't name; maybe it was hopelessness. "It doesn't matter."

I closed the distance between us. "It does too."

"I think you've always been the loneliest boy in the world," she said softly. "When you lived here and watched the world you wanted so badly to be a part of—and now, you're still not a part of it, are you?" She pulled her hood up. "You don't want to be a part of my world anymore, Haden. Trust me." She yanked on the necklace around her neck until it broke free. She held it out to me until I put my hand out. "If you have the feelings you say you do, you'll tell the others to stop trying to find me."

"Theia—"

She dropped the necklace into my hand. "Show them this. Tell them I'm happy here. That I don't want to come back. Not ever."

I clasped my fingers around the jewelry. It was warm. "I'm not going to give up on you."

She surprised me by grabbing my shoulders and stretching to me for a kiss. The press of her lips on mine energized every cell in my body. It was like coming home, only I'd never felt what that was like before now. My blood pulled in and out of my heart with a different rhythm, one that I knew instantly matched hers. I clutched her tighter, determined not to let her go. Not ever again.

And then I woke up.

CHAPTER TWENTY-FOUR

I didn't know if I'd ever been to a high school dance before, but I was pretty sure I would never go to another one.

The four of us—Gabe, Donny, Amelia, and me—stood in a corner holding cups of warm orange juice and praying for the clock to move.

"At least we look good," Donny conceded before she sipped her juice.

We did look good. Exceptionally good. Donny wore white—her idea of a joke, but the long dress molded to her body in all the right places with a slit up one leg and a dip so low in the back that Gabe made sure to stand behind her to block the view from other guys. Amelia went with an electric blue dress shorter than Donny's. Instead of jewelry, she dyed the tips of her hair blue and affixed some kind of sapphire jewels to the skin near her eyelids.

Ame was my date. Mike never manned up to ask her, and I knew Donny wouldn't go if Ame didn't have a date. And if

Donny didn't go, then Gabe couldn't go, and as far as I could tell, Gabe was the only one who really wanted to be there in the first place.

"Do you want to dance?" I asked Amelia.

She shrugged. "I suppose."

"Ouch."

She looked at me sideways and a small smirk curled her lips. "I'm sorry. It's just . . ."

"I know." I wasn't the date she wanted, and Theia was still living in a realm of the underworld.

After I came back with Theia's necklace and the unsettling news about the demon blood inhabiting her body, Ame had begrudgingly admitted she might have been a little hard on me. I obviously wasn't cheating on Theia—I was too busy staring at the talisman that had done nothing to protect Theia to even think about other girls. I put her pendant on a black cord and wore it every day. I didn't recall loving her, but I loved her all the same. It wasn't something I questioned anymore, not after that kiss. My brain may not have remembered, but my heart did.

"This is stupid," Gabe said, and we all looked at him. "This is probably as good as the four of us are ever going to look, and we can't even enjoy it."

"Theia would want us to have fun," Ame offered quietly.

"Theia would have hated this prom just as much as we do," said Donny.

The gym had been transformed into—well, not much. The music kept cutting out, the decorations consisted of a few banners with glitter paint, and the adult-to-student ratio was getting pretty close to two to one as the crowd thinned out.

"So, what do you want to do?" Gabe asked.

"I could eat," I said, reminding myself of Mike, but it was true. Food seemed like a really good solution.

"Pancakes would make this night salvageable," said Donny

"Oh, man . . . I could eat a pancake," Ame agreed, shocking us all—I'd only ever seen her eat salad.

Half an hour later, we stormed Varnie's front door in formal wear, carrying grocery bags of breakfast items. He came out of his room looking confused.

"Did I miss something?" He looked down at his shorts and tee. "Should I go put on a tie?"

"Please tell me you know how to cook," Donny said to Varnie, and he laughed when he took the bag out of her hand. Varnie ate a lot of sandwiches.

Instead, I answered, "I know how to cook."

"Riiight," Donny said.

"No, really."

It seemed odd to me too. Why would I know how to make pancakes? Were all demons fans of breakfast, or just me? But the knowledge was in my head, and so I put Donny and Ame on frying bacon, which might have been a mistake, Gabe on mixing batter, Varnie on setting the table, and I rolled up my sleeves and heated up the griddle.

Something happened in that kitchen as we worked around one another and tried to keep from spilling food on the girls in their pretty dresses. Donny kicked off her heels, making her look even hotter somehow. Ame chattered and giggled, unaware that Varnie stole awkward glances whenever possible, and that every time she laughed he smiled. Gabe and I played catch with a roll of paper towels in between my awesome flapjack flipping, and Donny kept telling us to knock it off. We all felt Theia's absence—but at the same time, I felt a part of something. I had a place where I belonged.

We sat at the table like a family, passing things and joking. I ate until I was so full I thought the button on my pants would give way. Everything just tasted so good.

Ame sat back. "Jeez, I'm stuffed."

"I don't even want to think about all those dishes," Donny said. "Hey, now that I believe in demons and magic spells, who's going to tell me about little dish elves that come and clean your kitchen while you nap?"

"There is a class of fairy called Nibs that will do it, but they come with their own set of issues. It's never worth the hassle of summoning them," Varnie answered.

"I was totally kidding, but . . ." Donny eyed him suspiciously. "Wait, are you punking me? There really is no such thing as Nibs, is there?"

Varnie smiled noncommittally.

"Ame, is there such a thing as Nibs?"

Amelia bit her lip to keep from laughing. "I've never heard of them, but that doesn't mean they don't exist."

"Amnesia boy?"

I held up my hands. "Yeah, sorry. Amnesia."

"You guys suck." She pouted.

It was fun to get her worked up. Donny lived so close to the surface that a few well-chosen words could spin her into a frenzy. Of course, sometimes that was a curse too.

Gabe looked at the table in disgust. "I'd almost rather do another one of those séances than clean up this mess."

Ame looked up. "We totally should. We haven't been able to try for a few days."

"I was kidding." Gabe sat back in his chair. "I hate those. It's creepy."

Amelia ignored Gabe and blinked sweetly at Varnie. "What do you think, Varnie?"

Varnie, the poor sap, would have leapt from a bridge if she'd asked him to with those pretty eyes. Donny cocked her head to one side and looked at Amelia very intently, and then she slowly tilted her head and looked at Varnie, her eyes thinning into slits. "Hey, wait a minute—"

Gabe cut her off with a kiss. I was beginning to think the guy had more psychic powers than Ame and Varnie combined. He acted like he was just along for the ride most of the time, but he always seemed to know exactly what wasn't being said. And how to handle Donny without making her . . . less Donny.

"We can do a locating séance, if you like, Miss Amelia. One more time couldn't hurt." Varnie blinked a few times, realizing he was acting like a pansy. At least I hoped he realized it. "*After* we clean up this mess."

We all groaned. After dishes, we took our places around the table in the war room. That's what Gabe had dubbed it to make it sound less freakish that we sat around a table chanting and looking into a crystal ball.

Next came quiet time. We all were supposed to quiet our minds. Mostly, we just tried to get serious and stop saying snarky things to one another—I don't know if my mind ever quieted. Quiet time usually lasted about two minutes.

Soon Varnie spoke. "Everyone, please close your eyes, open your mind, and breathe deeply."

I tried to relax. I was never comfortable in the room with

the crystal ball. And I hated those cards. They just seemed ominous to me. Predictors of disaster.

"Let your mind go. Think of the dark night sky and a blanket of stars. Imagine all the pinpoints of light—find one that speaks to you and focus on it." Varnie's voice deepened as he spoke. No longer the female impersonator or the surfer dude, he acquired a resonance that seemed to come out only when he was working like this. He led us on a trip through a galaxy in our minds. As we went further into the night inside our heads, Theia's necklace grew warmer on my skin.

"Everyone, please join hands. Once we have formed a circle, remember not to break it until I tell you."

That was an important step. If we broke the circle, bad things could happen. Varnie never elaborated on what bad things—but we were already freaked out enough that we didn't dare ask. "Bad things" was enough of a warning.

"I'm opening the channels," Varnie said next, not to us, but to the spirit world. "To ask—"

The table started bouncing. We all opened our eyes and looked at one another.

"All right," Varnie continued, his voice remaining calm. "Someone is already here, I take it."

The table thumped harder. The ball in the middle wobbled off its base and rolled towards me. My first instinct was to catch it, but I stopped myself. Donny and I used our joined hands to buffer the globe, keeping it from falling off the table.

The deck of tarot cards on the sideboard began shuffling itself as if an invisible entity were handing them side to side. Donny whimpered a little, and then, one by one, the cards began flying through the air towards us like missiles. We ducked, but one hit me in the shoulder hard enough to tear my dress shirt.

Ame stood, her hair blowing like she was standing against a strong wind. Without letting go of Varnie and Gabe or breaking the circle, she glared at the cards. "Stop." Her voice was calm but fierce, and the cards stopped their flight in mid-air. They just hung there. The invisible wind kept at her, but I think it might have been something she created, and not something aimed at her. It was like this weird energy that buffeted her, and consequently the rest of us.

Sweet, jokey Amelia looked like a goddess in a wind tunnel.

"I'm not enjoying this," Donny whispered.

"Yeah, me neither." Varnie cleared his throat. "We're going to go ahead and—"

Whatever he was going to say was cut off by letters forming on the wall in red, as if someone were spray-painting the wall with blood.

HADEN

As each letter appeared, my stomach dropped a little more.

Something began battering at the closed door and we all flinched with each bang.

"What the hell is going on?" Gabe asked.

Donny's hand trembled in mine. "I think we should stop. This isn't right."

I agreed. We'd never experienced anything so strong—or dark—before.

"Don't let go," Varnie reminded us. "We need to close the channels."

It was difficult to remain calm. The bloodred letters began to drip into elongated patterns, and the ramming against the door startled my heart with every bang. My muscles tensed, and I wanted to either hit something or hide under the table.

Amelia squeezed her eyes shut and the room exploded in a burst of white light. Like a flash of lightning, only warm as sunshine, the light seemed to illuminate every crevice where a shadow could hide. In that second of heat, the paint disappeared, the cards flew back to the sideboard, and the banging stopped.

Ame opened her eyes. "Whoa."

"Yeah, Ame, whoa," Gabe repeated.

A hush fell over the room. Our labored breathing was the only sound.

"Varnie," she whispered, "what did I just do?"

"I'm not sure, but I wanna say you just averted an apocalypse, Miss Amelia." His tone was dry, but his palm was not.

"Can we break the circle yet?" I was still scared, but I was also not enjoying holding wet hands with Varnie.

"You okay, babe?" Gabe asked Donny.

She was pale, really pale, and her lower lip trembled, but she didn't speak. We all broke the circle and instantly crowded around her chair. She shivered uncontrollably.

"Donny, what is it?" Ame asked.

Donny tried to talk but seemed to hiccup each breath.

"Babe?" Gabe shook her gently. "Please tell me you're okay."

Her eyes were glassy and a little vacant. I shared a concerned look with Varnie.

She gasped on a huge breath. "I saw her," she finally managed.

"Who?" Varnie asked.

"Theia! She was looking at me through the other side of a mirror. She looked so sad and then . . . and then all her skin shriveled up and she was this skeleton thing." She shivered again, and Gabe drew her into his lap.

Theia.

"It was probably a trick," Varnie said calmly. "Just like the noises and the message on the wall—tricks to scare us."

Or maybe it wasn't, I wanted to shout. I shot out of my chair and left the room in an effort to keep from exploding with pent-up rage. I was so tired of feeling helpless. Everyone was in danger, and it was all my fault. The writing was on the wall—literally.

And worst of all, I was jealous. I was pissed that Gabe could hold Donny when she was scared, and that Varnie could spend time with Amelia, even if she didn't have a clue that he was into her. And that the girl of my dreams was out of my reach.

That night I woke up, still in my room, barely able to breathe. It felt like I was under the tire of a car. I couldn't move, but I was acutely aware that I was awake and I was not alone. It was frightening, more frightening than my name in blood on the wall or even the ghastly faces in the tree bark. At least in the woods I could run.

I managed to blink until my eyes adjusted to the darkness.

It was then that I realized Theia was kneeling on my chest. I'd seen that before, in the demonology book Varnie showed me. That was how the mare demon took her prey. In the pictures, she was sometimes a beautiful maiden and sometimes a hag. No drawings ever depicted her looking as forlorn as Theia.

She was crying silent tears and her lower lip trembled. She looked away from me, like she couldn't bear for me to see her shame.

"I'm so very sorry," she whispered.

I couldn't speak or move. She was glowing a little—like she was edged in soft light.

"I don't want to do this, Haden. God, please make me stop."

And then she was gone, as if she had never been there.

And I wondered if she was already too far gone to save.

Theia sat in the corner of Haden's room, as small as she could make herself. The shame of what she'd become made her sick.

She'd just needed a taste. She'd needed it so badly. She lost all reason, all sense of herself.

She squeezed her eyes to cut off the memory, but it stayed just as sharp in her head. It was easy to make excuses, to put her needs ahead of everyone else's. Why shouldn't she have what she wanted? Hadn't she sacrificed everything? She didn't kill him, after all. And if she wanted to, she could make him enjoy the experience— exquisite pleasure, torturous delight.

Theia covered her ears. No, that was Mara talking. Mara whispering those things in her head. What she'd done was wrong. She'd let the demon in her win that battle. Haden was lucky she'd been able to stop. They both were.

Mara had played this one well. Promising Theia she could go out, she could see Haden, but there was a penance for the privilege.

Never again.

Mara's treacherous bargains meant that Theia lost, every time. She was waiting for Theia to make the mistake that would bring Haden back to Under forever. Theia would be stronger next time.

She had to be stronger.

CHAPTER TWENTY-fIVE

I was already sitting at the table when Varnie got up the next morning.

"You're up early," he said, getting his favorite mug out of the cupboard. He liked to hit the beach near sunrise on weekends.

I'd been staring into my coffee, long grown cold, trying to make sense of the séance, my dream that hadn't felt like a dream, and the fact that my girlfriend had tried to eat my soul last night.

"What's wrong?" Varnie asked, noticing my mood.

"Theia was here."

"Here? As in, she came here and you didn't go there?" He sat across from me. "Are you sure?"

I met his eyes across the table. "I think she was going to feed on me." Saying the words turned my blood cold. I wanted to panic, to explode in rage, to do *something*. Anything.

Varnie looked into his cup to avoid my eyes any longer. "Sorry, dude. That's not cool."

"Cool?" I echoed. "Varnie, we need to get her out of there. I need my memories back *now*. She stopped herself last night, but what if she can't the next time? She'll hate herself." *And next time*, I thought but didn't say, *what if it isn't me she goes after?*

"What do you suggest?"

I tunneled my fingers through my hair, the frustration a nagging ache. "I don't know. Can you hypnotize me or something?"

"I don't know how to hypnotize people." He left the table and came back with a cold slice from a pizza at least four days old.

"What about past-life regression or something?"

"Look, the best I can do is lead you into a very deep meditative state. But I'm not sure that's a good idea." He paused. "Of course, nobody ever listens to me when I say it's not a good idea, so I don't suppose you'll be any different."

"I can't do anything for her like this, Varn. If I could remember what I knew when I was a demon, maybe I could save her."

"Haden . . ."

"Please."

He nodded. "Fine. But when the world blows up in our faces again, I'd like it if at least one time somebody says, 'We should have listened to Varnie.'"

I exhaled the breath I'd been holding too long. "How do we do this?"

"Sit back in your chair and relax."

Right. I did what he asked, but I didn't think I'd be re-laxing anytime soon. I was too keyed up—my nerves were bouncing around like a sphere in a pinball machine.

"Deep breaths. Think about the air traveling into your nose and follow it down the length of your body. Visualize it being pulled all the way to your feet, to your toes, and then, exhale from your toes up again." And then he repeated it.

I did what he said, only I realized I was visualizing my body as completely empty except for the air because that was how I felt. I was a shell, devoid of life. Except that now I was a balloon.

Varnie kept telling me to look at things—stars in the sky again, blades of grass in a meadow, grains of sand on a beach. I was about to tell him it wasn't working, I wasn't relaxing, when I noticed I was in a graveyard of very old headstones.

The cemetery wasn't frightening or especially morbid. It also didn't feel like Under, but I was definitely lucid. I stopped at one stone surrounded by bushes of black roses and felt the fine hairs on the back of my neck stir to attention.

JENNIFER ANNE ALDERSON

Theia's mother. Just under my Adam's apple, the talis-man vibrated slightly. What did Mrs. Alderson have to do with getting back my memories? The only connection I could think of was that Theia had chosen her mother's necklace as the talisman that I now wore.

A talisman that had done little to protect her from me.

"Hello, Haden."

I whirled around towards the voice. A woman in a white

gown appeared in the mist. Her long, dark hair contrasted with the paleness of her skin, and her lips seemed redder than they should be.

"Hello?" I answered. I didn't recognize her, but then, I didn't recognize a lot of people.

She moved with an unnatural grace, and the mist billowed around her as she walked towards me. There was an ethereal quality about her, and I couldn't look away from her.

"I'm very worried about my daughter." She spoke slowly with a slight lilt. "She's in grave danger."

"Your daughter?" I looked back at the headstone. "You're Theia's mom?"

"Call me Jenny," she told me in a soothing voice.

Talking to a ghost was something I should have been used to after all the séances at Varnie's, but talking to the ghost of Theia's mother was a new level of strangeness. The spirits we'd reached had never seemed so real. They were transparent if you could see them at all. Theia's mother sort of shimmered, but she was corporeal.

"Why are you here?" I asked with no manners. This was supposed to be my subconscious, and yet there she was.

"My daughter is in a lot of trouble. She doesn't belong where she is."

My guilt overwhelmed me. "Mrs. Alderson, you have to know I never wanted this to happen to her. If I could switch places with her I would."

"You don't know how glad I am to hear that. What a fine young man you are." She smiled. "And, please, I meant it. Call me Jenny."

Jenny didn't resemble Theia in any way. Her cheekbones

were too sculpted, her hair too dark, and her mouth was all wrong. It was her lips, maybe, that weren't right. Theia's lips were plump and shaped like a bow, but Jenny's were thin and her mouth was wide.

Still, despite the differences, there was something very calming about her. I relaxed for the first time in what seemed like a very long time. Perhaps she was more than a ghost— maybe a guardian angel of some kind, because her presence was so peaceful to me. My muscles, my whole body, began to feel languid. Everything was going to be okay now. Jenny would fix it.

Jenny walked around me and sighed as she ran her hand over the headstone that marked her final resting place. "Poor Theia, trapped in that nightmare realm." She shook her head, her face a mask of worry.

"Can we get her out?"

"No, we can't." She looked at me like she was looking through me. "But *you* can."

The way she inflected her words filled me with a sense of calm purpose. *I* could save Theia. Suddenly, I felt like I was in a spotlight of warmth. Jenny looked at me like I could do anything. And I began to believe her.

Since waking up in the cabin, I'd felt unsure of myself. To be filled with such overwhelming confidence and peace was amazing.

"You can be her champion, Haden. You're the only one who can save Theia now."

Waves of courage coursed through me. She was right. I *was* the only one. "What must I do?" Whatever it was, whatever she asked of me, I would do it.

Jenny smiled, and it occurred to me again how different she and Theia were. Jenny's hair was almost black and Theia's curls were . . . and then the heated spotlight suddenly felt like a splash of ice-cold water.

Theia's curls were inherited from her *mother*.

Jenny's hair was straight as a pin.

Donny had told me all about how Theia used to hate her hair because it was so wild. She'd said she never wore it down until I came along. That I had somehow helped Theia make peace with her mom and the things about herself that were different from her father.

It was unlikely that a ghost spent an hour with a hair straightener before meeting me in a cemetery. This woman wasn't Jenny.

She was Mara.

I don't know how I knew it, but the clarity I felt seemed to shrug off the sense of purpose I'd had only seconds before. The calming, encouraging vibes were most likely manufactured by Mara to manipulate me. As soon as I recognized that, they were gone and I was left with only a knot of cold dread.

I swallowed hard and tried not show my fear. It was best if she thought I still believed her.

Mara blinked prettily at me, playing up her role as some kind of benevolent guardian sent to aid against evil. Only she *was* the evil. I didn't know how I'd missed it earlier. She was caked in impurity, visible only when you saw past her facade.

"I can help you remember, but first I need you to give me the necklace."

My hand went to it automatically. "Why?" Despite all reason, I felt safer with the protection of it against my skin, even though the talisman had not proven to be very useful.

"It's a symbol. Magic requires it."

My eyes darted around for an escape route. But was I really there or still at the kitchen table with Varnie? "What will you do to it?" I asked. "How will it return my memories?"

As I glanced around us, the rest of the graveyard disappeared. We were left on what appeared to be the summit of a mountain—just Mara, Jenny's headstone, and me.

"Haden, give me the necklace," she demanded, her voice no longer lilting and calm.

"Why do you want it so badly, Mother?"

Mara chuckled. "That's my boy. Even with no memory, you still recognize your own kind. It's time for you to come home, Son."

"I'm not a demon anymore. I'm not your kind."

Mara's pupils darkened. "We can fix that. Come home."

"Let Theia go."

She rolled her eyes. "I'm half tempted. Honestly, she's even more annoying than you were. Haden—" Mara pouted. "Come back."

There was nowhere to go at that moment, unless I felt like cliff diving, so I humored her, hoping she didn't want to kill me or eat my soul. How maternal were demons? I looked at the headstone again and wondered if my mother loved me. "What happens if I come back with you?"

Mara cocked her head, intrigued by my interest. "You get your memories."

"And Theia?"

"You get to keep Theia too." The venom was coated in sugar, but it was there.

I closed my eyes. "Let her go."

"You're getting tiresome, Haden. We all know how this is going to go. You and your friends are not powerful enough to stop me. Theia has made her choice, she promised herself to me, and now my blood runs in her veins. Trust me, everyone is much better off with her in Under."

"Why do you want the talisman?" I asked again.

"I told you. It's a symbol."

It had to be more than that. "How do I get my memories?"

She crossed her arms and arched her brow. When I blinked, I thought I saw her cheekbones protruding from her skin, but then her face was normal again. "Don't you find your human body limiting, Son?" Mara didn't wait for an answer. "You could have it all, you know. As a demon, you had more power than you can imagine right now."

The only power I wanted was the ability to save Theia, but I didn't dare voice my desire.

"You used to be special, Haden. Don't you miss that?"

It was as if Mara had plunged a knife into me and begun twisting it with each word. Yes, I did miss being special. I didn't remember what it was like, exactly, but I knew I used to be more. What I wouldn't have given just to be more useful to everyone.

"When you embraced who you were, you were stronger. Your friends would envy your speed and strength. They would be amazed at all the things you could do." She walked around me in a slow circle. "But instead you want to be a nobody. I don't understand it. You could rule this realm and your own, but you cower in obscurity and mope about a girl who will never be good enough for you."

My heart beat so erratically, I thought it might pound its way out of my chest. "If she's no good to you, why don't you let her go?"

"I made a promise to her just as much as she made a promise to me. I have to honor that, don't I? Besides, what on earth would you do with her now? You can't possibly control her, not in the unfortunate condition you're in. You'll need your other half or she'll eat you alive. Literally."

I looked down at my legs as vines circled their way up them. Picking up my feet did nothing to disengage the barbed stems. And then I couldn't pick up my feet anymore anyway. I was trapped, anchored to the ground with the mother of nightmares circling me like a predator.

"You're beginning to bore me, pussycat."

I tried not to panic, but I hated being immobile. "Where did the demon go?" I asked. "After they exorcised it?"

"It doesn't matter where it went, only where it is now." Mara pulled a necklace from her bodice. It matched the one Theia had given me. She smiled at my reaction as she dangled the twin talisman. "I'm a fan of symmetry."

I didn't know what she had planned to do. Maybe if I'd still thought she was Jenny, I would have given her the one I wore when she asked for it and somehow she would have switched them without my knowing.

"So, you're going to put that on me and I'll be a demon again," I said, even as I struggled against the vines that held my legs in place.

"It's not as simple as that. You have to accept it."

Accept a demon possession? "Then why tie me down?"

Mara shrugged. "Because it's amusing." She walked towards me, but her feet didn't touch the ground. She was gliding on air and getting closer and closer and . . .

And then I heard Varnie's voice, calling me back from where I was to where I needed to be.

Varnie's face isn't exactly what I usually want to see first thing upon waking, but at that moment I was really happy to see him.

"I was getting a little worried. You seemed a little deeper in the meditative state than I think is normal."

My throat worked for an answer. "Water," I said finally.

While he grabbed me a bottle from the fridge, I tried to understand what had just happened. The talisman thrummed with what felt like low voltage.

"I think I went to Under," I told Varnie after I drained half of the water.

"I don't think so," he said.

"But I saw Mara," I explained.

"Haden, I closed off the kind of channels that left you open for that. This was about you and your subconscious."

I knew what I had seen.

"Seriously, dude," he said. "Nothing else in or out."

"You weren't there."

"Neither were you. You were in your head."

I exhaled. "Varn—"

What if he was right? What if the whole thing was an elaborate scene set up by my subconscious in order to tell me something?

The talisman thrummed again.

Only you can save her.

You have to accept it.

When you embraced who you were, you were stronger.

As a demon, you had more power than you can imagine right now.

I clutched the talisman in my palm. Was it true? Would I be more useful if I accepted who I was born to be?

And then my palm burned. The talisman. I'd been living with it on my skin, never removing it and believing the whole time it had some kind of untapped power. I was probably right. It did have power.

My power.

The stone moved like it was alive.

"Varn, why did Theia have a talisman?"

He shook his head. "I wish I knew. Back when you were first sniffing around, I got a message that she needed a talisman, but that it wouldn't directly protect her. It didn't make much sense, which is nothing new. I couldn't decode the message, so I passed it on as best I could. Why?"

"I think I just decoded it."

He blinked, patiently waiting for me to explain.

Removing the necklace wasn't easy because my hands shook with the adrenaline coursing through my body. "The pendant can't protect her, but what's in it can."

"What's in the pendant?"

The one thing I'd spent more than a century wishing away. The one thing that would be strong enough to protect Theia from the nightmare of her new life. I set it in the middle of the table. "Me."

Varnie pushed his chair back a few inches, putting some distance between the talisman and himself. "The demon went in there?"

I nodded.

"How?"

"Mara must have done it. Maybe it went in there on its own. I don't know. I doubt Theia knew what it contained when she gave it to me. But that's what I figured out when I went looking for my memories."

"So we need to bury it or hide it now?" He looked as if he didn't want to touch it with a crane, let alone bury it.

"No, we let it out."

He shot out of his chair. "Are you insane?"

"Call the girls," I said. "We need to do another exorcism, this time in reverse."

DOWN IS UP . . . AGAIN

CHAPTER TWENTY-SIX

Theia

Everything changed again the night the burning man fell from the sky.

I scrambled from my covers and to the window.

This time he didn't look at me as he willowed past. His descent was slow, torturous again, and I know my heart stopped, catching in my ribs like a stone.

As I watched him, waiting for him to land, I relived his horror, my horror. Was it Haden? What was happening?

He didn't touch ground, instead disintegrating and dissipating into nothing in front of my eyes. I swallowed hard. And then my stuck heart began to gallop. I didn't know what to do, what to think.

Surely, if it was Haden, he didn't die. I didn't die the first time I came to Under, and he didn't die the first time he came to my world—so he was still alive. He had to be. I kept repeating it to convince myself.

But Haden shouldn't have to burn again, should he? I paced like a caged lion trying to work it out in my head. Was it someone else?

I tried the door but it was locked. It wasn't Mara who had locked me in; rather, it was one of the faceless butlers who had taken kindly to me. Some of the inhabitants in Under were still loyal to Haden, despite their fear of Mara. When I had explained to the butler that I didn't trust myself not to hurt his old master, he found a way to lock that door most nights.

Hours later, still unable to sleep, still pacing, I stepped onto the terrace. The view was never exactly the same; the mountains were always changing shape. One more thing to keep me off balance.

The night air was cool but a little balmy. It smelled like the sea. Sure enough, between two mountain peaks, an ocean not usually there was visible. Light from two setting moons glinted on the surface in a golden imitation of the sun.

I didn't let myself think about the beach back home. It was dangerous to want things. I turned to go back into Haden's room, my room, when I heard a noise. The hairs of my nape rose.

One thing I'd learned during my time in Under was that I couldn't cower. Fear was cherished and cultivated—my best weapon so far had been to imitate my father's formidable attitude in most situations. I straightened my spine and strode towards the ledge of the terrace, wishing I'd worn something more than one of Haden's "pirate" shirts outside. I took a deep breath and looked over the railing.

At the same time, Haden appeared, climbing up to the terrace. My first reaction was surprise, then joy, then fear. "What are you doing here?" I asked. What if Mara could sense him?

He vaulted over the edge in a practiced move.

"What have you done? How did you . . . ?"

"I've been sneaking in and out of my bedroom for half a century." His eyes flashed with dark humor. "There are strategically placed iron spikes from the ground up."

"You climbed the wall? What if you fell? You could have been killed." I paused as a new thought flashed across my mind. "Wait—you remember?"

Haden smiled. "I remember you. I remember every second." He reached for my hand, oblivious to the danger I presented to him, and kissed my fingertips in a gesture reminiscent of the Haden I remembered all too well. One that was both a demon and a boy.

Butterflies fluttered in my stomach, canceling for a sweet moment the ugliness I'd felt since the demon had taken residence under my skin. I wanted to warn Haden, to be strong and do what was right, but selfishly, I tightened my grip on the moment instead.

"You still have the way of moonlight about you," he said, reminding me of the thrill of our first meetings.

I felt beautiful when I looked into his eyes. He hadn't given up on me—on us. Not even when he couldn't recall that he'd loved me. I wondered if I had it in me to dare to hope again.

He looked over his shoulder at the waning light of the moons. "I've come to take you home."

"No, Haden, you should—"

"You will not wither here, not while there is breath left in my body."

"But your mother—"

"The night you made your blood oath to Mara. You promised you would never try to escape."

"I know. That is why you must leave. Now, before she finds us." Panic was rising in my chest. It was never a good idea for me to get too emotional. I had less control of the darkness inside me when I was overwrought.

"You won't break the oath if you are abducted."

I stepped back. "Haden, no."

"Good. Yes, if you fight me it will be even more believable. Try to run if you like." The wolfish smile was back. "I like a good chase."

I backed away from him. "This isn't a game. You have to leave. I can't go with you."

"I'm not asking, Theia." Haden's pupils darkened and it occurred to me that he was still dangerous. He lunged once and hefted me over his shoulder like a sack of flour.

The old Theia blushed at my precarious position. The new Theia rankled at the treatment. "Put me down," I commanded.

"Keep wriggling. This night just keeps getting better, lamb."

I pounded my fists on his back, but he never broke his stride. When the door didn't open, he kicked it. As we passed the shards of it in the hall, the situation began to get clearer.

"You're a demon again," I whispered, afraid to draw any more attention to my kidnapping.

"You're one to talk," he joked.

"How?"

"Later, Theia."

He took a set of stairs at the end of the hall, still carrying me as if I weighed nothing. They spiraled up and up the turret until we got to the tower room that held the looking glass into the portals.

He let me down, finally, in front of the window to the worlds. At first glance it was a simple gilded mirror, the only thing in the room. Looking into it, though, was always like breaking my heart.

"I can't go back there." In the reflection were Donny, Ame, Gabe, and Varnie holding hands, at the same cabin where I'd last seen them. "What if I hurt someone?"

He pressed his fingertips lightly over my lips. "Hush. Once upon a time, you told me we should fight to be together. You believed in me then, Theia. Could you find it in your heart to give faith one more chance?"

I wasn't the same girl anymore.

I was stronger.

I removed his hand from my lips. "Promise never to hush me again."

He laughed.

"I mean it, Haden. From now on, I say exactly what I want and no one tells me how I should or shouldn't feel or what I can or cannot say."

"All right," he promised. "Any minute we're going to crash back into that world, provided they get the spell right this time. Tell me, then, lamb, just in case we both lose our memories this time, is there anything you want to say to me?" His grin was full of dark promises and too charming by far.

"I want to say that you need to leave before you're caught."

"Not going to happen."

I looked at my friends. I so badly wanted to be reunited with them, but was terrified of trying to live on earth with the blood of a demon coursing through my veins.

"I know you're scared, but we'll find a way, Theia. Together."

I felt the pull of the spells, both the one from the other side of the portal and the one Haden was weaving around me.

I didn't know if I was strong enough to fight either of them.

"Don't let me hurt anyone."

"You hurt us all by staying away."

I looked longingly at the door. *If I could find the courage to run* . . .

"Theia," he pleaded, his palms cupping my jaw gently and turning me back to him. He leaned into me, and I to him. His eyes searched mine and, finding what he looked for, his lips followed suit.

His kiss was tender but full of a yearning I recognized from my own heart. I began to drown in everything he offered—love, hope, faith. It was all there, even though it was mixed with a heavy dose of the darkness that lived in me now.

It wouldn't be easy. And Mara wouldn't give up. That was certain.

But Haden had turned away from the thing he wanted most, to be human, to come for me. I couldn't fight him, didn't want to. Instead, I gave myself to him and to the dragging tide of his heart. We kissed as our bodies became weightless and we were pulled into another world.

And together we fell under.

ABOUT THE AUTHOR

Gwen Hayes lives in the Pacific Northwest with her real-life hero and a pack of wild beasts (two of whom she gave birth to). She is a reader, writer, and lover of pop culture (which, other than yogurt, is the only culture she gets). Visit her on the Web at www.gwenhayes.com.